"I am what I am. T

"Since I am given a c
I am not stupid. I know it is not because you care for me that has prompted you to ask me to be your wife—not even pity or guilt—that it is only Violet you want."

He shook his head. She was right. He would not insult her intelligence by denying that, and as proud as she was, her pride would make her oppose him. "I care enough about you to be hurt and angry by the appalling way you have been treated by your neighbors. You do not deserve that."

"No, I don't—and I thank you for your concern. Your honorable nature is to be applauded, but you don't have to feel under any obligation to marry me."

"I don't."

Melissa's chin lifted and she glared at him. "I told you I do not want to marry you. Do you, in your arrogance, assume I will change my mind?"

"It has been known for some women to do so."

"And I am telling you that I am not most women."

Author Note

I do hope you enjoy reading this, my latest book, *Wedded for His Secret Child.*

When the unworldly, innocent Melissa Frobisher decides to visit the Spring Gardens on her eighteenth birthday, she encounters Laurence Maxwell, who is unable to resist her quiet beauty and independent spirit. After spending a delightful interlude in the deepest shadows of the gardens, they part, unaware that their romantic encounter has sparked a situation that will explode at some time in the future.

Melissa's reputation is completely ruined—more so when their daughter is born after nine months. Twenty months later the lovers meet again. Melissa's feelings for this handsome lord are unchanged. Laurence is shocked to discover he has a daughter he knows nothing about, and for the sake of their child they decide that marriage between them is the most sensible course to take.

The early days of their marriage are fraught with problems. While Laurence wrestles with his inner demons, Melissa must confront the ghost of the woman who came before her—his wife, whom she believes he had loved and lost...

HELEN DICKSON

Wedded for His Secret Child

HARLEQUIN
HISTORICAL

ISBN-13: 978-1-335-50577-4

Wedded for His Secret Child

This edition published by arrangement with Harlequin Books S.A.

For questions and comments about the quality of this book, please contact us at CustomerService@Harlequin.com.

Harlequin Enterprises ULC
22 Adelaide St. West, 40th Floor
Toronto, Ontario M5H 4E3, Canada
www.Harlequin.com

Printed in U.S.A.

Helen Dickson was born and still lives in South Yorkshire, UK, with her retired farm manager husband. Having moved out of the busy farmhouse where she raised their two sons, she now has more time to indulge in her favorite pastimes. She enjoys being outdoors, traveling, reading and music. An incurable romantic, she writes for pleasure. It was a love of history that drove her to writing historical fiction.

Books by Helen Dickson

Harlequin Historical

When Marrying a Duke...
The Devil Claims a Wife
The Master of Stonegrave Hall
Mishap Marriage
A Traitor's Touch
Caught in Scandal's Storm
Lucy Lane and the Lieutenant
Lord Lansbury's Christmas Wedding
Royalist on the Run
The Foundling Bride
Carrying the Gentleman's Secret
A Vow for an Heiress
The Governess's Scandalous Marriage
Reunited at the King's Court
Wedded for His Secret Child

Castonbury Park

The Housemaid's Scandalous Secret

Visit the Author Profile page
at Harlequin.com for more titles.

Chapter One

1794

Violet was not yet one year old when Melissa rode out one fine day in spring. She rode astride, with her daughter in front of her, her favourite hound bounding along beside her.

Violet had the natural healthiness of an infant. Despite the passing of time Melissa remembered the man who'd sired her as if their brief encounter had been yesterday. She saw his likeness every time she looked at her daughter. The moment she had cradled her baby in her arms she knew nothing in her life would be the same again.

She was amazed by the outpouring of maternal love she felt for the tiny human being. A protective love, the kind of which she had never known, had engulfed her. With each passing day this new presence in her life left a trail of comfort as though coated in soothing balm. She insisted on doing everything for her—even feeding her, much to her mother's horror. She had wanted to employ a nursing woman to take over the task. Melissa had even insisted that the crib be brought from the nursery and placed in her room, beside her bed.

Violet soon became the centre of attention both inside and outside the house, fussed over and adored by everyone. Everyone felt the need to touch her dark, glossy curls and proclaim they had never seen a happier child.

Melissa's mother, who, despite her initial reservations about her daughter keeping the child, had fallen in love with her. She was horrified that Melissa insisted on taking her out in this improper fashion, telling her that Violet should be in the nursery in her cot, not bouncing about atop a horse, but Melissa would have it no other way. Nestling in a sling fastened around Melissa's waist, the infant was secure and in no danger.

Warmed by her cloak and with her dark hair loose about her shoulders, she rode along happily. Here was a damp, earthy smell on the air and on either side of the narrow lane the bare hedgerows provided shelter for rabbits in their burrows. Beyond the hedgerows the empty fields were ploughed, each ready for planting. She couldn't wait for spring to arrive when everything would burst into life. So deep was she in her thoughts that it was a shock when a galloping horse and rider appeared suddenly round a bend. Fortunately they didn't hit her, but in the rider's attempt not to, his mount swerved and reared up, throwing the rider from the saddle where he landed in an ungainly heap on the ground. Melissa held on to the reins and pulled her frightened horse to one side. For several heart-stopping moments she was occupied soothing its terror and holding on to Violet. It was the man's voice and the barking from her dog that jerked her from her ministrations.

'In God's name, get this damned dog off me.'

Seeing the wild tangle of dog and man, Melissa slid to the ground, still clutching Violet. The dog, of indeterminate pedigree, big, floppy and excitable, was barking ecstatically. There was mayhem as she tried to restrain the dog, who seemed intent on licking the poor man to death.

'Do you usually take up the whole road?' the man reproached harshly, trying to push the dog away, but the dog was having none of it. 'How the devil I managed to avoid you I'll never know. Didn't you hear me coming or are you deaf?'

'I'm sorry—'

'Sorry! Is that all you can say when you've just frightened my horse to death?'

'It was not my fault. I was riding well in.' Melissa was indignant that this infuriating stranger thought he was in the right. 'You were riding much too fast. This lane has many twists and turns and is often used—and there is certainly nothing wrong with my ears.'

'Then you should ride with more care,' he barked, while the dog continued to pant in his ear, 'especially when in charge of an infant. To have her bouncing about in front of you like that is both dangerous and irresponsible. And here, take your damned dog. He's totally out of control.'

'No, he isn't—and his name is Bracken. He's simply pleased to see you. He usually comes with me when I am riding.'

'Why? Do you feel you need protection? I suppose I have to be thankful I haven't been mauled to death. Is he fierce?'

Managing to hold on to a wriggling Violet, who was straining her neck to see what all the fuss was about, Melissa merely nodded. Let him think what he liked, even though Bracken was more likely to greet a newcomer with lots of tail wagging and affectionate slobbery licking. She watched the man—a gentleman by the cut of his clothes—get to his feet and seize the reins of his trembling horse before brushing his clothes down and running his hand distractedly through his thick black hair. His tall hat had fallen off and lay upside down on the ground.

'I trust you are not hurt from your tumble,' Melissa said.

'I've suffered worse,' he grumbled.

'I'm glad to hear it. Now if you are quite sure you are all right, I'll be on my way.'

That was the moment the man raised his head and looked at her for the first time. On meeting those glacial silver-grey eyes recognition jolted through Melissa like a lightning force, rendering her speechless. There was a vibrant life and an intensity in those piercing eyes that no one could deny. They were beautiful, she decided, and they made her shiver slightly at their intensity. Her breath caught in her throat. He had a knowledgeable face, a face that had seen life. It was strong and slashed with swooping black eyebrows. His mouth was firm and hard, but it had a lift at each corner which spoke of sensuality. There was an aggressive virility about him, an uncompromising authority. His chin was thrusting and inclined to arrogance.

He was astonishingly handsome, as handsome as she remembered. It was as if the Lord had decided that his face was too perfect and placed a smudge—a small birthmark close to his right ear—like the dab of purple paint from an artist's brush. Her heart was pounding in her ears and there was a short, humming silence as the man took a closer look at her face. His brow furrowed as his eyes narrowed searchingly and then widened with disbelief.

'Melissa! Good Lord! What the hell…?'

Melissa's arms tightened around her daughter and she stepped back, having no idea what to say or how to react now she was face to face with the man who had occupied her waking thoughts for the past twenty months. She realised at once that nothing had changed. Her feelings were just the same and her whole body yearned towards him. Her face flaming at the meanderings of her mind and what had occurred between them in the Spring Gardens in London, she shook her head free of the memory of their coupling, focusing her eyes on him.

He stepped closer, taking firm hold of the reins when she was about to turn away. Sweeping her with a bold gaze, those incredible eyes that were so like her daughter's delved into hers before narrowing as remembrance began to dawn on him. He raised a single, questioning eyebrow. 'When we parted I never thought I would see you again. It was in the Spring Gardens when I'd just got back from France—perhaps twenty months ago. We—'

'Please don't go on,' Melissa was quick to retort, stirred by a sudden tumult of emotions and having no wish to hear what she had done on that beautiful night put into words. She was conscious of an unwilling excitement. In fact, much to her annoyance, she was very much aware of everything about him—the long, strong lines of his body, his face strong and handsome—and she saw faint lines of weariness on his face which aroused her curiosity. 'I'd rather you didn't.'

Her embarrassment—the soft flush that sprang to her cheeks and the way she lowered her eyes—brought a crooked smile to Laurence's lips and a knowing glint to his eyes. 'I wouldn't dream of embarrassing you if that's what you are afraid of. But I do remember everything about that night—and it may surprise you to know that after we parted I tried to find you.'

'You did?'

'Yes. I wanted to make quite sure you were all right. We made love. You were a virgin and I was not in the habit of deflowering virgins. My conscience smote me and I found myself turning back to look for you with mingled feelings of regret and concern.'

His words—that he had tried to find her, that he had been concerned about her—touched Melissa. She bit her lip and clamped down on her emotions which threatened to surface—despair, hopelessness and fear of laying eyes on this man again. When they had parted, a finger of disappointment had traced a delicate path down her spine. It had left her bewildered, for how could she have enjoyed such intimacy with a man? Why had she done something so reprehensible, so contrary to her upbringing that it would court a malicious scandal?

No one was allowed to see what festered inside her, the deep yearning which just would not die. She felt the intensity of his gaze fixed on her face. Her feelings for him were unchanged, all dominating, obscuring the pain of their parting. She could actually feel the tears welling up inside her, but she would not weep in front of him. He was looking at her with such shock and surprise, but no distaste, that to her own amazement and horror she wanted nothing more than to be gathered once more into his arms. What he said next quickly banished these tender feelings.

'You aroused my curiosity,' he murmured gently. 'You could have secured a king's ransom for what you lost to me, yet you came willingly, without even attempting to bargain for your worth. You then disappeared without a trace.'

Melissa stared at him speechless, unable to fully comprehend the impact of his words.

'You wore the attire of a servant and yet you seemed gently born and not the type to be wandering the gardens with other ladies of the night seeking pleasure. It was the sound of your laughter above the music and chatter of the crowd that drew my attention. It was a joyous laugh, young and infectious, as though nothing had ever troubled you.'

Melissa threw back her head and glared at him, mortally offended by his words. 'Ladies of the night? Is that what you thought I was? You were mistaken. I was not peddling my wares—far from it. I was in London for such a short time and, having escaped my mother's watchful gaze I was simply there to experience the delights of the gardens—until I encountered you.'

In the face of her ire, he looked deep into her eyes, frowning deeply as he began to wonder at the repercussions for what had occurred. 'Dear Lord, I had no idea—and who would have thought I would meet you here of all places.'

Melissa opened her eyes wide, then blinked rapidly, but Laurence had seen the moisture which shone in her eyes. It encouraged him and his face softened into a smile. 'You are upset—and see, you are upsetting the child.' His gaze dropped to the squirming bundle in her arms. 'What have we here? Good Lord! Your child is nothing but a babe.' He glared at her accusingly. 'Have you no sense holding on to such a young child on a horse?'

Melissa stiffened in what appeared to be offence and her face, which had been ready to crumple with her angry tears, hardened and her lip lifted in contempt as she put up a defence, determined to pull herself together. 'I assure you she is perfectly safe with me. See—she is secure in the sling.' Standing up straight, her head held high, her jaw thrust forward, she pushed the heavy mantle of her hair back from her face with her free hand. 'And I am not upset. I am angry because you almost knocked me off my horse with your recklessness. If the child is upset it is because you frightened her—didn't he, Violet?' she said, looking down to smile brilliantly, heartbreakingly, at her daughter.

Raising her eyes, she was struck—as she had been the first time they'd met—by how different he was from all other men she knew. There was something in his face, in his whole demeanour, that set him apart. As he continued to scrutinise her she wished more than anything in the world that she wasn't attracted to him, that she could keep her eyes from straying to that mouth that had once explored every curve and hollow of her body. She had vowed many times to put him behind her, but it was easier said than done. The brief time they had spent together making love was etched on her soul and nothing could erase it however hard she tried.

'She is your child?'

She nodded, averting her eyes. 'Yes.'

'She is very bonny. Your husband must be very proud of her.'

'I—I have no husband.' Raising her head, Melissa saw something move in the depths of his eyes—as if a thought had taken hold.

'No? How old is your daughter?'

'Eleven months.'

Violet was curious about what was happening around her and strained her neck to look at the stranger who had appeared from nowhere and disrupted their ride. The effect on Laurence was instantaneous.

'Give her to me.'

Reaching out, he pulled Violet from the security of the sling and held her at arm's length. The child did not turn back to her mother and kept her eyes, curious and searching, fixed on the man. He continued looking intently at Violet, grey eyes meeting grey, locking, the older eyes searching, probing, the young eyes inquisitive, thoughtful. Watching him closely, Melissa watched his changing expression, her heart beating frantically. It was as if a sudden pain twisted his heart—as if it had been pierced by a sharp blade.

As he cradled Violet in the crook of his arm, a thought clearly suddenly struck him and he pushed back her bonnet, gently lifting the tumble of hair that stood about her head in a froth of light, to reveal the small, tell-tale mark just above her ear. Melissa almost felt his shock.

'Well, well,' he said softly, 'what have we here?' He continued to scrutinise Violet, in no hurry, it would seem, to hand her back to her mother.

Melissa began to feel uncomfortable. 'I—I'll take her. I must be getting back.'

'Back? Where is back?'

'Home—to High Meadows. Baron Charles Frobisher is my father.'

'Is he indeed.' Raising his head, he looked at Melissa. The still, bright silver of his eyes was enigmatic, revealing nothing of his feelings. 'Violet is my daughter. She has the mark. There can be no dispute over it.'

With two identical faces looking at her it was a statement of fact Melissa could not deny. Even their expressions, audacious and compelling, were the same and with a tilt of humour at the corners of their lips.

'She—she is my daughter,' he reiterated. 'It takes two to make a child. We—you and I—made this one.'

'Yes,' Melissa whispered, wanting to snatch Violet from his arms and ride for home. She could see he was finding it hard to comprehend that this was happening. Not only had he made love to a sexually innocent girl from a respectable family, but he had impregnated her.

'Violet,' he said, speaking softly. 'It's a pretty name.'

'I think so,' Melissa murmured, swallowing down the hard, emotional lump that had appeared in her throat. 'When she was born her eyes were blue which quickly turned to violet. I thought they would remain so, but as you see they are no longer violet.'

'Has she been baptised?'

'No—not with her being illegitimate.'

'Then she will be. Every child should be baptised.'

Melissa looked at him steadily. 'What is it to you? You do not know her.'

'Through no fault of my own. It is something I

intend to rectify. I am responsible for her existence. I want to help.'

'Violet is my daughter. That means that I make the decisions concerning her.'

Laurence looked at Melissa as if he was about to explode. 'We'll see about that. You cannot bring a child up on your own.'

'I have my parents to help me.'

'They won't always be there. You and I—what we did, Violet is the innocent result,' he said, handing Violet back to her.

Melissa felt a sudden surge of anger when she recalled how disappointed she had felt when he had left her in the Spring Gardens. How stupid and naive she had been. Despite the feelings he had stirred in her she was ashamed that she had been such a willing participant. Her sexual innocence and lack of knowledge regarding the male species had led to her undoing. But perhaps this was nothing out of the ordinary and he was used to making love to ladies whenever the fancy took him. After all, she thought bitterly, how would she know? She regarded him coldly, her face showing no trace of emotion. With pride and self-respect she held her head high.

'That night in the Spring Gardens dealt me a cruel blow, but I was determined not to be the victim of circumstance. Despite what you must have thought at the time, I did not have your experience. Apart from yourself, no other man has touched me—either before or since,' she told him with simple honesty, giving him further insight into just how truly innocent she was.

'Thank you for telling me. Now I know Violet, have seen her, I cannot walk away from her.'

Melissa could think of no immediate reply. Panic rose into her throat, her heart beating so loudly that she felt it must be audible. How far was he prepared to take his responsibility? What would he do? Take Violet away from her? It was a situation she could not allow. She could not endure any more humiliation. With an urgent need to escape she took a step back, but then she stood, transfixed by the power in his eyes that held hers.

'There is no need to fear me, Melissa.'

'I don't,' she replied. But she did. She feared even more what he would do. 'And me?' she asked the question quietly.

Laurence looked at her directly and the impact of his gaze was potent. He took a step closer, his powerful, animalistic masculinity immediately assaulting her senses. Melting inwardly, she felt her traitorous body offer itself to this man—in that moment they both acknowledged the forbidden flame that sparked between them. He raised one well-defined eyebrow, watching her. He seemed to know exactly what was going on in her mind.

'As to that we shall have to see. Does the idea of me being involved in Violet's life strike you as distasteful? It is customary for the father of a child to be a part of its life.'

Melissa almost retreated from those suddenly

fierce eyes, but she steeled herself and held her ground. 'I do not find the idea of you in any way distasteful and as much as you want to be a part of Violet's life you must understand that ever since I realised I was with child the decisions that have been taken where she is concerned have been mine and mine alone. I cannot help it if I find the idea of sharing the responsibility with someone else—difficult.'

He looked at her hard, then nodded and cupped her chin in his hand. 'I do understand—more than you realise. I can see that you have not had an easy time of it. But our daughter is a beautiful child, a credit to you, and I thank you for what you have done for her in my absence. Believe me when I tell you that had I known of her existence I would have come to you before now.' Dropping his hand, he drew her horse forward. 'You live nearby, I take it?'

His touch had been like a caress. She had felt a frisson of warmth glow inside her and she hadn't wanted him to pull it away. She had embraced it. 'Yes, about a mile away.'

'Then I will ride there with you. No doubt you have had some difficult questions to answer. How did your parents react when they found out you were to bear an illegitimate child?'

'My mother with anger—which was understandable. She was mostly concerned with what others would think. She didn't want friends and neighbours to ridicule my situation. My father was upset. My mother wanted me to go away, to have the child and let some needy couple adopt her. I couldn't do that. To give away my baby was anathema to me.'

A silence stretched between them, filled with the intensity of the emotion that suddenly linked them.

'Thank God for that,' he said calmly after a short pause in which neither of them seemed to want to break the silence. 'I'm relieved you remained strong and fought for her.'

'I couldn't do anything else. My mother is a formidable lady. It was a huge relief when I won the battle to keep Violet. But I couldn't let her go. I wouldn't hear of it. When my mother realised I was serious, she suggested that I went away and when I returned with a child tell everyone that I had married and my husband had died.'

'I take it you didn't want to do that either.'

'No. I couldn't spend my life living a lie. When I got over the initial shock of my condition, my duty was to the child. I decided to look to the future, to my new life with all the responsibility due to that child who would grow up without knowing her father—life was too short to squander on what ifs and wherefores. My day-to-day life would change, I knew that, and that I would be ostracised and shunned by friends and neighbours. But after much soul-searching I discarded any resentment and self-pity I felt about my situation. Now I spend as much time with my beautiful daughter as I possibly can.'

Laurence gave her a look of admiration. 'It appears to me that you are a capable young woman. I can only apologise for not being there to support you. When we parted that night, I had no idea who you were or where you lived. I truly believed you were a servant.'

'I know. That was what I wanted you to think. It was my birthday—my eighteenth—and when my maid told me she was going to the Spring Gardens with her friends, I could not resist the temptation to go with her.'

'I see. I did not know you.'

'Nor I you—apart from your first name.'

'And I yours.' Retrieving his hat, he brushed it down and placed it on his head. 'Let me help you on to your horse.'

They rode slowly back the way Melissa had come. The house became visible through the trees lining the road. She knew he could not fail to register the overgrown gardens and the years of neglect showing on the house with its patched roof and peeling paintwork, which her father could not afford to repair due to mismanagement and their ancestors being forced to sell off land to settle debts accrued at the gaming tables. She saw the look on Laurence's face and chose to ignore it. It was best that she knew his opinions of her home and her family, but she wished he had not made it quite so obvious.

'This is your home?' he said.

'Yes. As you can already see, it has been somewhat neglected. My ancestors thought their own amusements were more important than keeping the house in order, but I would not wish to live anywhere else.'

Having halted in front of the house, Laurence took Violet while she dismounted. 'This unfortunate state of affairs was brought about by me. I'm not proud of myself for what I did to you at the Spring Gardens. Had I known who you were, that you were the daughter of a gentleman, I would have sought you out and apologised to your family—even though your father would have been within his rights to call me out. I fully intend to do what is right.'

Melissa bristled at his words. 'And if I had not been the daughter of a gentleman, but only a servant?'

'My responsibility to the child would be the same regardless of the mother's station in life,' he said, handing Violet to her as a groom appeared to take her horse. 'Obviously matters cannot be left like this. I will speak to your parents—'

'Oh—are you coming in?'

'Not now. I have to consider how best to proceed. I shall call on them tomorrow.'

With no further word he looked again at a gurgling Violet before turning his horse and riding away. Melissa watched him go, wondering in what way he wished to proceed. Perhaps he would offer some kind of financial settlement for Violet's future. If so, Melissa's mother would certainly not object. The only other way she could think of that would put things right would be if he were to offer her marriage, but somehow she doubted he would do that.

As Laurence rode away from High Meadows, his encounter with Melissa Frobisher had given him much to think about. He could not equate the elegant young lady with the amazing amber eyes and wealth of dark hair with the frivolous girl he had dallied with in the pleasure gardens all those months ago. He felt a deep stirring of compassion mingled with admiration for the manner in which she had coped with her situation—a combination of emotions that was completely foreign to him. Hers was not a situation he would have inflicted on a gently bred lady of character—or any other female for that matter—and it pained him to contemplate the tribulations she must have gone through.

He remembered her as being a young lady who had been so sure of herself. Dress her in fashionable clothes, coif her hair into ringlets and curls, and she would not have been out of place at Almack's. He remembered her as being so direct it was easy to forget that she was so young. He supposed it came with being left to her own devices. He recalled how impressed he had been by her and how grateful he had been that she had been so unexpectedly capable of breaking down the barriers he had erected around himself since the death of his wife. And yet he caught himself up short, chiding himself for having misread the situation so entirely and for his callous disregard of her future when their short yet pleasurable liaison was over.

So, what was to be done now? His life at this point in time was fraught with problems—he had no time for marriage and affairs of the heart. A man who loved too well was vulnerable—something he had learned to his cost. Certainly in the past he had yielded to the desires of the flesh as much as the next man, but he had never doted on any of them—except one, a beautiful, callous woman called Alice, a woman he had made his wife, a woman who had deceived him with another, leaving him and taking their son with her, only for it to end in tragedy. Now, almost three years on, he was confronted with a serious dilemma.

When he had encountered and made love to Melissa Frobisher, how could he have known she was something other than a servant? He'd fallen into the oldest trap in the world, made weak by his own maleness, and the trap unwittingly set by this woman's own female body which hadn't even known what it was about. He had done so much harm to her who, at the time, in her innocence, had likely confused sexuality with infatuation or even love in her mind. But whatever the facts of the matter he must, for the sake of the child they had heedlessly made, put it right. However awkward that might be, he must pay the price of his passion. Already he was taking steps with regard to his child.

When he had taken Violet in his arms, he was rewarded with a smile that lit up the darkest corner of his heart. She had looked into his face with interest, as if she, too, was affected by the poignancy of the moment of their meeting. The new life he held seemed like a miracle after all he had suffered after losing his son. The memory of the pain he'd felt when he had been told of Toby's death, the harrowing, crucifying agony, had lessened a little with time, but it had not gone away. It never would.

He'd wanted to find something there to give him pause, to remind him why he'd vowed on the death of his son never to father a child again, because should he lose another, the pain of it would be impossible to bear. But he had found nothing except the trusting eyes of a child, his child, a child he could not, would not deny. He had stepped over an invisible line and wouldn't be able to step back again. He could only move forward. On discovering that Violet was his daughter, hope had flared within him, a great shining hope...

Dear Lord, was he mad letting his thoughts wander as they were doing, when all his senses, every warning bell, every instinct for self-preservation that his human body possessed told him to back away, not to be tempted a second time? But Violet was his daughter and he would not. Could not.

It was the next afternoon and Melissa was outside with Violet, awaiting the arrival of their visitor. Holding her daughter close, as she walked in the garden she gazed at the old house with great affection. Unlike so many large houses, High Meadow had not withstood the passage of time well. Melissa's great-grandfather had built the house to impress, with no thought of restraint, but from the day the builders had moved out the house had begun a long and steady decline.

Melissa's once prosperous ancestors had been part of a merchant class, but after a series of poor investments there was little money left to inherit. But there was something eternal in the mellowing walls and gardens overgrown with creepers and vines. It was set in a deer park, serene and untouched, though a large portion of the land and farms High Meadows depended on for its income had long since been sold, along with much of the house contents. The income from the few remaining tenants was meagre and Melissa's mother worked tirelessly trying to make ends meet.

Melissa missed her brothers terribly. Robert had married a hard-headed businessman's daughter from the north of England. She was no great catch, but from her mother's point of view and their own impoverishment, she was not a disaster. Henry, two years Robert's senior, was a lieutenant in the Royal Navy. She thought often of the time when they had been children, when they had run up and down the wide staircase and slid down the wooden banister, the sound of their voices, the playful squabbling and boisterous laughter, filling the house.

That was all gone now and the spacious rooms felt empty and bereft. She knew her parents missed her siblings, especially her mother, who had doted on her handsome sons, often at the expense of Melissa, who had often felt rejected in favour of her brothers. When Robert and Henry had left home to seek their independence, her comfort had come from her father's beloved horses, who loved her for who she was.

Her mother was always concerned with doing the right thing and with protocol and rules for this and that, insisting that they should be followed religiously. She certainly made up for her father's easy-going manner. Very little disturbed him unless it concerned his horses. This often infuriated her mother, who wasn't a cruel woman, just bitterly disappointed that she was buried alive in the rustic Hertfordshire countryside instead of being part of the London scene.

Melissa was watching with interest as a dead beech tree which had been felled by two woodmen was in the process of being sawn into logs that would be taken round to the stables and stored. Violet was having great fun trying to scramble over one, gurgling with glee as she managed to perch on top. The two men laughed at her antics, clearly taken with the child.

'Ah, keeping an eye on Violet, I see.'

Melissa spun round to find herself confronted by Laurence. He had dismounted from his horse and was holding the reins loosely in his hand. She hadn't seen him arrive and his sudden appearance put her on the alert. 'I always do.'

Unfortunately Violet chose that moment to tumble off the log. Laurence made an exclamation and started forward, but at the sound of his voice Violet picked herself up and grinned, all thoughts of her tumble forgotten as she crawled towards the man who had made such a big impression on her the day before. With a gesture that tugged at Melissa's heart and astonished the two woodcutters, Laurence dropped the reins and swung the child up into his arms, hugging her close and kissing her rosy cheek.

'I trust you have informed your parents of my

visit—and the connection I have to Violet?' he asked, looking at her over the top of Violet's head.

'Yes. It was—difficult,' she told him, which was true. Her mother had been struck dumb and her father had gaped at her in absolute astonishment before bombarding her with questions until her head ached. 'They are expecting you.'

'Indeed! Lead the way.' Handing Violet to her, he instructed one of the woodcutters to look after his horse. 'The sooner I make their acquaintance and get this situation under control the better.'

Without a word he strode towards the house ahead of her, his long legs eating up the ground with considerable speed. Melissa followed at a slower pace, her nerves a jangled mass of discordant vibrations. She was reluctant to face what awaited her inside when Laurence had introduced himself to her parents as their daughter's seducer, father of Violet, and told them whatever it was he intended to do.

It was no fault of his that he hadn't been aware of Violet's birth. Had she known his full identity and where he lived, she would have notified him, but this had not been the case. However, now he did know it was to his credit that he wanted to rectify matters, but, she couldn't help wondering, where did she fit into his order of things?

The door was opened by the white-haired Bradley, an old retainer whose duties were butler, her father's valet, carriage driver, general servant and anything else when there was a job to be done.

Melissa strode in ahead of Laurence. 'Are my parents in the drawing room, Bradley?'

'They are, Miss Melissa,' Bradley confirmed, glancing curiously at her companion. 'Shall I announce you?'

'Good heavens, no. They know to expect a visitor. I'll announce myself and…'

She turned and lifted a questioning eyebrow.

'Lord Laurence Maxwell, the Earl of Winchcombe,' he obliged with a twinkle in his eye, as if to humour her.

Melissa raised her eyebrows even further. 'My word!' she breathed. 'An Earl! Now, *that* will impress my mother. Please come with me. The sooner we get this over with the better—although you must prepare yourself for my mother's temper. Papa is a gentle soul, but Mother is a different matter entirely. Woe betide anyone who gets on the wrong side of her. Is that not so, Bradley?'

'If you say so, Miss Melissa,' he replied, prepared to agree to anything she said.

Laurence's face hardened. 'Lead the way—and thank you for the warning.'

'Don't mention it. It's best that you are forewarned.'

Melissa marched towards the drawing room and without ceremony opened the door. She existed in a state of jarring tension as she fought to appear calm, clinging to her composure as best she could as the dreaded moment when she would have to introduce Laurence to her parents came closer. Her father, small, stout and always rumpled looking, was reading a paper in his favourite chair by the fire, his feet propped up on the brass fender, while her mother sat drinking tea. On seeing Melissa followed by a tall gentleman, she took a sip from her teacup and set it down, dabbed her lips with a cloth napkin and then rose to greet the visitor with a smile. The Baroness was a formidable middle-aged woman, slender to the point of being thin, with sculpted cheekbones and as regal a nose as one would ever see.

'Why, Melissa. I was beginning to wonder where you could have got to.' Her eyes went beyond her to the gentleman with interest. 'Our visitor has arrived, I see. Aren't you going to introduce us to the gentleman, my dear?'

'Of course,' she said, juggling Violet in her arms, who was straining her neck to see the man who appeared to have made such an impact on her. She looked at Laurence, who looked completely relaxed, yet there was an undeniable aura of forcefulness about him, of power. 'This is Laurence Maxwell—Violet's father.' She turned to Laurence. 'I would like to introduce my parents.'

The silence that fell was complete. Dispelling the prolonged silence, Laurence stepped forward with a respectful bow of his head.

'I am Lord Laurence Alexander Maxwell, the Earl of Winchcombe. My home is Winchcombe Hall in Surrey. I realise my appearance will come as something of a shock to you both, but you must believe me when I say that, had I known of your daughter's situation, I would have come before now. I would understand your reluctance to admit me into your home. I am a stranger to you and have done nothing that entitles me to an acknowledgement from you. I came upon your daughter by chance while out riding yesterday.'

Remembering his manners, with a stony expression on his face the Baron stepped forward, unsure how to greet this visitor—a titled gentleman who had ruined his beloved daughter—but he considered it necessary to be amiable if the man was to offer reparation. He executed a stiff bow.

'Baron Charles Frobisher at your service.' He looked at the illustrious visitor closely. 'Is it correct what Melissa has told us—that you are Violet's father?'

'Apparently that is the case.'

'Well,' the Baroness said, not quite sure how to receive the man who had seduced her daughter—a handsome one at that and an earl to boot—but she managed to hold on to her composure. She held her head high as she considered him coolly. 'I cannot deny that it was indeed a surprise when Melissa told us she had met you and that you intended to call on us. Naturally my husband and I are interested to hear your reason for coming here now. When I recall your less than gentlemanly treatment of Melissa on your previous encounter, you must forgive me if I appear somewhat bemused by your presence. When gentlemen find their indiscretions have landed them in hot water, they usually take to the hills rather than face up to their responsibilities.'

Hearing the sharp, patronising voice, Laurence was already regretting having come to her, yet he was impressed by this woman who had managed to keep her wits and composure despite the circumstances. Any other woman would have either gone to pieces or flown at him in anger for the ruination of her daughter.

'I suspect your feelings have run to something stronger than bemusement, Baroness, and all things considered I cannot say that I blame you. However, I am not one to shirk my responsibilities and I trust you will have the goodness to hear me out.'

'Indeed! You certainly owe my daughter that consideration after what you have done. If you'd had an ounce of common decency—whether she was a servant or noblewoman—you would not have done what you did. You ruined her—a decent, vulnerable girl.'

'I'm not proud of myself, which is why I am here now—to make amends.'

'Well, I have to say that I am relieved not to have to plead for her salvation from the man who destroyed any chance she had of making a decent marriage,' the Baroness said.

'I cannot do more than humbly apologise for my conduct and offer recompense.'

'You don't have to do that,' Melissa interjected with a frown, hoisting her wriggling daughter to her shoulder. 'I was equally to blame. What happened between us was by mutual consent, so please do not think you have to make any recompense.'

He looked at her intently. Yes, she had been willing. It was what they had both wanted. He'd felt it in her supple body, in its yielding, which had melted in that certain way women had when they were ready to take what they wanted, knowing what it was he had to offer. But she had been so young, a mere girl, really, and therefore she was absolved of all blame.

'But I do. I did you a great discourtesy for which I ask your pardon. What I did was inexcusable. It was unpardonable of me. You are very beautiful—sweet... but I know that is no excuse. The fault was undoubtedly all mine. I cannot leave without coming to an arrangement with you.'

'An arrangement,' the Baron said quickly. 'Kindly explain what you mean by that.'

Melissa was looking at him directly, holding his gaze with her own. Not one of his servants would look at him so, for her look was telling him that she could read his mind, that she knew what he had come for, what he wanted and the answer was no. Still holding her daughter, she moved closer to him, holding herself straight as she glared at him.

'I know what it is you want,' she said, her voice shaking with anger. 'You want Violet for yourself, don't you? You want to take her away from me. Indeed, I know I am right and I can tell you now that you are wasting your time. Have you any idea what it would do to her—to suddenly have her mother disappear from her life for no other reason than that you want her for yourself? Have you any idea how selfish that makes you appear? You have no right. She belongs to me. I will not allow you to take her.'

'She is my daughter,' he said with an inbred arrogance and certainty that said it would do no good to argue with him. 'If that was what I wanted, I would have every right.'

'I will not part with her. Don't you dare ask that of me. Had you told me of your intentions yesterday it would have saved you a visit to my home, wasting both your time and mine. What is it you intend, to buy her?—because if so I will tell you now that I don't want your money. There isn't enough money in the world that could buy my daughter.'

'You do realise that I could take Violet away from you by law, but that would mean exposing us all to publicity and I don't believe that either of us want that.' It was true, Laurence did not want that—not after the damning, shaming publicity he had been forced to endure when his wife and son had died. He turned to the Baron and his wife. 'Do you have anything to say?'

Melissa watched her parents, knowing exactly what her mother was thinking, that if he were to offer them money for Violet it would enable them to live well, as never before. The house, which was in such a miserable state of repair, could be done up at long last and the Baroness would be able to buy the latest fashions when she went to town, which she hadn't been able to afford for more years than she could remember. But knowing how her mother had become deeply attached to her beautiful granddaughter and knowing how Melissa doted on her, she was confident that her mother would support her in her decision.

For just a moment, the softening of the Baroness's face indicated that she might be tempted if he were to offer significant recompense and persuade her daughter to see sense, as money always won, until the Baron spoke up.

'Violet will not leave this house,' he said firmly. 'My daughter is right when she says there isn't enough money in the world that could buy her. Life has not been easy for Melissa, I grant you—and Violet's birth has created its own gossip in the neighbourhood—but she has weathered the worst of it and I am proud of her. Violet is my granddaughter and this is her home for as long as Melissa wants it to be, so let there be no more talk of you taking her away. Violet will not leave this house without my consent.'

Chapter Two

Melissa gave her father a grateful look and went to stand by his side. She was unable to think, unable to feel. How could Laurence ask her to give up Violet? If that was indeed what he wanted. Of course she wouldn't hear of it. She would never let him take her daughter away from her. She couldn't believe how besotted she had been on her first encounter with him—it felt as if her life had started to go wrong the day she met him and she was beginning to realise how naive, how stupid she had been to keep his memory alive all these months, calling herself all kinds of a fool for her unrealistic illusions. Despite the intimacy of their previous encounter he was still a stranger to her. Now she had become reacquainted with him and seen his arrogance and authoritarian manner, getting to know him better held little interest for her now. Though a small vestige of pain still lingered, she no longer felt foolish, she felt free, as if a great weight had been lifted from her shoulders.

'I don't think there is anything further to say,' she said, hoping the matter was resolved. 'If you do not have a wife, then perhaps you should get one—one who is prepared to give you a child.'

Something dark shifted in Laurence's eyes, but his face remained expressionless. 'I am a widower. My wife died in unfortunate circumstances almost three years ago.'

Melissa stared at him. His reply affected her deeply and it was strange that at that moment she should feel regret that she couldn't help him—unless, of course, he were to offer her marriage, which wasn't beyond the bounds of possibility if he had no ties and really did wish to do his best for Violet. There was a fleeting look in his eyes, an expression of loss she couldn't begin to understand. 'I'm sorry. I didn't know.'

'How could you? The worry of it is that a child was the result of our brief coming together and I cannot ignore that fact. I cannot walk away. In which case, if I want to be a part of my daughter's life—and I do, passionately—then there is only one course open to me. You are mistaken if you thought I wanted to take Violet from you. You were too ready to jump to the wrong conclusion. It is my wish to have my daughter close to me, but I would not dream of parting her from her mother. That would be a despicable act I could not condone. I have seen how it is with you when you look at Violet. I admire the way you prepared yourself in advance to openly give birth to an illegitimate child and I know you are fiercely protective of her and would not be prepared to let her go under any circumstances.'

'No, I would not. Then what is it you want?' Melissa asked.

'The offer I would like to make includes you, Melissa.'

'Oh—I see.'

Laurence captured her eyes. 'I want Violet with me. If it means marrying her mother, then that is how it will be,' he said, confirming Melissa's fears that Violet was all that mattered to him. Shifting his eyes to the Baron and his wife, he said, 'I am willing to marry your daughter. If it is acceptable to you, then you have my guarantee that she will be supported in a manner suitable to her upbringing and want for nothing.'

The Baroness's lips stretched into a smile. 'How extremely generous of you, Lord Maxwell. Naturally my husband and I will be happy to agree to a marriage between you and Melissa.'

Melissa stared from Laurence to her parents and back to Laurence, unable to believe what she was hearing. He was offering to marry her. That was what he had said. But why did he have to sound so dispassionate about it? She tried to block out the images of their meeting in the Spring Gardens from her mind, but it was no use. They paraded across her mind, tormenting her with vivid images of a star-struck, infatuated girl, mindlessly besotted by a handsome stranger.

She saw herself gazing up at him like a doe-eyed girl, thinking he was the most wonderfully handsome man she had ever seen and had fallen instantly in love with him. And when he had taken her in his arms she had almost swooned as her feelings and emotions got the better of her. How nauseating it all seemed to her now as the wonderful afterglow of their passionate union finally went out. She felt anger and frustration rising within her like a hot tide. This man had intruded into her life and her mother were talking as if she had no say in the matter whatsoever.

'Please do not discuss my future as if I am not in the room, Lord Maxwell. I have not agreed to any of this, yet you appear to have decided my future without even asking me what it is I might want. You cannot expect me to simply do as I am told just because you are accustomed to having people do your bidding, so please don't use my daughter to manipulate me. I do not want to marry you.'

Laurence could not have been more surprised if it had been the dog which had spoken. She still dared to argue, but it was in him to agree with her. 'Forgive me. I am only acting in the best interest of the child.' He crossed to where she stood and looked down into her turbulent face. Her eyes were glowing as her temper rose.

'I gave birth to Violet without you,' Melissa went on, 'and yet suddenly here you are, full of good intentions. You have decided to marry me because it's the only way you can get your hands on Violet. I am obliged to you, but you have no right to inflict your authority on me. I have no doubt that you are used to instructing people to do your bidding and having every expectation it will be done.'

'Then you must excuse me for I cannot alter the habits of a lifetime.'

'I would not ask you to.'

'Good, because I am what I am. Take it or leave it.'

'Since I am given a choice, I will leave it, my lord. I am not stupid. I know it is not because you care for me that has prompted you to ask me to be your wife—not even pity or guilt—that it is only Violet you want.'

He shook his head. She was right. He would not insult her intelligence by denying that and, as proud as she was, her pride would make her oppose him. 'I care enough about you to be hurt and angry by the appalling way you have been treated by your neighbours. You do not deserve that.'

'No, I don't—and I thank you for your concern. Your honourable nature is to be applauded, but you don't have to feel under any obligation to marry me.'

'I don't.'

Melissa's chin lifted and she glared at him. 'I told you I do not want to marry you. Do you, in your arrogance, assume I will change my mind?'

'It has been known for some women to do so.'

'And I am telling you that I am not most women.'

'I know that,' Laurence said, staring at the scornful young woman who was regarding him down the length of her pert nose and felt a glimmer of respect that she would dare to take him to task over what he was offering, which was to her advantage. 'I am aware that arrogance is one of my least attractive points, but I assure you I do have some good qualities to counter-balance the bad.'

'Really! I would not have known. Looking back on our encounter in the Spring Gardens, I cannot deny that I was equally to blame for what happened between us. But I was just a girl with no experience of what life was like away from my home.'

'You are no simpleton, Melissa. You must have thought of the consequences.'

'Consequences?' There was a distinct edge to her voice. 'I did—fleetingly—but marriage to a man of substance who would treat me with all respect and cherish me into the bargain did not enter my head. And I am convinced that at the time my vested interests did not come very high in your thoughts. I am sure I need say no more. You knew your state of mind better than I.'

Laurence had the grace to look abashed as he took her meaning.

'When I saw you I confess I was instantly smitten...' she laughed bitterly '...and how ridiculous is that? How stupid does that make me sound? How could I have known that I was about to fall prey to a degenerate libertine?'

Laurence's face tightened. 'As I recall you were not averse to my advances. But it's too late for recriminations. The deed is done and there is no going back.' He looked at her hard. 'I have many faults, Melissa, but walking away from my mistakes is not among them. You have already expressed your reluctance to have anything further to do with me quite frankly. Do not go on to impugn my honour as a gentleman.'

She looked away, then back again. 'I apologise.

My criticism was unwarranted. I did not mean to insult you.'

'I mean what I say. You are mistaken when you accuse me of trying to inflict my authority on you. Nothing was further from my mind. The way I see it you gave birth to my child—my daughter. I cannot walk away and pretend she does not exist. Whatever your thoughts, Melissa, I am not here to hurt you. I am here to make amends. I am older than you—a man of the world. You were a naive young woman. I should have known better and I deeply regret what I did. I have no desire to see you disgraced. What I am suggesting is a fair offer.'

'Fair?' she retorted, her heart beating so fast as she prepared to argue her case further. 'You haven't even had the grace to ask me formally to be your wife. Despite what we—what we did,' she said, almost choking on the words and embarrassed to be speaking of something so intimate in the presence of her parents, 'you are still a stranger to me. I don't know if I want to marry you.'

'Then I trust you will let me know when you have made up your mind. It is of great concern to me.'

'Yes, I suppose it is, but we were doing nicely before you came along.'

'For now, maybe, but what of the future?'

'Future? What future?'

'Your future. Violet's future.'

'We'll manage.'

Laurence looked down at the proud young woman in her worn gown cradling her child. He could feel the noose of matrimony tightening around his neck—a noose of his own making. 'It is a dilemma, to be sure. I took the innocence of an inexperienced girl which effectively destroyed all your chances of having any sort of respectable life of your own. With no husband to lighten your load, you will be carrying the burden of what we did for as long as you live. Unintentionally I have inadvertently, but effectively, destroyed your future. I am Violet's father. I would like us to raise her together.'

Melissa frowned, giving him a hard, sceptical look. 'Why? I will not have my destiny or that of my child dictated by circumstance. Is it pity or guilt that has prompted you to asked me to be your wife—to do the honourable thing?' she demanded.

He shook his head. 'I might have known you would suspect this—and as proud as you are, your pride would make you oppose me. I care enough about you to be hurt by all you have had to endure since you discovered you were to bear my child—and from what I have seen of our daughter—well, what can I say? Only that now I have seen her I cannot bear the thought of not having her in my life—to see her grow.'

'You don't have to marry me to do that. I will not stop you seeing her any time you want.'

Having heard enough, the Baroness stepped forward. Behind the face of dignified respectability, the ambitious mother had taken over, wanting only the very best for her only daughter and determined both to avoid further scandal and to make the best out of an intolerable situation.

'Be sensible. Melissa. It is because of your disobedience in the past and your determination to flout the rules that govern the lives of respectable young ladies that you find yourself in this unenviable situation in the first place. By any moral code you are disgraced. If you imagine for one minute that any self-respecting gentleman will consider marrying you in the future then you are mistaken. The way I see it there is only one way out of this. If you want respectability then you must take what Lord Maxwell is offering and be grateful.'

Melissa stiffened with indignation at her mother's harsh rebuke. She had become accustomed to the fact that she would never marry, that no man would take on a woman who had fallen so far from grace and given birth to an illegitimate child. Now, out of the blue had come this force, this transformation which had caused her heart to perform a whole new beat, to be moved by one man and no other. A man who did not want her. A man who was prepared to marry her for no other reason than to get his hands on her daughter—their daughter. It was not to be borne—she could not.

'That is not fair. You are asking me to enter into a binding contract that will change my life—to wed a man I don't know.'

'You knew him well enough to let him get you with child,' her mother reproached pointedly.

'You must see what I am suggesting is sensible,'

Laurence pressed. 'I am asking you to do this—if not for yourself or your parents, then to do it for our daughter. Will you be my wife, Melissa? There really is no way out of this for either of us.'

Melissa looked at him, her emotions running riot inside her. He was staring down at her, his profile harsh, forbidding. She knew what a shock all this must be for him and she had no doubt that from the moment he had discovered that Violet was his daughter he had been thinking hard for some way out of the situation he had inadvertently created all those months ago when he had answered the call of his lust and wandered off with her into the trees of the Spring Gardens. She also suspected that there was an anger simmering away beneath that tautly controlled façade of his.

He didn't want her—she had no illusions about that. For reasons of his own he wanted Violet. While most men shunned their illegitimate offspring, Laurence Maxwell quite obviously felt quite differently about it.

'Your wife?' she uttered quietly, his words causing her more shamed anguish than anything he had said to her. 'But how can you want that? How can you respect a woman who was so deficient in morals that she could give herself to a man as I did?' This was true. No woman of any class would ever be so forward as to do what she had done, to encourage the advances of a man who was a stranger to her.

'If I had any doubts about your morality or that Violet is not my daughter, then I would not be here now.'

Laurence looked down at his pink-cheeked daughter and touched her cheek. 'But you were innocent and she has the mark—that's proof enough that she is my daughter—and see, she's smiling at me. She does not share your aversion to a marriage between us.'

Melissa looked down at Violet. She was indeed smiling at him—and gurgling. Traitor, she thought, scowling at her daughter. How could she do that? She felt betrayed by her own daughter. 'Don't flatter yourself. She smiles at everyone.'

Never had she imagined she would be envious of her offspring when Laurence caressed her daughter's cheek—but, no, she thought defiantly, she didn't want him to touch her ever again. Something inside her snapped, something small and rebellious. Raising her head imperiously, she was aware that a tiny part of her was tempted to fall in with his plans, to do anything to please him, but she would not be bullied. Looking at her parents' expectant faces, she knew they wanted nothing more than for her to agree to what Laurence was suggesting, but she was not so easily won over.

She asked herself why she was being like this? Laurence should have been her prince, her knight in shining armour, come to rescue her from the scandal of raising a child—his child—unsupported by a husband. But he did not in the least care for her and he never would, and her heart was laid waste in a pitiless manner by knowing that. But so what? Her heart could not reason, so she sought the logic of her mind instead. Yes, she was hurt, aggrieved by his indifference to her, but would life be so terrible if she married him? She was never going to love anyone else, that she was sure of, and she had Violet to consider in all of this.

The stigma of her child's birth had struck a bitter note in the local community. People they had known for years avoided them. Their closest friends had grown guarded. Innocence, she had learned, was a technicality when loose morals were involved. However many times she told herself to live in the moment, at High Meadows there was little escape from the impact of the past. Did she want her daughter to grow up without a father to guide her, to love her? No, she could not do that to Violet, so why would she not want to take this way out?

Melissa knew it would be a great joy for her father and a triumph for her mother if she accepted this strange proposal of marriage, something the Baroness could boast about in her circle of friends, and she silently reprimanded herself for feeling put out by it. Perhaps it would be good for Violet to be raised elsewhere.

'Isn't marrying me a bit extreme?' she said, continuing to argue, though not as forcefully now. 'Is not the custom for men in your position to pay women off for what we did? I will accept your support for Violet, but marrying you is something else entirely and wholly unnecessary to my mind.'

He frowned. 'Is that what you want, Melissa—for me to pay you off as I would a mistress? Believe me, there is nothing respectable in that. In fact, quite frankly, I find it rather vulgar to even consider it.

Marrying me is the only possible solution. If you wish to continue the argument, then consider Violet. She will have to partake of the disgrace of her illegitimacy and any hope she has of marrying well in the future will also be dashed. Can you live with that on your conscience as well as depriving her of her father?'

She hesitated, struggling against the insidious feeling of surrender which was steadily crushing her. Then came the realisation that she had no option other than to agree with him.

'We will be married,' he said abruptly, clearly reading her acquiescence in her face. Her expression turned to one of resentment. 'Don't look so put out. It may not be so bad. We may rub along well together, but the child must come first. You do see that?'

It was not what she wanted to hear. *Rub along!* That was not how she saw a relationship between a husband and wife, but she relented. 'Yes—yes, I do.'

'What passed between the two of us doesn't matter now. I don't matter and neither do you. But Violet didn't ask to be born and she does matter. I cannot abandon my own child and still live with myself.'

'Nevertheless I cannot quell the feeling that a marriage based on such a beginning—without love—is a prelude to disaster,' she muttered.

'It needn't be. Are you afraid of me, Melissa?'

Regardless of the raw emotions quivering through her, Melissa shook her head. She wasn't afraid of him—she was suddenly afraid of herself. 'No,' she said. 'I'm not afraid of you.'

'Good, because you have no reason to be. Love has

no place in marriage. In our world, marriages are generally arranged for profit and gain—but I grant you there are exceptions. Our marriage will be what you and I make it. We must make sure the advantages far outweigh any difficulties that may arise.'

They regarded each other in silence. Melissa felt her stomach sink. It would seem that her position was inescapable. She took a steadying breath. There was little point in worrying about marriage to him and what it would mean for her and Violet just now. She was in this situation so she would have to make the best of it. The whole farce of this marriage was to secure Violet's future. Her mother was right. Violet would need her father and Melissa's own personal feelings were not a priority. She was the first to concede defeat with a sigh and an imperceptible inclination of her head.

'Very well. I will do as you wish,' she said, reluctantly yielding to his authority as her future husband and the father of her child. 'Now please excuse me. Violet is tired. I must put her down for a nap.' She moved to the door, saying over her shoulder, 'I will leave you to discuss the details with my parents.'

Most put out that Melissa had walked away from him, Laurence followed her, halting her as she opened the door. She fixed him with a gaze that was full of confusion and fear—fear of what? The future? Of him? It was also naked and sad. 'Must you leave? My business is with you. Do you think this gives me any pleasure?' he asked quietly, so her parents couldn't overhear.

'No,' she replied equally softly, her expression bland. 'I don't suppose it does.'

'Melissa, look at me.' He waited until she raised her head and met his gaze before speaking. There were shadows and lines of strain around her lovely eyes. No doubt he had put them there and he hated himself for it. 'We should talk,' he said gently, 'without pretence or dissimulation. Please believe me when I say that I only have your best interests at heart. You must realise there is no compulsion. I may have sounded decisive and forceful in what I think is the most sensible course to take regarding our future together, and I can imagine how alarmed you must feel, but do not feel that you are under any obligation—your wishes do matter to me.'

His approach and understanding of her feelings went a little way to putting Melissa at her ease and she found herself able to quell the sense of panic which had begun to tighten its hold. 'Yes—thank you.' At least he didn't utter words of love he didn't feel. Neither had he proposed to her with any show of sentimental affection, so she had accepted his proposal in the same unemotional way it had been offered.

'I am in the county visiting my good friend Sir Antony Bentley. I expect to be here another two weeks. You are acquainted with the family?'

Melissa had heard of the Bentley family. Apart from fleeting glimpses at one county event or another, she didn't know them. They were an old established family in the area and much respected. 'I know of them. We have met occasionally on hunts and so forth, but we do not socialise with the family.'

'I have known Antony all my life. Our mothers were friends and Antony and I attended Cambridge together. He was with me at the Spring Gardens when we met.'

Realisation dawned on Melissa. She recalled seeing him with a gentleman and that the gentleman had seemed familiar to her. She could not believe he was none other than their neighbour, although she had only seen him on occasion and thought nothing of it. 'Yes—I remember now. He seemed familiar at the time, but I could not place him then.'

'He will attend me at the ceremony. I will send to London for a special licence and the wedding will take place within the next two weeks—before I have to return to London. I would also like Violet to be baptised at the same time. At a later date I will formally adopt her as my daughter. Does that meet with your approval?'

Melissa stared at him, hesitating for a moment before she replied. He was looking at her with a gentle understanding and concern, yet he was completely different from the man who had made love to her with such intimate tenderness. They were not the same two people who had come together in the Spring Gardens when they had claimed nothing from each other but the pleasures to be enjoyed in each other's arms. That night she had been living purely for the moment. She hadn't fully realised that what was about to happen would determine her whole future.

'Yes. I can see no reason why not.' On that note she went out.

Living at High Meadows with no other thought than country pursuits, she had seen so little of the world at large and knew so little of men. She had attended just a few sedate gatherings on her visits to her Aunt Grace in London with her mother, but had not attended dances like most girls of her age. All she had to measure Laurence Maxwell against were her own brothers. But this man was not like either of them.

Laurence stood for a moment, looking at the closed door. Before coming to High Meadows he had thought long and hard about the steps he was about to take. In the end he had decided that if he wanted to know his daughter, there was only one thing that could be done. He must marry Melissa. In this he knew he must tread carefully. He could not deny that there was something about her that tugged at his senses and imbued him with a chivalric instinct to protect. He was entirely to blame for what had occurred between them. He should not have been foolish enough to interfere with an innocent and inexperienced girl. It could not have been easy for her being vilified for what he had done to her.

Returning to the Baron and his wife to discuss arrangements for the wedding, he thought it strange that the tension that had built within him since the previous day's encounter with Melissa was already dissipating, leaving him tired, but more at ease. He had not realised how much her criticism of him had hurt, had undermined his certainty that what he was doing was right.

Laurence insisted on a small, private ceremony, even though the Baroness had pressed for a larger ceremony to impress her friends. She did not approve of such haste, but, ultimately thankful he was willing to take responsibility for dishonouring Melissa, she relented before he left the house, conceding to his every wish.

As he rode away from High Meadows, he groaned as he relived the manner of his proposal of marriage. He had handled it like a thoughtless, heavy-handed idiot, without finesse or sensitivity. He understood only too well the chasm that stretched before them. There was so little common ground between them and no depth of acquaintance to hold them steady against adversity. He and Melissa needed time alone together to smooth out the issues between them. Nothing would be resolved otherwise. But he continued to brood as he rode, conscious that for the first time for many months, the face that filled his mind was not that of Alice.

Laurence arrived at Beechwood House at the same time as Antony, who had been visiting one of his neighbours. After handing their horses over to a groom, they proceeded to make their way to the house. Antony was Laurence's closest friend, a jovial good-natured man with a shock of sand-coloured hair and as different as night and day from Laurence. He was warm hearted and possessed of an enormous amount of charm, which endeared him to everyone and was the reason why he was invited to every fashionable occasion.

'How were things at High Meadows and your meeting with Baron Frobisher and his charming wife?'

'Pretty well as I expected,' Laurence replied. 'It could have been worse, I suppose. Baroness Frobisher came over as something of a dragon and rightly reproached me most severely for ruining her daughter. I'm not proud of what I did, Antony, and I can't blame her for being angry—although when I proposed marriage to Melissa she became more amenable.'

His statement was met with outright disbelief and then irrepressible humour. 'So, Miss Frobisher has succeeded where many others have failed.' He did not hide his delight.

'It would appear so.' Antony had been with Laurence at the Spring Gardens when he had met Melissa. When Laurence had returned from his ride the previous day he'd told him of their encounter—he'd also told him about Violet. To say that Antony and his wife Eliza had been surprised was an understatement. Laurence was pleased when Eliza stressed her delight and her eagerness to meet Melissa. They had known when he set off for High Meadows earlier that he intended to put things right, that he was honour bound to do the right thing by Melissa and propose marriage.

'Eliza will be delighted. She had high hopes that you would marry again one day. All I can say is, thank God! Do I congratulate you?'

'If you wish.'

'Then I do, most heartily. I well remember that night in the Spring Gardens. You had just returned from France after setting your business to rights in Marseilles. You hadn't been back in London twenty-four hours and already you were eyeing up the fairer sex.' Antony's face wrinkled into lines of humour and a wicked twinkle danced in his eyes. 'You made no secret of your interest in the young woman we now know was Melissa Frobisher—a neighbour of mine had I but known it. I did not recognise her—although I wouldn't, never having been introduced. So—are you ready to wed again—after Alice?'

Laurence considered Antony's question as he avoided his probing gaze. The answer was no, he wasn't. Widower and self-proclaimed single man from bitter experience, who, ever since the death of his wife and young son, regarded all women as being dispensable and irrelevant. In the wake of the death of his beloved son and the troubles that had erupted in France, his life at the time he had met Melissa was a disaster and there was little he could see in his future that would make it any brighter.

'Whether I am ready or not is irrelevant. I have no choice,' he replied brusquely. 'There was a time in my naive youthfulness when I had dreams and yearnings which I carried into adulthood and married Alice, foolishly believing she would make all my dreams of marriage and children come true. How stupid I was, how incredibly gullible.' Suddenly he grinned, a hint of the old wickedness in his eyes that Antony had not seen in a long time, but the underlying bitterness that had bedevilled his life since his marriage to Alice remained. 'I thought I might have a few more years of debauchery to enjoy before I settled for one woman, but things change—and Violet is quite adorable.'

As they made their way to the house the two friends made light conversation. Laurence appeared calm, but appearances could be deceptive, for there was a look behind his glacier grey eyes, like a volcano that was dormant but liable to erupt at any moment. He was used to women falling at his feet. Before his marriage to Alice he'd never been without a beautiful woman by his side and often they'd called him cold-hearted and disrespectful when he'd moved on to someone else. After the tragedy of Alice's accident, when her carriage had overturned, killing her and their son outright, everyone believed it was this that had made him steer clear of forming any new relationships, but it was something far simpler than that. Laurence had just never met anyone who could hold his interest for any length of time.

'You are to return to London soon,' Antony said, striving to match Laurence's long strides. 'How long before you go on to Winchcombe?'

'I'm not sure. I have business to take care of that can only be done in London. After that, we'll see. I intend to marry Melissa within two weeks. That will give her time to get used to the idea.'

'Eliza and I are also due to return to London shortly. She wants to extend her wardrobe and you know how she loves to shop.'

'You will be staying at Mortimer House?'

'With my own irascible brother-in-law? Of course we will, Laurence. Eliza sees little of Gerald as it is. I know what he did to you—and I cannot blame you for the way you feel about him, but for Eliza's sake I must be agreeable towards him.'

Something savage and raw stirred in the depths of Laurence's eyes, before they became icy with contempt. 'Of course you must and thank you, Antony. I appreciate your understanding.'

Antony and anyone else who knew Laurence and Sir Gerald Mortimer—two men who used to be as close as brothers—were well aware of what had induced the unconcealed dislike between the two; Gerald Mortimer was responsible for the breakdown of Laurence's marriage to Alice, which had ultimately led to her death. For a long time afterwards everything had ceased to matter to Laurence except the sensation of loss. He'd immediately taken ship for France where he didn't have to face the shell he'd become nor answer the unanswerable questions of grieving friends and relatives. In fact, he hadn't entirely wanted to live either. That time was a blur. He'd trusted his future to his business and fate.

'Eliza intends inviting a few neighbours over for dinner one evening before we all go to London, Laurence. Shall we extend the invitation to the Frobishers, do you think?'

Laurence thought about it and then nodded. 'Yes, I am sure they would appreciate that. It will also give me the opportunity to get to know Melissa a little better.'

* * *

Confused by all that was happening, by the changes that were suddenly turning her life upside down, a listlessness settled over Melissa on the approach to the wedding, unlike her mother who was openly delighted with the developments. It was all turning out far better than she had dared to hope for.

In a moment of desperation Melissa told her mother of her doubts about the marriage. She would have appealed to her father had she thought she would receive his support, but it would be useless. Life was much easier for him if he went along with his wife's wishes. He would simply dismiss Melissa's entreaties and retire to the stables. Her mother, who, unable to think of anything else but preparing for her daughter's prestigious marriage—more so when a fortune and a title were being dangled in front of her like a carrot to a donkey and was rushing forward instead of back and jumping in with both feet—was adamant that the wedding would go ahead.

'It is all arranged,' she told her firmly, unmoved by her passionate pleas. 'Be grateful. If it is love you are looking for, then I advise you to forget it. It is nothing but an unrealistic adoration that renders humans blind to life's unpleasantries. I am immensely fond of your father, as you know, but I have come to realise that it is wealth and power that protect us from life's hardships. Sometimes, Melissa, I cannot understand you. I cannot understand why you are against this. Most girls would give anything to marry a man of Lord Maxwell's ilk with a fortune and a title. From what

I understand he could buy his friend Antony Bentley fifty times over and never miss the cost. And his title—the Earl of Winchcombe—is vastly superior to anything I could ever have hoped for. Your marriage will put you at the forefront of wider society.'

None of that interested Melissa, but she grudgingly realised that marriage to Laurence was the most sensible course to take. She owed it to Violet—and there was no doubt that her parents would benefit from it in the long run. Half the time she was afraid to think about Laurence—certainly to feel more for him than she could possibly help.

Seeing him again had brought back many emotions and memories, memories to be avoided and ignored, but which could not be denied. Laurence Maxwell was capable of invading her mind in ways that could destroy her if she did not push the emotions down and bury them deep inside her. In truth, she'd wanted to run away when she'd recognised him. She had remembered his smile, how it had felt for him to hold her in his embrace as if it had been only yesterday. She'd been engulfed with memories of the months she'd spent thinking of him and now there were no words to describe how she felt about him. How could she have known that night in the Spring Gardens that she had sparked a situation that would eventually explode in her face?

But throughout it all the one thing, the one emotion, that refused to be silenced was regret. She would never regret the birth of her beautiful daughter. She would accept all Laurence was offering for the sake of Violet. But an unknown future loomed ahead for her.

Melissa tried to quell the nervous fears that were mounting inside her as the time for her to marry Laurence drew nearer. She was surprised when an invitation came for her to dine at Beechwood House along with her parents. She shuddered at the thought of it.

'I cannot do it. I cannot face everyone. It's bad enough when I meet people in the village and at church, having to endure judgemental looks and condemnation—but to be present at a dinner at Beechwood House is a step too far.'

'You can do it and you will,' her mother said, not to be denied the opportunity or the pleasure of socialising with their more affluent neighbours. 'Your father and I will be with you and you have the spirit to withstand whatever they will put you through. If you are seen out and about as the future wife of Lord Maxwell, it will soothe the gossip your scandalous conduct has caused and help stem the gossip as to your future until the next unfortunate young lady falls from grace and they will lose interest in you.'

And so Melissa gave in.

Chapter Three

Beechwood House was the residence of the Bentley family. It was the first time the Frobishers had been invited to enter. Situated in a low valley, it presented a stirring sight. The Baron and his family were honoured to be invited as Lord Bentley's guests. Baroness Frobisher was in her element. Attired in their best finery, they travelled in their carriage, approaching over a hump-backed bridge that spanned a wide stream and approached up a long, curved drive to the front of the house. The closer the carriage carried Melissa to Beechwood House, the more vulnerable and weakened she became, feeling this was very much Laurence's environment, rather than hers.

Servants assisted them out of the carriage and escorted them into the house. Looking around her, Melissa stood in the splendid oak-panelled hall already filled with guests—maybe thirty or more—and with servants flitting among them. Some she recognised as neighbours. Those who did not wish to distance themselves from her parents were polite and courteous, but Melissa couldn't fail to notice the censorious way people looked at her. Painfully aware of the extent of her disgrace, she responded mechanically to the few cold greetings addressed to her.

Determined to put on a brave face and keeping her head high, in a state of consuming misery she stood beside her parents, watching everyone greet each other, while drowning in humiliation and making a magnificent effort to pin a smile on her face and avoid the malicious eyes that made her skin burn. Being part of such an elite gathering made her realise all the more that an alliance with Lord Maxwell would be a remarkable triumph for her mother. Her nerves were already at full stretch as she watched Lord Antony Bentley approach them.

After greeting her parents warmly, he then turned his attention to Melissa.

Melissa dropped a conventional curtsy, lowering her eyes, her eyelashes touching the soft flush which had suddenly sprung to her cheeks. Knowing Antony Bentley was fully aware of the events in the Spring Gardens between her and Laurence made it impossible for her to conceal her embarrassment. Seeming to read her mind and to put her at her ease, he reached for her hand, his handsome, boyish face breaking into a brilliant, reassuring smile and his blue eyes twinkling with delight.

'Your servant, Miss Frobisher,' he said, bending over and pressing a gallant kiss on the back of her hand. 'And may I say I am truly delighted to meet you at last, having heard all about you from Laurence—and being neighbours, so to speak. In fact, I'm most surprised we haven't had occasion to be introduced before now.'

'Thank you for inviting us tonight,' Melissa replied. 'It was thoughtful of you.' She liked Antony Bentley at once. He was both amiable and charming and his eyes sparkled with humour.

'Not at all. Consider this a betrothal celebration if you like,' he said quietly so as not to be overheard by over-attentive ears. 'I was pleased to oblige. Ah, this is Eliza, my wife,' he said, taking the hand of an attractive woman who had appeared by his side. He drew her forward. 'I am sure you two will become well acquainted. Laurence will no doubt tell you how my wife keeps us all on the straight and narrow,' he said on a teasing note, casting his wife a fond look.

Melissa looked at the tall, slender young woman dressed in a fashionable gown of saffron silk, wishing she had paid more attention to her own appearance. Sir Antony's wife was a pretty brunette, with a delicately arched nose and winged brows over light blue eyes, lively and interested.

'What a pleasure it is to meet you at last, Melissa—I may call you Melissa?'

'Yes—I would like that.'

'Thank you—and you must call me Eliza. Laurence has talked about you so much that I feel as if I know you already.'

'Oh,' Melissa said, smiling. 'Well, that must have been very boring for you, so I apologise.'

'Not at all. It's obvious how much he admires you.'

'Really? Forgive me if I seem surprised. You see—I am sure it will come as no surprise that Laurence and I have been thrown together wholly by circumstance. He—does not know me at all well.'

'There is no need to explain to me how you and Laurence met,' Eliza said, lowering her voice to a conspiratorial whisper, 'when he caught the eye of a pretty girl in the Spring Gardens. I am well aware of it and have to say that it beats the usual, boring form of courtship. But however it came about, I cannot suppress my exultation that, by your actions, it has prompted Laurence to take a more serious interest in marriage once more.'

Try as she might, Melissa couldn't suppress her smile. 'The circumstances were such that he was left with little choice. I—am aware he is a widower, but I know nothing about his first wife.'

The smile melted from Eliza's lips and a sadness entered her eyes. 'I am sure you will come to know all about her in time. Laurence must be the one to tell you about what happened to Alice, but I must advise you that it is painful for him to reflect on the past.'

'So you will not enlighten me?'

'As I said, it is not for me to do so.' Eliza took a breath and shook her head, as if she wanted to say more.

There was some history there, Melissa thought, and she was tempted to probe further. But it wasn't her business and she knew there was no point in pressing Eliza to reveal more than she wanted. If she felt like talking, she would, probably at some time in the future and when they were better acquainted.

'I understand. I would not ask you to betray his confidence.'

'It may surprise you to know that you are the first woman he has shown a serious interest in since Alice's unfortunate death. I am well pleased that you and Laurence are to be married. I can imagine it will draw considerable attention in London—and at Winchcombe—in fact, it has happened with such speed that I cannot believe it myself. You have a daughter also, I hear. I am eager to meet her.'

'Violet. She is quite adorable, even though I do say so myself.'

'She is very dear to you, I am sure. I understand that you are to go to London the day after the wedding. We will be travelling down ourselves so I look forward to seeing you there before Laurence whisks you off to Winchcombe—which is a beautiful house. You will love living there.'

Melissa was completely taken with the easy friendliness of this attractive woman and accepted the feeling as mutual as Eliza's slender fingers squeezed her own before releasing them and excusing herself.

Laurence stood at the top of the stairs, a solitary, brooding figure looking down with a bored expression on his handsome face at the scene below him, then he saw Melissa enter with her parents and his heart lurched. Though he had made every effort to resist her appeal, he could feel the meagre store of his resolve waning. He paused to observe her. From a distance, witnessing her humiliation at first hand and knowing he had had a hand in her downfall, he realised just how difficult her situation was and was mortified that it was because of his doing. It was indeed brave of her to come here tonight, showing herself in the face of so much hostility. As a result of her transgression, she was at the mercy of an unforgiving society and, had he not offered her marriage, then she would probably have lived out her life in shamed seclusion at High Meadows.

Attired in a gown the colour of deep rose and decorated with lace and ribbons, which he suspected had been worn on many an occasion, her dark hair gleaming beneath the candles' glow and drawn up and away from her face and arranged in simple curls, she looked incredibly lovely. But standing behind her parents, she seemed on edge, her face pale. He was glad to see Antony and Eliza make themselves known to her, but seeing how their other guests favoured her parents and shunned her, he was furious. Proceeding to descend the stairs, he managed to appear superbly relaxed, for if he was going to make things right for her it was important to play out a perfect charade and appear casual. Since he couldn't stop the malicious tongues vilifying her, he had to turn it about, to ensure the attention on her was directed in a way he wanted it to be since she was to be his wife.

Melissa's heart skipped a beat when she saw Laurence approaching at a leisurely pace, experiencing the thrilling depths to which her mind and body was stirred whenever she was in his presence. Radiating a strong masculine appeal, he was unsmiling, his dark hair and the immaculate black clothes he wore making him seem like a sinister-looking figure indeed. Every inch of his tall frame positively radiated raw power, tough, implacable authority and leashed sensuality. He walked with an easy stride until he stood before them, inclining his head in polite greeting, his silver-grey eyes as clear as crystal. The trouble was, now she had agreed to be his wife, it was as if everything inside her was out of control, but where this man was concerned she couldn't help herself. She was not unaware that his interest in her had drawn everyone's attention.

When he halted in front of her he bowed, smiling at her, but it was to his friend that he spoke. 'I see you have made Miss Frobisher's acquaintance, Antony.'

'It has been my pleasure,' Antony replied, 'and you were right, Laurence. She is quite charming. I do believe your lovely lady has drawn everyone's attention.'

Laurence glanced around and noticed as he did so several people turn rapidly away in embarrassment at having been caught gaping.

'Now—please excuse me,' Antony said, looking towards his wife, who was moving about the guests. 'My wife is beckoning.'

Melissa watched him walk away. For what seemed an eternity, she stood perfectly still, existing in a state of jarring tension, clinging to her composure as she waited for Laurence to speak to her. At that moment she was sure that there were no eyes in all the world that shone brighter than those which looked down into hers. As she stared into the translucent depths, it was easy for her to imagine a woman being swept away by admiration for him without a single word being uttered. A slow, appreciative smile worked its way across his face as his eyes leisurely roamed over her body. The unspoken compliment made her blood run warm. Taking her arm, he led her away from her parents.

'You look entrancing,' he said in a quiet voice. 'I'm delighted you were able to join us. I can imagine the invitation came as something of a surprise. I should have warned you, but there was no time. Eliza was keen to meet you before the wedding.'

'It was kind of her. I thought it was your doing.'

'I implied I would appreciate them making your acquaintance before the ceremony. It was Eliza who suggested a dinner—inviting some close neighbours would give your father the opportunity to announce our betrothal. Would you approve of that? After witnessing their treatment of you, I think it especially needful tonight.'

Inhaling deeply and taking a firm hold of herself, she nodded. 'As you wish. It will certainly please my mother to have it out in the open.'

'Personally I don't care a damn what people think, but, no matter what you believe, it is not my wish to cause more gossip that will hurt you.'

Her face working with the strength of her emotion, which had, for the moment, got the better of her, Melissa gazed up at him. His eyes shone softly down into hers. His words, spoken quietly and with gravity, touched her deeply. 'I'm afraid it's a little late for that. You have seen how I am being treated. When Violet was born, they might as well have tarred and feathered me and tied me to a tree.'

At any other time Laurence would have laughed at the image her words conjured up in his mind, but now he would not insult her by doing so, for the strain of what she had gone through—was still going through—was there on her lovely, troubled face for him to see.

'You have been treated harshly. You did not deserve that. For what it's worth I am sorry and I am determined to do my upmost to put it right. I will speak to your parents before we go in to dinner.'

'Sir Antony and Eliza have made me feel welcome. I appreciate that.'

'They were astonished when I told them we are to be married—although they cannot fail to be taken with Violet when they meet her. When they were made aware of the circumstances that have brought about our betrothal, they agreed that I am doing the right thing. Now come and meet some of the other guests before we go in to dinner.'

She hung back. 'Do I have to?'

His slow smile held the charm that had drawn many a lady into his arms before his marriage. Taking her hand, he tucked it into the crook of his arm. 'Consider it necessary—to please me.'

Laurence seemed blind to the conspiratorial smiles Antony and Eliza exchanged and his manner was that of pride as he calmly presented Melissa to the house guests—a polite, friendly gathering—who were suddenly willing to set aside their displeasure concerning Melissa's past conduct in the face of such a distinguished and wealthy gentleman's preference for her company.

The meal was a relaxed, informal affair and extremely civilised. Melissa found herself seated beside Laurence, who was attentive to her every need throughout the meal. The gay and constant chatter lightened the mood somewhat. Looking for unease on Melissa's face, Laurence found nothing but calm and the soft glow of light in her lovely eyes. Despite her inexperience, she spoke easily and with confidence to those around her. There was surprise followed by congratulations when Baron Frobisher announced the betrothal and it pleased Laurence to see how his future wife became lively and amiable, a lovely young woman in possession of a natural wit and intelligence.

Seeing her as she was tonight, her face flushed after partaking of a small glass of wine, her eyes sparkling in the light of the chandelier suspended above the table, Laurence thought she was still a girl in many ways. A girl he was intrigued by, a girl who had it in her to entice and arouse him—a young girl who had been hurt and paid the price for what he had done to her. He had not set out to seduce her, nor she to trap him. She had thought she loved him, deeply and sincerely and with all her young heart. And so they had come together in that age-old way and he had taken her from girl to woman. The simple truth was that he had amused himself with her and for that he was deeply ashamed.

'Are you glad you came?' he asked, bending his head close to her ear.

Turning, she met his eyes and saw a kindly warmth in the silver depths. 'It's turned out better than I could have hoped.'

'And no doubt you're wondering what all the fuss was about.' He chuckled at her questioning bewilderment. 'Your mother told me you were concerned about appearing among your neighbours and that you took some persuading to come tonight.'

'My mother has an unfortunate habit of saying too much and speaking her mind far too often,' Melissa said crossly.

'Think nothing of it. I can see you have set the gentlemen agog and tomorrow all the ladies' tongues will be wagging, telling their neighbours how delightful is the lovely Melissa Frobisher after all. So you see, some success will have come out of tonight. Now, since I know virtually nothing about my future wife, tell me about yourself.'

Melissa stared at him. 'Why—what is it you wish to know?'

'Anything—anything at all about your life before we met. I've always prided myself on being a good judge of character and I'd like to know if my assessment of you is correct.'

Melissa laughed, making the loose curls about her head dance as she shook her head. 'I think we will have to live together for some time for you to do that. If I don't want you to think ill of me, then how will you know that what I tell you will not be out of self-interest?'

His shadowed smile was lazy as he held her gaze. 'Try me. I am not gullible enough to believe an interpretation of events that are untrue. Besides, I've already decided that you are a woman of passion and opinions, that you have the most stubborn nature and that good behaviour hasn't always been an abiding principle in your life.'

She sighed and looked at him with mock gravity. 'That is a fair assessment. I cannot argue with it. I have always been contented and blissfully unaware of the vicissitudes of life. It may shock you to know that having decided from an early age that I had no use for the lessons in French and sums, or improving my writing and tuition on all the things a young lady of quality should learn, often evading my governess, I would saddle my horse and ride to places where no one could find me.'

'I suppose galloping hell for leather all over the countryside was your idea of fun.'

She flashed him a smile. 'It was exactly that—although I've had to rein in my enthusiasm since Violet came along. In exasperation, my mother would scold me most severely, wondering why it was that her wayward, wilful daughter caused more ructions, more aggravation than her two older brothers put together. They were both even tempered, whereas I possessed a strength of will my mother called stubbornness. Only my father, who found me good-humoured, lovable, maddening and frequently defiant, understood me. Mother frequently accused him of letting his daughter run rings around him.'

'And did you?'

'Yes...' she laughed '... I'm afraid I did.'

Her laughter was a husky, rich sound and Laurence remembered how it had drawn him to her in the Spring Gardens, when she had danced and laughed and tossed her head, her lovely amber eyes aglow with warmth. In the space of time they had been seated at the table, this enchanting young woman had made him feel more light-hearted than at any time in the last three years. Her manner was not flirtatious, but rather the result of naturally high spirits. Her eyes sparkled with merriment that was contagious. She fascinated him. In fact, he couldn't remember being so intrigued by a woman for a long time.

After she'd drained a small glass of wine, her inhibitions no longer as restricted as they had been when she'd arrived, Laurence was amused to see her wade through the delicious courses that were placed before her.

'For a young lady of such slender proportions, you have a remarkably robust appetite.' His eyes narrowed and one dark eyebrow rose in amusement.

'I didn't realise how hungry I was.'

'So it would seem.'

'Please don't mind. I've eaten nothing all day. I

was too nervous about tonight to eat—and I've been busy.'

'Doing what?'

'Getting ready for tonight. I couldn't make my mind up what to wear—not that I have an extensive wardrobe, you understand, but I wanted to look my best.'

'I can't imagine it taking that long, although I must admit that I find the end result extremely pleasing.'

His compliment brought a flush to her cheeks and she liked the way he was smiling at her as he said it. There was a curl to his mouth which she was not quite sure how to decipher, as if it gave him immense delight to tease her—not to be hurtful, but with a wicked smile and a glint in his eye which she could not interpret. She sensed he was a complex, deep-layered man who allowed no one to see the hidden fathoms of himself.

And then the evening was over. When they had said goodnight to their hosts and her parents had climbed into the carriage, Melissa hung back a moment to say a private goodnight to Laurence. Gazing at the cool, dispassionate man standing before her, looking so powerful, aloof and completely self-assured, she smiled up at him.

'Not only are you an accomplished businessman—oh, Eliza lost no time in making me aware of your accomplishments,' she told him when he raised a surprised eyebrow, 'you also appear to have a gift for strategy and subtlety. Why, who would have thought that these are the same people who have shunned me for the past twelve months. I have not seen Mother look so animated in a long time. She could not be more delighted at the way things have turned out—for which we have you to thank.'

Taking her hand and raising it to his lips, he smiled down at her, relieved that the evening had gone well and a beginning had been made to their future relationship. 'I do my best,' he replied. Unable to resist the temptation she presented him with, he drew her close, savouring her warmth and her softness. So alluring was the curve of her lips that he was tempted to prolong the embrace, but he chose instead to keep it gentle and persuasive, merely brushing her lips with his own.

'Goodnight, Melissa. When we see each other again it will be at the church.'

On the journey back to High Meadows Melissa was content to sit back and let her thoughts drift while her mother talked non-stop about the evening, seeming unaware that her words fell on deaf ears. Melissa's head was filled with thoughts of her betrothed, unable to really believe that very soon she would be his wife. She found herself contemplating what her future would be like married to Laurence Maxwell. Had she really agreed to be his wife? She wanted it, this came to her in a blaze of honesty, but at the same time she shrank from the prospect.

Out of curiosity she wanted to know more about Alice. She wondered what kind of marriage he had enjoyed with his late wife. He had mentioned her, but told Melissa nothing about her, which could mean that he had loved her to distraction or quite the opposite. Never having experienced the loss of anyone close, she imagined that the death of a loved one had deep roots and cast long shadows. Its impact could be stored away, but not forgotten. Nothing would ever be the same again. Melissa was afraid of failing in her duties as a wife—and afraid that Laurence would measure her unfavourably against Alice.

'I am to commit my entire life into the keeping of a man I do not know—except in the carnal sense,' she said to Daisy, her personal maid, as she helped her prepare for bed. 'Oh, Daisy! When Violet was born I gave up thinking I would meet a man who would want to marry me—and certainly not Violet's father. I cannot believe this is happening to me. I have to ask myself if I am doing the right thing.'

'Of course you are, miss. You are about to marry the most handsome man I have ever laid eyes on. There are plenty of women who would give their eye teeth to be in your position, so don't even consider changing your mind. You must look on this as a golden opportunity. Don't let it slip through your fingers. If you do, mark my words you'll live to regret it. Besides, you can't deprive Violet of her father. She would never forgive you.'

Melissa sighed. 'I know.' Her eyes clouded over and her face became serious as she quietly contemplated Daisy's words. 'He would not be marrying me were it not for Violet, Daisy, I know that. I have to wonder what marriage to him will be like. He is so proud and arrogant and intimidating at times—but I think deep down there is so much more to him than that. He is duty bound to right the wrong between us and he simply adores Violet. As young as she is, she already has him eating out of her hand.'

'And who wouldn't, miss? But it is scarcely to be wondered at that he is proud and arrogant. A man as rich as he is, and with everything in his favour, can afford to be. I have heard that among his friends he is an agreeable, good-humoured man—but I have also heard he has the most violent temper. You would do well not to aggravate him before you are married, otherwise he might change his mind and marry someone else instead.'

Melissa gave her a sharply suspicious look in the mirror. 'I doubt it. He's not prepared to miss out on the chance of being Violet's father. And anyway—how do you know so much about him all of a sudden?'

'I just happen to know some of the servants at Beechwood House, miss. He's often visited in the past and the staff have got to know him quite well.'

Melissa knew how Daisy with her lively disposition loved to gossip and socialise in her time away from her duties at High Meadows, when she contrived to learn what news she could about people, so if anyone knew anything about what was going on in the area it was Daisy. 'What else have you heard about him? Is there anything I should know about before I pledge my life to him?'

'Not really—only that he was once married, which you already know about. His wife, who I believe was a great beauty, died several years ago, leaving him a widower.'

'I wonder what happened?' Melissa wondered aloud. 'No doubt I shall find out in time. I'm glad you're coming with me, Daisy. I don't think I could bear it if you didn't.'

Daisy laughed, drawing the brush through Melissa's long, curling hair. 'I can't wait to see what Winchcombe Hall is like, miss. Your life is going to be so different from what it is now. I wouldn't miss it for anything.'

Melissa sighed wistfully. Daisy was right. Laurence was handsome. In fact, he was the first man to stir her emotions and set her body aflame with desire. She wasn't sure she liked the way her heart was inclined to race when she recalled the occasion in the Spring Gardens when they had been together, when he had spoken smooth endearments into her ear, for it made her realise how vulnerable she was to his charm.

Over the following days everything was hurried along—what her bridal gown would be, clothes gone through that would be suitable for the new Lady Maxwell to wear—until her husband provided her with a wardrobe befitting his wife. There was no time for Robert and his family to journey from the north, or Henry from his ship, to see her wed.

The wedding took place at midday in the small village church where Melissa had worshipped all her life. Here she was to become a Countess—Lady Maxwell. The realisation of the title struck her anew. She rarely considered the fact that on their marriage, Laurence's status would become hers. Perhaps it was because of the uncertainty she still felt.

The local pastor presided. The special licence Laurence had obtained eliminated the necessity of the reading of the banns. Stiff and unsmiling and with a strange sense of unreality, Melissa walked down the aisle of the small village church with her arm through that of her father's. At the outset, Laurence had said he did not care to surround the ceremony with undue pomp. This suited Melissa perfectly, for she did not want to attract further attention to herself. But it was not the marriage she had envisioned. There were to be no festive celebrations and her gown was not the lavish extravagance of a bride. It was ivory and pale blue silk gauze, a gown that was not new, there being no time to hire a dressmaker to outfit her in the latest fashion, so she'd had to make do.

Melissa stood beside Laurence at the altar, aware of nothing but his close proximity. Glancing up at his darkly handsome features, and with his tall, powerful frame attired in a superbly tailored midnight-blue coat that accentuated his lean elegance and flawless white cravat, she thought that on the whole he was a man any woman would be proud to have for her husband—or lover. She fought the memory that thought aroused. Sometimes she forgot the incredible things they had done but then, at the mere mention of his name, they would come rushing back.

On this day, the most important day of a woman's

life, she thought that she had never felt so happy and content. With Laurence by her side she could not fail to continue to be so. Was it love she felt for him? Never having experienced anything of that nature in her life before she had met him, she had nothing to compare it with, so she thought she must be. It was the truth and she wanted to tell him that she loved him, but until he felt the same she would hold back. It was important to her that she was loved equally in return.

A quietness of expectation fell. All eyes were focused on the bride and groom. Even the pastor beamed at Melissa, in spite of the fact that he had joined in with the voices of condemnation of her transgression when Violet was born out of wedlock. Time stood still as they were swept into the marriage ceremony, but it seemed only a moment before Laurence was sliding a gold band upon her finger. It was a solemn, joyless affair, but thankfully all went smoothly as the pastor intoned the words that would bind her to Laurence for ever, although there was an aura of strain and unreality about it. There were a few raised eyebrows from friends and neighbours who had only recently been made privy to her betrothal. Just a handful of her parents' close friends attended, along with Eliza and Sir Antony Bentley.

And the pastor pronounced them man and wife in the eyes of God. With a smile, he then informed them that it was customary for the groom to seal the marriage by kissing the bride.

Laurence turned and looked down at his wife, his eyes gleaming with something that was so intense that

Melissa stiffened when he drew her towards him. His fingers moved around the delicate bones of her jaw. Bending his head, he claimed her mouth in a gentle kiss that brought a smile to the lips of all those present. At last his grip slackened and she could breathe. The ceremony was over, signed and sealed and legally binding until death did them part.

'Now it is time to baptise our daughter.' Taking Melissa's hand, he led her down the aisle to the font, where Daisy was holding a sleeping Violet. She did not open her eyes until the cleric poured water on her head, which she took exception to and began crying loudly. Taking her into his arms, with soothing words Laurence dabbed the water away.

Then the carriage was taking them back to High Meadows where the Baroness had laid on a small wedding breakfast. Alone with Melissa for the first time that day, from beneath hooded lids Laurence allowed his gaze to dwell on her. Melissa was his wife. He must not forget it, even though he knew nothing about her. It was his responsibility to care for her comfort and well-being. He remembered the vision he had seen walking down the aisle towards him bathed in sunlight, snatching his breath away, and he had been unprepared for the pride that had exploded throughout his entire body until he ached with it, for no bride had ever looked as lovely.

When he had offered her his hand, she had lifted her own and placed it in his much larger one. He had felt the trembling of her fingers and saw the anxiety in her large amber eyes. Immensely relieved that she hadn't decided to pull out of marrying him, he had given her hand a little squeeze in an attempt to reassure her. When they had sealed the vows that they had just made with a kiss, her lips had been pleasurably warm and had softened under his caress.

'How does it feel to be my wife—Lady Maxwell?'

As Melissa met his gaze, her mouth curved in a little smile. 'If you must know, I don't feel anything at the moment. It's difficult to take it all in. I feel no different to how I did before I left home.' She arched her brows in question. 'Should I?'

'I can think of plenty of females who would.'

'I don't doubt that, but I am not one of them. Titles are meaningless to me.'

He nodded slowly. 'Of course not. After all, you had no idea of my identity when we first met. You are very beautiful, Melissa,' he murmured, for so she was, and he watched as the colour flowed delightfully beneath her pale white skin and her eyes darkened with warmth.

'So are you,' she breathed.

Laughing softly, he reached across and took her hand, raising it to his lips. 'A lady is not supposed to say that to a gentleman.'

'Not even when that gentleman is her husband?'

'In which case, perhaps she can be excused. I thank you for the compliment.'

Back at High Meadows the guests partook of the wedding breakfast—savouries and delicate cakes washed down with champagne. Laurence wished for something stronger to drink, but repressed the urge just as he forced himself to receive the congratulations and polite good wishes of the guests he had not met before today.

Antony glanced at Laurence and Melissa and raised his glass in a gesture of a toast. 'To your future years together and wedded bliss.' He grinned.

Laurence cast him an ironic glance, but other than that, his features were perfectly composed. He always kept his emotions effortlessly under rigid control. At that moment, as he lifted his glass to his lips, he was feeling nothing stronger than a certain impatience to be away from the stilted conversation and tortuous celebrations among the handful of guests and the stifling atmosphere of High Meadows. He was impatient to leave for Beechwood House with Antony and Eliza where he was to spend the night without his bride. He was to return to High Meadows early the following morning, when he would leave for his house in London with his wife and daughter.

They had to make an early start if they were to make London before nightfall. Melissa bade a tearful farewell to the servants she had known all her life. It was particularly hard say goodbye to her parents, but they promised to visit Winchcombe as soon as it was convenient for them to do so.

By the time they were in the coach, Melissa was wondering if it was all a dream. Accompanied by Daisy and a fretful Violet, who didn't care for being so confined, they travelled to London in Laurence's large travelling coach. Thankfully, with the rocking of the coach, the child eventually fell asleep. Laurence occupied himself with some papers he had brought with him and absorbed himself in them most of the time.

Seated across from him, when she wasn't looking at the passing scenery Melissa found her gaze settling on him. Not for the first time she wondered what lay in store for her in London and her curiosity about his first wife grew. He seemed reluctant to talk about her and Melissa didn't want to pry. They didn't know each other very well and she felt there were limits to how much one should know about another person's life quite so soon. In the future when they knew each other a little better, there would be opportunities for him to tell her.

Seeing Daisy's eyes were beginning to close, Melissa took the sleeping Violet and settled her on her lap, telling Daisy to have a nap. The maid took no persuading and within seconds had joined Violet in sleep. Laurence set aside his papers and looked across at her.

'It must be hard for you leaving your parents. Is this the first time you have been without them?'

'Yes. I shall miss them, I know—and they are going to miss me and in particular Violet. You will have seen how they adore her.'

'Who could not? She is exquisite. You have brothers—two, I seem to recall you telling me.'

'Yes. Henry, who is the eldest, is a lieutenant in

the Royal Navy. He loves the life and has no intention of leaving the sea.'

'He is the son and heir?'

'Yes, but ever since he was a boy he's been in possession of a spirit of adventure. He was always lively and full of mischief and I loved him dearly. He always wanted to go to sea. I cried for weeks when he left. I missed him so much. Involving himself in the running of High Meadows and country matters held no interest for him. The war with France gives us constant worry that something might happen to him.'

'I can fully understand that. The war also affects merchantmen. I have it on good authority British merchant vessels and their cargos have been taken by privateers, which is a constant worry for me since I have vessels trading European goods with the West Indies.'

Melissa's opened wide in astonishment. 'Goodness! You have ships of your own?'

He laughed in the face of her surprise. 'It's what I do and it often takes me away for long periods. Tell me about your other brother?'

'Oh, Robert is quite different. He was more studious and serious than Henry. He is married to Charlotte and for the present is living in the north of England with her family. Her father does not enjoy the best of health and with Charlotte being the last of his offspring living close to the family home, he has become somewhat dependent on Robert. It's unusual, I know, but Henry has relinquished his claim as Father's heir. Robert will inherit High Meadows when the time comes. He loves it more than Henry. He's keen to return to put some order into it.'

'And you? Did you go to school?'

'Oh, no, nothing like that. I had a governess.'

'And what was she like—about a hundred, a tyrant who rarely spoke of anything other than the rudiments of education?'

'Good heavens, no.' Melissa laughed, a sound which was cool and crystal clear to Laurence. 'She was nothing like that. Miss Stanhope was a strict disciplinarian, but there was nothing to dislike about her. I have much to be grateful for, where she is concerned. I missed her dreadfully when she left—and she was nowhere near a hundred.'

'I was jesting,' Laurence said, his eyes twinkling, strangely unwilling to let her stop talking about her past. 'And your parents? You told me they are going to miss you and I can understand why.'

'Yes—especially Papa.'

'You are close to him, I could see that—and very much like him.'

'Papa has a penchant for anything with four legs. His passion for prime horseflesh is well known. In that we are alike.'

'Your mother doesn't share his passion?'

'No, she doesn't ride and rarely goes to the stables. She's susceptible to bites and stings and any creepy crawlies cast her way—which is her excuse. Do you keep horses at your London house?'

'You'll be happy to hear that I do—carriage horses—and I do take the opportunity to ride out in the park when I can. I'm sure there will be a mount there to your liking.'

'I imagine there will be. Do you come to London often?'

'Yes. Why do you ask?

'No reason—only—with Winchcombe as your family home in Surrey, does the time you spend in London justify you keeping a house there as well? There are hotels you could stay in.'

He smiled. 'What you say is true, but first of all most of my business is taken care of in the city and there is something to be said about maintaining one's investments—property prices are always rising and houses in Grosvenor Street are always popular. Another reason is because I can afford it and I don't like hotels.' This was true. Tough decisions and being ruthless in business and long-term investments had made him a wealthy man. He had taken a hit with the war in France, where he had warehouses in the south of the country, but he had foreseen the troubles and got out in time. 'I also have to take my seat in the House of Lords occasionally—more so with Europe in a state of turmoil.'

'Indeed. But you are not a politician in the professional sense?'

'No. It is simply that all peers of the realm have been trained to regard it as our right and duty to participate in governing the country. We enter Parliament as we do university and gentlemen's clubs.'

'It all seems very grand to me. And what do you debate in the House of Lords?'

'The issues at this time are many and varied—and of an extremely serious nature. But I am not required to spend all my time in the House of Lords—which is a relief since I am heavily committed to my business affairs.'

Chapter Four

It was a relief to all when they arrived in London in the late afternoon. Violet had woken from her sleep and was quite perky. Laurence looked at Melissa, knowing how anxious she was about entering the house and meeting the staff.

'Try not to worry,' he said softly. 'Try to relax. Though you might find your life here in London and later at Winchcombe different to your own life in Hertfordshire, remember that the people I employ are friendly and understanding. You will like them, I promise you.'

Melissa smiled at him nervously. When she stepped from the temporary haven of the coach, she would be stepping into a new world—which was evident when she entered the house. Like every other residence in Grosvenor Street, Laurence's town house was an imposing building. The door was opened by a footman and they walked into a high, spacious hall with an elegant staircase rising to the upper floors and a black and white marble floor. Melissa could not restrain an exclamation of approval, which brought a smile to Laurence's lips.

'My goodness!' she exclaimed. 'What a beautiful house.'

Laurence grinned. 'I'm glad you think so.'

Her arrival with Violet was expected. With great excitement servants were hovering in the hallway and leaning over the balustrade on the upper floor, hoping to catch a glimpse of their new mistress and the master's child—although how he came to have a daughter at almost a year old and everyone none the wiser was a mystery. They knew very little about their master's private life since the tragic death of his first wife. None of them realised that his new wife was quite unaware that her daughter was to take up residence in the nursery which had been occupied by the master's first offspring, Master Toby.

A tall, handsome woman in a plain black dress came to the fore, smiling broadly. 'I am Mrs Evans, the housekeeper. Welcome to your new home, my lady,' she said with a gracious smile. 'Did you have a pleasant journey?'

'Yes—thank you,' answered Melissa, her nervousness beginning to disappear.

'Perhaps your maid would like to take your daughter to the nursery. I have taken the liberty of appointing a nursery maid to look after her. Her name is Tansy. I am sure you will approve.'

Taking Violet from her mistress, Daisy carried the bright-eyed gurgling child—who was delighted by all the attention she was receiving—up the stairs to the nursery, leaving Laurence to introduce his wife to the staff.

Melissa tried to make a mental note of all their names, which, being so many, was no easy matter. They eyed her with a great deal of interest and with all the curiosity a stranger produced—especially when the stranger was their new mistress.

'Now come along,' Laurence said, taking her arm. 'Let me show you to your rooms.'

They went up the curving staircase to the landing where they had adjoining suites. Laurence disappeared into his own to prepare for dinner, leaving Melissa alone with a young maid called Sophie. Daisy was to continue as her own personal maid, but she was settling Violet into the nursery. With a wry smile on her lips, her eyes made a sharp assessment of the gown Sophie had quickly unpacked from her trunk and for the first time since entering the house felt a sharp twinge of disappointment. How she wished she had more fashionable attire to do justice to her new position.

When she was ready, Mrs Evans came to take her to the dining room, where her husband was waiting.

'It's a beautiful house, Mrs Evans,' she said, pausing to take a closer look at the paintings adorning the walls as they descended the stairs.

Reaching the bottom, she paused to look a little longer at the painting of a young woman in a beautiful scarlet gown, who seemed to be looking out of the painting straight at her. Her heart flipped over, for she knew immediately the identity of the subject. The perfect features, the deep blue eyes shadowed with dark lashes, which seemed to be laughing at the artist with obvious pleasure. It was painted by the hand of a master to catch all the vital beauty of the sitter. It was Alice, the woman Laurence had loved and lost. How plain and uninteresting Melissa thought she was in comparison—the woman who had been forced on Laurence through a sense of duty. Poor Laurence. What an unfortunate bargain he had made in order to secure his daughter.

'That was the master's first wife,' Mrs Evans explained.

'She was very beautiful, Mrs Evans.'

'Yes, she was. It was a tragedy what happened to her.'

'And who do we have here?' Melissa asked. For some reason which she could not explain, she had no wish to hear about her predecessor's attributes just then. Plenty of time for that later. She shifted her attention to the painting of a young boy which had been given pride of place. He was holding a puppy in his arms. Seeing a likeness to Violet in the small face, she said, 'I see Violet looks very like her father when he was a boy—if this is my husband.'

'Oh, no, my lady. This is Master Toby. Such a sweet boy.'

'Oh—a relative?'

'The master's son.'

Melissa drew a sharp breath and sent a shocked

look at the housekeeper. For a moment a deathly hush fell upon the hall. The word *son* caught Melissa's blurred attention. Her heart contracted. She stared with dazed shock at the painting, trying not to let Mrs Evans see how affected she was by this. But Mrs Evans was looking at her intently, as though to assess the effect of the bombshell she had unintentionally just dropped on her.

'Oh, dear! You didn't know he had a son?'

'His son?' The revelation shocked her deeply. She wanted to ask her more, to know where this child was now, but, feeling it was important that Laurence told her himself, she shook her head. 'No, Mrs Evans. I didn't know.'

'Oh, I see.' Clearly feeling that she had betrayed a confidence, Mrs Evans's expression became guarded. 'Well—things have happened in such a rush lately—what with the wedding and everything. He will not have kept it from you intentionally—he isn't like that. Lord Maxwell has had so much to contend with of late, but I am sure he will tell you all about Toby.'

Mrs Evans's answer was what Melissa would expect of a faithful servant. Her loyalty was evident and her defence of him intense. 'And the first Lady Maxwell? It must have been hard for him losing his wife.'

'It was a terrible time. He took her loss hard. He wasn't the same afterwards. As soon as the funeral was over he took off for France—he has business over there, you see—and with the troubles breaking out in that country to knowing how it would affect fury he had felt at the time boiling up inside him now just thinking about it, of how the discovery of his wife and son's deaths had sent a wave of emotion crashing over him, flooding his mind with a turbulent mixture of guilt, frustration, loss and love—guilt because he had not been there to protect his son. She looked at his handsome face with its stern, sensual mouth and hard jaw, but what she saw was a man tormented by the loss of his wife and son. Her heart ached for him. A lump of poignant tenderness clogged her throat and she moved to stand before him.

'You must tell me about him, Laurence.' Her mouth went dry and her heart began to beat in heavy, terrifying dread as she sensed that he was about to withdraw from her. 'I cannot imagine how you felt, but if anything should happen to Violet I would never recover from it. I know you are a very private person, but I am your wife. If you cannot open up to me, even if it is just a little, then it bodes ill for the future.'

He turned and looked at her. His face was expressionless. His eyes were empty, a glacial silver-grey remoteness that told her nothing of what he felt. 'You are right. You should know about Toby—but not now. Now is not the time.'

'And Alice?'

His face hardened. 'Not now.'

'Of course. I understand that losing both your wife and your child have left deep scars,' as yet unhealed, she thought sadly. It was an emotional burden he clearly still found difficult to bear. 'I can see

him, it provided him with something else to focus his mind on.'

Melissa stood for a moment, staring blindly at the painting of the child. Had Laurence's grief over his wife's death been so great that he hadn't wanted to live without her? Where was Toby now? She desperately wanted to know the answers, but she would not ask Mrs Evans to supply them on so personal a subject.

Melissa entered the candlelit dining room off the hall. Laurence was standing by the sideboard, pouring red wine into two glasses. Melissa was struck by his stern profile outlined against the golden glow of the candles. She saw a kind of beauty in it, but quickly dismissed the thought. It was totally out of keeping with what she had just learned. He turned when she entered and moved towards her, his narrow gaze sweeping her with approval. She closed the door and leaned against it. Her insides had gone cold with dread. Laurence glanced towards her.

'I hope you approve of your rooms. They...' He faltered. The grim expression on her face made him wary. 'Melissa? What is it?'

'When were you going to tell me about Toby?' she asked, trying not to think of the woman—his first wife—who had died not so very long ago, a woman who had borne him a child—a woman he must have loved and whom he still mourned. The thought was so immediate that she didn't even want to think about it, but she knew she must. 'Is it true that you have a son?' She expected him to refute her question, but he didn't. He stiffened, his jaw clenched so tightly the corded muscles stood out. He looked at her, his eyes turning to ice.

'Yes, I do—I did.'

No slap in the face could have hurt so much. Failing to understand just then what his words implied, a sudden weight fell on Melissa's heart at what was happening. She was stunned, bewildered, and a thousand thoughts raced across her brain and crashed together in confusion. Slowly she walked towards her husband, so distracted by her own rampaging emotions that she never noticed the sudden hardening of his face as he looked at her, as if he were bracing himself to meet a firing squad.

'I would have preferred you to tell me yourself instead of finding out from your housekeeper. You must have known you could not keep such an important matter from me. What were you thinking? Did you intend to hide him away from me?'

'I have not hidden him away.' Laurence's voice flared with what could have been pain. For a man usually so mentally astute, Laurence was too stunned to move. He shrank from the pain he suddenly had to confront and the hostility he was encountering in his wife.

Halting in front of him, she was trembling with anger, her hands clenched into fists by her sides. 'You have a son, Laurence—a son! Why have you kept this from me? For what reason? Or did you simply forget to tell me?'

'I didn't forget,' Laurence ground out, his face white with his own anger and emotions he was fighting to suppress. 'I should have told you, but it's a discussion I preferred not to have at present.'

'I see,' she said, determined to stand her ground. 'You have a son and yet you did not think I had a right to know when you asked me to marry you? How old was he when he posed for the painting in the hall—the little boy I thought was you when you were a child?—the features so like our daughter's. For heaven's sake, Laurence. I don't mind that you have a son—I welcome it, in fact—a brother for Violet is quite wonderful.'

Laurence's face twisted and darkened. 'He posed for the painting when he was three years old—just six months before he died.' Pushing a hand, which trembled through his thick hair, he took a step back, his face quite blank now. He felt that he was on dangerous ground. He'd kept everyone at arm's length for so long that he dreaded letting down his guard now. Strangely, since meeting Melissa again and making her his wife, another part of him was calling time on the endless solitude.

His words stunned Melissa. Embarrassed and ashamed for speaking with such bluntness and insensitivity, she drew a fortifying breath. Pain clouded his eyes. 'I'm so very sorry, Laurence. Please forgive my harsh words. I did not know.'

'My son died in a tragic accident—it was so totally unnecessary.'

Melissa had no notion of the same uncontrollable

my questions have revived painful memories for you and I regret my curiosity.'

'You are right, they have. However, because you are likely to find out sooner or later, I would prefer to tell you the circumstances of their demise myself rather than you hear of it from the servants—as you will eventually. Alice and Toby died together in a carriage accident. Now I would be grateful if you could leave it at that. My late wife is not your concern, so please quell your curiosity. You are newly wed and there are other things to focus your mind on.'

Melissa was shocked into silence. This was not what she had expected to hear. It was indeed a tragedy. She could hear the anger in his tone, but behind that she detected an abject sadness. She felt that Violet's very presence was bringing back painful memories for him, but on reflection she realised how her being in his life might also help him. 'Laurence, I am sorry.'

He smiled ruefully. 'Don't be. It's not your fault.'

Nevertheless, Melissa felt regret at being the source of his pain and that she had intruded into his memories and his home. He paused and looked at her, his loss still evident in his eyes. 'When you are ready to talk about it, I am a good listener.'

Turning from him then, she moved away. 'I see a table has been set for dinner. I think we should eat. I confess to feeling quite famished.' Her throat ached and her eyes burned, but she would not cry. She held herself steady as she walked across the room, resisting the urge to go back to him. But she could not. He had married her for Violet's sake and for no other reason. She must not allow herself to forget that. She was Lady Maxwell now. If Laurence still loved and mourned his first wife to the exclusion of all others, then she must accept it, but the scars of the wounds he had suffered were still raw. What she felt for him went deeper than compassion.

He was a troubled man and his quiet, anguished suffering aroused her protective instincts. She wanted to help him, to soothe and comfort him. But most of all she wanted to love him—and for him to love her. The attraction that had drawn them together in the Spring Gardens, the desire, was still there. She could feel it and she knew it was reciprocated. Hopefully, given time, that desire would draw them closer.

Dinner was a strained affair. Melissa managed to maintain an outward show of calm, despite the tumult raging inside her. A cold thrill ran through her as she ate, an awful sense of shock invading her entire being, although why she should feel this way puzzled her, for she had never really given much thought as to what had become of Laurence's former wife. She took a sip of wine, hoping the meal would be over quickly so she could escape.

'You said you were hungry,' he said. 'I hope you enjoy the dinner.'

'I shall endeavour to do so,' she replied, spreading a napkin on her knees.

'As long as you don't upset Cook by not eating. Mrs Russell is very efficient—and, being a woman, she is extremely temperamental and takes it as a personal criticism if anyone refuses to eat.'

'What! Even you?' Her eyes sparked with humour.

'Even me.' He smiled in response.

The food was delicious, excellently cooked, but Melissa's appetite appeared to have left her. Laurence talked amiably about what to expect when they reached Winchcombe in Surrey and describing the surrounding countryside, giving Melissa a brief insight into the people who lived and worked around the village of Winchcombe. When they had finished Laurence suggested they sit by the fire before retiring. As much as Melissa would have preferred to escape to her room, she complied. His mind had been preoccupied since she had asked him about his son and she would like to clear the air between them before they retired. Drawing a long, shaky breath, she clasped her hands together in her lap and met her husband's cool, assessing stare, determined to try to ease the tension that existed between them.

'Things do not have to be difficult, Laurence. There is no need for there to be discord between us,' she said quietly, cautiously. Encouraged by his lack of argument, she continued. 'I realise how inconvenient marrying me is for you—as it is for me marrying you—but surely nothing that has happened should make us treat each other badly.'

Laurence relaxed into the chair across from her, meeting her gaze, unable to resist the soft appeal in those huge eyes of hers. He sighed, his expression becoming more relaxed as he capitulated a little. 'No, of course not. And you are right. We must strive to make the best of things.'

Melissa had to suppress the urge to utter a deep sigh of relief. 'Are we to stay long in London?'

'Two or three weeks—maybe a month,' he answered. 'In the meantime it is important that you are fitted with a new wardrobe. You will be advised which fashionable shops to visit and all the best dressmakers, who will measure and fit you.'

'That is extremely generous of you.'

'Generosity doesn't come into it. As the lady of Winchcombe Hall it is important that you dress accordingly. Antony and Eliza are travelling to town today—she may have told you of their plans. As she is always at the forefront of fashion Eliza has kindly offered to take your wardrobe in hand.'

'She did mention it when we met—as soon as can be, in fact. Do they have a house in town?'

Laurence's face tensed and he avoided her eyes. 'No. They will be staying with Eliza's brother.'

'I see. Does he resemble Eliza?'

He frowned. 'There is a likeness.'

Melissa was surprised by the harshness of his reply. She watched the subtle change to his face, the way a shadow seemed to pass across it. The way the lines in the corners of his eyes deepened, despite how he tried so very hard to control his features. 'Why—what is it, Laurence? Do you not see eye to eye with Eliza's brother?'

'I do not,' he answered abruptly. 'He is a man who has nothing to recommend him in either character or manner and I do not want you to go anywhere near him. Eliza is a different matter. She is a woman of consequence—she shamelessly adores forcing society to bend to her will, as well as her husband.'

Melissa decided not to pursue the issue of Eliza's brother, but Laurence's aversion to the man stirred her curiosity and she couldn't wait to find out more.

'Antony is quite besotted with his wife,' Laurence went on, 'and always has been. I feel I must tell you that Eliza was Alice's close friend.'

'Oh—then I can only hope that she won't resent me—although she was very kind when we met at Beechwood House.'

'You've made a conquest. Eliza likes you—she made a point of telling me so. Where you are concerned I do not think it will do any harm for her to help you with your wardrobe.'

'She—did tell me that she is aware of the circumstances that brought us together.'

'Yes—and I have to say she was surprised and felt she had to question your suitability as my wife.'

'Really? She gave no indication of that when we met.'

'Then you must have won her over.'

Melissa fixed him with a steady gaze. 'I'd like to think so. No doubt I shall get to know her better—and you, Laurence. I still know so little about you.'

'I imagine Eliza will give you a rundown of my character. While I am in London I have a great deal of business to attend to so I shall not be able to give you my full attention. You will be glad of Eliza's company. She will accompany you wherever you want to go. News of our marriage will have reached London by now, so I have no doubt you will encounter curious strangers who will watch your every move.'

'Indeed I shall—no doubt looking for something to gossip about,' Melissa retorted tartly.

Laurence's heart turned over when he saw the wounded look in her glorious eyes. 'Worry not, Melissa. Content yourself with the fact that you will not have to face them alone. I will be by your side when we attend our first society event. At other times you will be with Eliza.'

'I can do little else. Will you tell me more about what to expect when we reach Winchcombe? What have you told your servants?' she asked, fully prepared to be met with abject disapproval and hostility when she came face to face with them. 'Do they know about Violet?'

'Of course. It is hardly the kind of thing that can be concealed. I sent instructions ahead to have rooms prepared for you and the nursery for Violet.'

'I imagine they were shocked,' Melissa murmured, feeling quite wretched.

'I imagine there were some raised eyebrows—which is to be expected. But their relief over me marrying again and having a new mistress at Winchcombe will outweigh the shock and any objections they will feel on learning I have married the mother of my illegitimate daughter. If it makes you feel any easier, no one knows of the circumstances that brought us together, which are known only to your family,

Antony and Eliza and ourselves. I would like to keep it that way. I am sure you will agree that it is a matter that needs delicate handling.'

'Of course. I understand,' she said quietly. 'At least I shall know what to expect and I must thank you for sparing further damage being done to my already lacerated reputation. Were the sordid details of our meeting to be made known then my humiliation would be complete.'

'My housekeeper has been telling me for some time that it is high time I looked for another wife.'

'Then I can only hope they approve of me—although I must warn you that my skills at managing a large household—especially one as large as I imagine Winchcombe to be—are sadly lacking. I have never applied myself to any task of such magnitude. My mother did try to train me in the duties she said would be expected of me when I married, but I was too busy helping Papa in the stables.' Then again, Melissa thought, Laurence might not wish for her to take responsibility for his home. He had married her to become close to Violet. But she was proved wrong by his next words.

'You will soon learn to oversee the household and to be a gracious hostess for our guests. Mrs Robins, the housekeeper at Winchcombe, will help you. You will soon fit into your role—as I will fit into mine as your husband.'

'I hope I will have plenty of opportunity to ride out. Papa is going to arrange to have Freckle sent on for me.'

'There will be time enough for that. You will soon be dashing about the Surrey countryside as you did at High Meadows. But please don't underestimate your position. You are mistress of Winchcombe Hall. The servants will look to you as they did to my mother—and later, Alice—on all matters to do with the household.'

'I will do my best, but your mother and your…your first wife did things their way. I have been raised in a certain way and I ask for your patience. I will not change from who I am or what I am. I like the way I am, but I promise you that I will try my utmost to familiarise myself with the household. But, I ask you not to compare me with your first wife or your mother, Laurence.'

'I will not do that. Winchcombe was my mother's life—as was my father. They had a good marriage.'

'I don't doubt it. She would not have behaved as I have done—and got herself with…' She fell silent, biting her lip, holding back the words that were hurtful to her to say, but Laurence had already heard them even though they had not been spoken.

'You are right, Melissa. She did not get herself with child before she married my father. However, you are too harsh on yourself. You did not get pregnant alone. I played an equal part.'

'Yes, you did, but no well-bred young lady, who would normally be seen exclusively among the company of the social elite, would have been seen dead attending the frivolities of the Spring Gardens in the guise of a servant to gratify her need for fun, nor would she have risked her reputation by indulging in such wanton behaviour that would damage any chance she might have of making a decent marriage.'

What she said was perfectly true, but when Laurence had first seen her he had wanted nothing more than to make love to her, until he had discovered that she was unsullied, untouched by any other man, and that had suddenly posed a threat, a danger to his peace of mind. She was different because never having belonged to another man made her so, gave her added appeal.

'You are my wife—and more importantly the mother of my child. So while you are resisting like an untamed horse against the reins which marriage to me will impose on you, I ask you to stop. I have told you that there will be times when my business affairs will take me away, maybe for weeks at a time, so for the time we are together we will spend it getting to know each other better.'

Getting to his feet, he held out his hand. Tentatively she placed hers in it and rose, a wariness in her eyes. He smiled.

'I have often thought about the short time we spent together in the Spring Gardens. I remember it clearly,' he said, 'and with good reason,' he concluded quietly, meaningfully, without further elaboration. 'What we did…' He smiled again as he opened the door. 'It is worth remembering.'

'It was many months ago, Laurence. Do you believe we are the same two people we were then?'

'Why, what is this, Melissa? Do you have reservations about what is to happen between us tonight?'

'I don't know. Everything has happened at an alarming rate.'

'Then perhaps I should warn you that when I have you in my bed I will focus all my attention on breaking your reserve. Do you think I can?'

Suddenly hot faced and bewildered, Melissa stared at him. She had never known a man to be so perplexing and she was suddenly shy of him. There was something in his eyes tonight that made her feel it was impossible to look at him. There was also something in his voice that brought back so many stirring memories of their first encounter that she did not know what to say. When she would have turned her face away he placed a gentle finger on her chin and forced her to look at him.

'No. Don't turn away. Look at me, Melissa.'

Would he break her reserve? Could he make her forget herself and accept the demands of her body as she had before? His deep voice saying her name made her senses jolt and a treacherous warmth was slowly beginning to seep into her body.

'You could have walked away when we met in the Spring Gardens. But you didn't. You stayed because you wanted the same thing as I did. We wanted each other.'

'What we did was dangerous—and foolish,' she protested.

'And wrong? Do you really think when you look at Violet that what we did was wrong? Neither of us has anything to gain by pretending that what happened between us is forgotten,' he said bluntly. 'Marrying each other proved that it wasn't over, if it proved nothing else, and it's never been forgotten. I've remembered you all this time—and I know damn well that you have remembered me.'

Melissa wanted to deny it, but she couldn't. He would know she was lying and hate her for the deceit. 'No,' she said shakily. 'I've never forgotten you or what we did. When Violet was born, I couldn't forget it even if I wanted to.'

He smiled at her retort and his voice gentled to the timbre of rough velvet. Before she could step away, he had taken her in his arms. 'Stay where you are,' he murmured.

'Why?' she whispered, her gaze settling on his lips.

'So we can continue with what we started in the Spring Gardens. I won't force you,' he said quietly, 'nor will I force you to do anything you don't want to do once you are in my bed. I will not ask you to do anything that is against your will.'

The effect of his words was a combination of fright and excitement. She felt her flesh grow warm. His nearness and the look in his eyes, which had grown darker and was far too bold to allow a small measure of comfort, washed over her. His gaze dropped to her lips, riveting there, and Melissa felt her body ignite at the same instant his mouth claimed hers. With a soft moan she slipped her hands up his chest, her fingers sliding into the soft hair at his nape, her body arching to his. A shudder shook his powerful frame as she fitted herself to him and his lips crushed hers, parting them, his tongue driving into her mouth with urgency, as their dormant passion finally exploded. Laurence encouraged her to give him back the sensual urgency he was offering her, and Melissa began to match his pagan kiss. They kissed again and again, their breaths mingling, and still they carried on, gentling the kiss and then starting again.

Melissa was a young woman with no more knowledge of the erotic arts than what she'd gained that night in the gardens, but there was that mysterious something inside her to entice and arouse Laurence and he was soon sinking into the hot chasms of delight she seemed to be offering him, delights he had denied himself for so long. Out of sheer preservation, an eternity later Laurence lifted his head and looked down at her flushed face and smiled, gently touching her moist lips with his finger. Her dazed expression drew a laugh from him.

'Until now I had managed to convince myself that the memory of the passion between us all those months ago must be faulty, or at the very least grossly exaggerated. But that kiss surpassed even my imaginings. I promise you that you won't be disappointed when I take you to bed.'

The impact of his closeness and potent masculine virility was making Melissa feel altogether too vulnerable. In fact, she was in danger of becoming hypnotised by that silken voice and those mesmerising silver-grey eyes—the fact that he knew it, that he was deliberately using his charm to dismantle her emotions, stirred her to action.

Drawing herself up straight, she playfully poked her finger at his chest and pushed him away from her. 'I think I should go to bed and let your opinion of yourself, especially your ego, get some sleep. It will have another arduous day of imagining to deal with tomorrow.'

'Oh, it will—but not imagining, Melissa. Reality. Go on up. I shall give you adequate time to prepare and then I will join you. We are man and wife. How else are we to get through the night if not the way we started—with a meeting of the senses, and sating the physical needs of our bodies?'

Melissa felt a sudden quiver run through her as she left him, a sudden quickening deep within her as if something came to life there, something that had lain dormant for a long time. Knowing he was watching her, that he stood in the doorway, his arms folded and a shoulder resting against the frame, she went up the stairs in awed bewilderment, feeling his eyes burning holes into her back as she went.

Laurence continued to watch her until she had disappeared. During their wedding yesterday, he had sensed her tension and her inner confusion, and he realised, as if for the first time, just how difficult she must be finding this situation. This was the day after the most important day of a woman's life, their first day as husband and wife. She had left everything that was familiar to her in order to face a new way of life at the side of a husband who was still a relative stranger to her, a man who, through his restrained manner, he realised with a twinge of regret, must have given the impression that he was indifferent to her. Suddenly, without pausing to question the reason why, he wanted to make things easier for her, to show that he was willing to give their marriage a chance.

Despite the time they had been apart he found her stimulating and was drawn to her. He admired her beauty and her spirit, the warm depths of her eyes, the occasional flash of scarlet indignation on her cheeks when things weren't going her way and she tried to defy him, and he felt a twinge of pleasure. She was the lively girl he had met in the Spring Gardens, the one who had amused him, who had flirted and laughed, tossing her bright head, her eyes deep and glowing and her lips wide and soft and ready to be kissed.

From the very first moment of meeting her, his mind had been locked in furious combat. Perhaps it was because she was so unlike Alice as it was possible to be. Everything about her threw him off balance. Melissa's mere presence resurrected emotions he thought had died when he had finally seen Alice for what she truly was. Melissa had stirred his desire as no other woman had succeeded in doing for a long time. Just now, when he had seen the passion in her eyes brought about by their kiss, he wondered why, from the very first, she had been able to affect him like no other woman had in a long time and why he felt this consuming need to possess and gentle her without breaking her spirit.

Chapter Five

Daisy was waiting for Melissa when she reached her bedchamber. With quiet respect she helped her undress. All the while Melissa's eyes were drawn to the huge bed with its velvet curtains and turned-down covers. Garbed in her concealing white nightdress, she sat at the dressing table while Daisy removed the pins in her hair and brushed it over her shoulders. When this was done she turned down the oil lamps and added more coals to the glowing embers in the hearth.

Her duties done Daisy turned to her mistress. 'I'll leave you now—unless there is something else you require.'

'No—no, thank you, Daisy. Go to bed. It's been a long day for all of us. Violet might not be able to go to sleep without me,' she said, donning her robe as she went to the door, 'and with a stranger looking after her she might fret—although Tansy seemed to know what she was about.'

Melissa was satisfied that the young nursemaid appointed to look after Violet was more than capable, but Melissa wanted to make sure her precious daughter was settled. The nursery was a lovely room of reasonable size, simply and elegantly furnished. It was cosy and warm, with all the requirements for taking care of a child. Toys spilled out of boxes and a handsome white rocking horse occupied one corner. It was fortunate she had gone to check on her because Tansy was indeed having difficulty putting Violet down. She was tearful, her eyes awash and her cheeks red from crying. On seeing her mama, she reached out her arms. Melissa took her and held her close. The familiar contact and soft, loving words soon turned the child's sobbing to snuffles.

Through the door connecting their rooms, having changed into a floor-length robe of maroon velvet, Laurence entered his wife's chamber, expecting to find her waiting for him. He was taken aback when he saw she wasn't there. Daisy was about to go to her own chamber.

'Where is my wife?'

'Oh—sir—you startled me. She—she was concerned about Violet and has just gone to check up on her.'

Relief tore through Laurence. Of course she was concerned about their daughter—her first night in a strange house. He should have known that was where Melissa would be.

Laurence entered the nursery. The unfamiliar

scene made him stop and catch his breath. The light was dim and his wife was slowly walking back and forth across the carpet, a sleepy Violet's head resting on her shoulder. It was a lovely scene, one of homeliness and contentment, and something deep and profound stirred within Laurence. He stood for a moment, watching her. He had never seen anything more delightful or touching than Melissa's closeness to their daughter. It was plain to him that Violet was everything to her and he couldn't help feeling a surge of male protectiveness towards both her and their daughter and the weight of responsibility for having drawn them into his life.

Unbeknown to her he continued to watch. Attired in a deep pink robe, her feet bare and her dark hair unbound and resting on her shoulders, she looked at Violet, her expression one of melting softness. He recalled how he had taken a fancy to her the moment he had set eyes on her and enjoyed every single moment of the short time they had spent together. He had thought she was quite lovely, strong and brave of spirit, but at the same time like a delicate fluff of swansdown to go in whichever direction the wind sent her, with her liquid amber eyes, the fine ivory and rose of her skin and the lovely proud tilt to her head which he'd particularly liked. There had been a delicate quality about her, wary but not cautious exactly, with the air of one who expects dangerous, exciting things ahead but is prepared to meet them head-on regardless.

She was warm and good-humoured and he found

her pleasant to be with. He liked her natural intelligence, passion and empathy and the fact that she was unconcerned by social structure or setting out to impress. He had once believed she was a young woman who was no stranger to intimate, casual encounters, but he now knew she'd had no more knowledge of the erotic arts than a young girl, but she'd still had it in her to arouse and entice him.

'So this is where you are. I thought you had flown the nest,' he murmured, moving further into the room and concentrating on the tiny face of his daughter. 'Is she asleep?'

'Almost. It's been a long day for her. She usually sleeps in my room. I thought she might be confused by the strangeness of the nursery and everything that's happened. It was fortunate I came up. She was crying.'

Laurence reached out and stroked Violet's face with his thumb. 'She's tired.' Her eyes started to close. She fought sleep for another minute and Laurence and Tansy watched silently as Melissa continued to walk slowly to and fro, then stopped as she snuffled into a contented rest.

'She should settle now.'

Placing her in the cot, Melissa gently smoothed the hair from her daughter's damp brow and followed the caress with a soft kiss. Laurence came to stand beside her and gazed down at his daughter. She was lying on her back, her hands on either side of her face, her chubby palms open. Reaching into the cot, he touched one of her soft cheeks with the tip of his finger. The fan of her dark lashes shadowed her plump rosy cheeks. Her rosebud lips were soft and pink and slightly open. He found it difficult to believe that she was his daughter, flesh of his flesh. Something stirred in him, drawing quite dramatically into an emotion he did not at first recognise but which, when he'd studied it further, he was certain he would find gratifying.

He was quite unprepared for the feelings and the emotions that almost overwhelmed him as memories of his son's birth assailed him, remembering how he had held him in his arms shortly after he was born. He breathed deeply, dragging air into his tortured lungs, fighting for control. Everything that had any meaning had been taken from him when Toby had died, leaving a great emptiness which could never be filled. But now he had Violet and the void left by his son was suddenly filled with hope.

Seeming to sense his struggle, Melissa looked at him and smiled and moved a little closer. It was as if she had the urge to reach up and press her lips to his cheek. With difficulty she appeared to resist, but, as if wanting to make some kind of contact, instead she touched his cheek with gentle fingers, the lightest of caresses. It was her first unsolicited gesture towards him and it took him aback. As it did her.

'I sense what you are feeling, Laurence. I do understand how difficult this must be for you.' She looked at Tansy. 'We will leave Violet now, Tansy, but if she should wake and be inconsolable you must come and tell me.'

With a wistful glance at the sleeping child, reluctantly she let Laurence lead her out of the room.

'Violet will be fine, Melissa. Try not to worry about her.'

'I know. It's me—just being silly.'

'No. It's you being a loving and devoted mother.'

He noted the tension in her body when he took her arm. Frowning with concern over the apprehension he saw on her face, suspecting it was not entirely concern over Violet that was troubling her, he halted outside her room. 'I am not a monster, Melissa. I suppose you could say this is our wedding night, but I have told you that I will not force you to do anything you do not want to do. You have my word on that. Everything has happened with such speed that I never courted you in the way that you deserved, or gave you the consideration of which you are worthy. We can sleep apart for the time being, if that is what you prefer.'

'Thank you,' she said, her tension easing a little on hearing this, but she did not move away. 'You won't have to do that.' She leaned slightly towards him.

As Laurence looked at her, the sight of her warm amber eyes, her soft cheeks and fragile neck aroused in him a violent and unfamiliar desire, such as no woman had aroused in him since they had come together all those months ago. As she sighed deeply and stretched her spine languidly, like a cat beneath the sun's warmth, the slender, graceful length of Melissa was outlined beneath her robe. The fabric strained over her breasts, rich and full. Her figure was taut and trim. All at once Laurence felt unbalanced by the strength of his emotions. Sensing a softening in her and her hesitation to open the door to her room, he did it for her, drawing her inside and closing it.

'I don't have to leave,' he murmured, drawing her into his arms, relieved that she didn't resist, 'unless you want me to. I only have to walk through that door over there and I will be in my own bedchamber.'

'Or you could just stay here with me,' she suggested.

'That is what I hoped you would say.' Brushing the hair from her eyes, he smiled down at her. 'I knew you wouldn't be able to resist me.'

'Resist you? What exactly did you have in mind?' Melissa raised her eyebrows.

'Why don't you let me show you?'

Laurence lowered his head and his mouth captured hers, soft and flower-like beneath his own. She was warm and pliant in his arms, her body and hair sweet-scented. His senses began to flee away and his breathing quickened. He loved the feel of her in his arms as her body moved against his and she moaned quietly. Lifting his head, he released her arms which had found their way round his neck. Taking her hand, he led her to the bed. Again he bent to place a soft kiss on her lips, then drew back.

'I think we should get rid of this.'

Quickly he unfastened the ties of her robe, tossing it into a chair. All the while he stared into her eyes. Melissa stood still, keenly recalling the desperate longing that had haunted her since the night she had met him. All she could think about were the things he would do to her and the pleasure she would feel. Even now his eyes were burning into her.

Without a word he removed his own robe. His strong, muscular body, eternally masculine, proud, savage and determined, gleamed in the soft light of the lamps. Seeing him thus, a tremor of admiration seared through Melissa.

Unable to resist taking her in his arms once more, Laurence kissed her again. His body was beginning to take over his mind and he took a moment to divest her of her concealing nightdress, exposing her body to his gaze. The firelight and shadows added a glow to her flesh. Her hair fell loose down her spine and he revelled in sifting his fingers through the thick tresses before drawing her down on to the bed, his eyes drinking in in her beauty. He stretched out alongside her, his hand and mouth caressing her breasts. They were full and high, like ripe, firm fruit, thrusting themselves into his palm, the nipples hard. He was staggered by the wave of possessive lust and desire that rioted through his veins. Ridiculously potent, it stunned him with its intensity.

'Explain to me why we waited and didn't do this last night?'

'That's easy,' Melissa said, sighing happily as she closed her eyes and relaxed against him, loving the heat of his mouth on her body. 'You preferred to spend our wedding night in the company of your friend—or it could be because I am worth waiting for.'

'I'm not going to disagree with that,' he breathed,

kissing her again, teasing her lips with his own as he ran a warm hand along the pathway of her firm stomach, pulling her body closer to meet his.

There was a haste in him now to know and to touch every part of her, to reacquaint himself with her body, to claim her as his own. Melissa felt devoured and it took an effort of her will to remain pliant beneath his probing eyes. He tasted everything which was being freely offered to him. He took one of her nipples between his lips, his hands caressing where they touched. When he kissed a tortuous path between her throat and breasts, she stretched, inviting him to touch, to linger, to delight in curves and hollows. His long-starved passions flared high and his blood spilled through his veins like molten lava as his lips wandered at will over her flesh, the sculpted hipbones that defined her sides and the inside of her leg.

For them both it was a time of reconciliation and revelation, that they could enjoy such intimacy, respond with such freedom. Melissa's thoughts fled as his fingers found the most tender part of her. A whisper of a sigh escaped her as, with an eagerness born of the pleasures that were creeping into her body, she raised her head to kiss his eager lips. Laurence's sanity finally deserted him. Rising above her, he lowered his hips between her thighs, his maleness piercing her body in an act of simple, unrestrained passion. He filled her fully, thrusting deeply, possessively, touching all of her. It was incredible and, as she began to move as he moved, beauty and something wonderful began to happen to them both.

With a physical effort Melissa forced her eyes open and looked at him. His face was hard and dark with passion. It was the same in his eyes, yet there was as much tenderness in them as there was desire. Her fervent hope was that he could feel all the exquisite things he was making her feel.

Any apprehensions Melissa had previously had vanished beneath the scorching heat of their mutual desires, as they were merged into one being, husband and wife, wrapped in the absolute bliss of their union. They were two beings fused together in a spiralling eddy of passion. And then ecstasy as they came closer still and Melissa felt his seed erupt, spilling into her, their lives merging.

Holding her close with his lips against hers, Laurence waited until the flame that had ignited them both subsided and they relaxed. Sated, a fine film of perspiration glistening on his body, his hair damp, his breathing deep, he moved his weight from her and pulled her into his arms as he came down from the unparalleled heights of passion she had just sent him to. He felt the final shattering of a door he had kept locked and bolted in his mind for a long time—at least since their coming together in the Spring Gardens. His wife was innocence and wantonness, passionate and sweet.

Melissa sighed and melted into her husband's embrace, unable to believe that she could feel such joyous elation quivering inside. And yet, with honesty, she recognised that she had held something of herself back from the heat of sensation that had begun deep inside her, when, with his gentle touch, he discovered and tormented the secret delights of which she been taken unawares. But she dared not allow it to overpower her, so at the end she had turned her mind from what was happening to her, from the treacherous demands of her body, from complete dependence on him.

Laurence leaned over her, gently smoothing her tumbled locks from her face, tracing his finger down the soft curve of her cheek, surprised to see her eyes awash with tears. Yet he had sensed her withdrawal from him, from succumbing to her ultimate pleasure. It had left him strangely disappointed, even though his own satisfaction had been overwhelming.

'No matter how unconventional our beginning, or what the future might hold, we will always have this. How do you feel?' he asked, his voice gentle, his gaze so tender that Melissa's heart contracted.

'Like your wife,' she murmured, placing her lips gently on his chest.

'Then why are there tears in your eyes?'

'It's happiness that makes me weep,' she reassured him.

'It only seems like yesterday when we met in the Spring Gardens. Why did you allow me to seduce you?'

'At that time I had no experience of the world away from High Meadows. Believe me when I say I did not set out to trap you. Nothing could have been further from my mind. But—seeing you, I was dazzled. I was drawn to you sincerely and with all my naive young heart. I didn't know what I wanted from you—only that I wanted it quite badly.'

'And I took it.' He was encouraged by her willingness to respond to his passion, but he realised she would have to learn to trust him. 'You learn fast, Melissa, but I still sense within you a reticence. One day I will break through that reticence and make you tremble in my arms. When the strangeness of the past two weeks are over, you will learn to trust me and you will give me more. It was unpardonable of me to make love to you on our first encounter, but you were quite irresistible as I recall. I know that is no excuse for what I did.'

'Irresistible? Dear me—was I?'

'Yes, my love...' He was sorry at once that he had used that endearment, which had automatically slipped out.

'But I am not your love, am I, Laurence?' Melissa said quietly. 'I am not Alice.'

Laurence stiffened and then moved away from her. She had obviously touched a raw nerve.

'No, you are not Alice. You are nothing like Alice. I told you I have no wish to discuss her, especially not here, in our bed.'

The words wrenched Melissa's very soul. How she wished she had never mentioned his first wife, but after what had just happened between them she refused to be downgraded and was prepared to argue. As she tilted her chin her look was one of pure defiance. 'I am your wife now, Laurence.'

'So you are and you would do well to remember it.'

'I'm not likely to forget.' He turned and looked at her, his expression giving her no reassurance. His eyes were slits of explosive anger in his grim face and she could almost feel the effort he was exerting to keep it under control. 'You're angry, Laurence, but you have no reason to be. My intention was not to give offence, but if your reaction to any mention of your first wife is to fly into a rage, then I will not speak of her at all.'

'That would be the sensible thing. I think it's time I went back to my own bed. Eliza will be here shortly after breakfast. You have a busy day ahead of you.'

'Really?' Her voice was ragged with emotion as she fought to control her anger, feeling the fragile unity they had shared moments earlier beginning to slide down the slippery slope of clashed wills. She propped herself up on her elbow when he got out of bed. 'It didn't seem to matter to you when you took me to bed.'

'Melissa!' He looked down at her face, flushed from their lovemaking, and the wild tangle of her hair falling about her naked shoulders. His gaze took in her slender body, the firm rose-tipped swell of her breasts and narrow waist. She looked so very young, even though she was nearly twenty. Then his heart was strangely moved, for that's all she was, despite the birth of Violet, a young woman who had been hurt by what she saw as his rejection of her. 'Try to get some sleep.'

He crossed the room to the connecting door, turning to look back at her. He didn't want to hurt her any more than he had, but the truth was that if he didn't leave her, he would be tempted to remain all night. She had the smell of a woman aroused. He could still taste the sweetness of her, still feel the softness of her breasts as he had caressed them. Before they had made love he had wondered if it would be as good as he'd remembered. He had not been disappointed. Why was it that he remembered it so clearly? he wondered perplexedly.

'Do you not care for me at all, Laurence?' she asked quietly. She had not asked him if he loved her—she was wise enough to realise that he didn't.

'Melissa, of course I care for you. How could I not? You are a beautiful woman.' He was looking for an excuse, not wanting to tell her the truth, not wanting to hurt her with it, that when he had met her that first time he'd been doing nothing more than amusing himself with her and he was ashamed. And now, after what they had done, how could he shatter her woman's pride and self-respect, her belief in herself and her own remarkable quality that was quite unique? What had just happened between them was the only time they had met on common ground. It wasn't a meeting of the heart and mind, but a meeting only of the flesh. How could he tell her he did not love her—could never love her—that he was incapable of feeling that way about a woman ever again?

Melissa did it for him. When two people loved each other to the exclusion of all else and entered into a commitment of marriage as a fulfilment of that love, then it could not help but succeed. That was not how it was between her and Laurence. Getting out of bed, not even bothering to cover her nakedness, picking up his robe from the bed she marched to the connecting door and opened it, standing aside and thrusting his robe into his arms.

'Here—take it. You don't want to catch a chill,' she remarked in a frozen tone.

'What's this?' he said quietly. 'Has my wife gone cold on me so soon?'

'It's complicated. I said I felt like your wife—I'm no longer sure that I do. I'm sorry if my remark about your first wife upset you. You have my word that I will not mention her again. I feel that already you are regretting your decision to marry me. You did so to be a father to Violet and for no other reason, I know that, and I am sure you see me as a responsibility you could do without—that I am nothing more than a pitiful nuisance.'

'Those are your words, not mine,' he replied harshly.

'Nevertheless,' she seethed, her eyes blazing while her voice was like splintered ice as she wondered how they could have come to this in such a short time, when just moments before she had been languishing in his arms, 'that is how you think of me—how you feel—and if that is so then I feel I should remove myself from your house forthwith.'

'Like hell you will.'

Laurence spoke quietly, but Melissa could hear the anger in his voice, a slow vibration. They stood glaring at each other. Laurence was very close to her, but he didn't touch her. She could have walked away, but neither of them seemed capable of moving right then. The moment was too intense.

'I will give you a warning, Melissa, and heed me well,' Laurence said in a low, terrible voice. 'Do not even consider leaving this house with the intention of leaving it for good. You are my wife and you will not leave without my permission—and you will certainly not take Violet from me.'

'You, you, you!' she retorted angrily, in an outburst that astonished him, not only because she dared to speak to him in such a way, but also because it was the first display of real emotion he had witnessed from her. 'This is not all about you, Laurence. You may be my husband and Violet's father, but I am still her mother and know better than you as to what is good for her. You are quite the most arrogant man I have ever known and clearly care nothing for my feelings.'

'As a matter of fact I do care and, like you, I feel Violet is the most important thing in my life. Which is why you will remain here with me until such time as we go to Winchcombe. Do not dare disobey me.'

Fury was quick to flare in Melissa's eyes. 'How dare you say that to me? I will not submit to any man. I do not need your permission to do anything and if I wanted advice, I would not ask you. I will not be unquestioningly subjected to your whims, however charismatic you may be. In the eyes of the law you might own me, but you do not own my spirit.'

His eyes narrowed and a murderous glint shone out at her. Only one woman had dared to speak to him so defiantly and look at him with sparks shooting from her eyes. There was a deep and dreadful silence, a silence so menacing, filling with an unwavering determination of both of them to hurt, to destroy one another, that the tension was palpable.

'Do not goad me, Melissa, and do not defy me. Do you forget so soon that you vowed to obey your husband?'

Melissa's voice held nothing but contempt. 'I do not forget. I am not your chattel and I will not be treated or spoken to as such.' The expression on her husband's face was difficult to read, but some new darkness seemed to move at the back of his eyes. 'Of late everything has happened so quickly I've hardly had time to draw breath. We need a while to get to know each other better, so I think we should take each day as it comes.' She met his gaze levelly. 'For the time being I wish to be left alone—to go to bed alone. I think you know what I mean.'

'You are my wife and I have a legal right to touch you—to share your bed any time I choose. But worry not. I'll control my lustful urges and not allow my base instincts free range.'

'I'm glad to hear that.'

They looked at each other in silence, a silence so deep Melissa thought they would never climb out of it, then, with a simple dignity which moved Laurence in its restraint, she walked back to her bed and got in, turning away from him. She did not stir when he went into his own bedchamber and closed the door quietly behind him.

* * *

Alone in the huge bed that a moment before had been the place of so much loving, Melissa pulled the covers over her head and drew her legs up to her chest. She knew Laurence didn't love her and it was unreasonable of her to expect him to. Tears welled in her eyes. He had done his duty towards her by making her his wife. He was telling her without saying the words to be satisfied with that. In the deeply wounded depths of her soul and known to no one but herself, she could never be, but it was something she must endure and count herself lucky.

What had Alice been like—the woman, his first wife, who had woven her web about him with such intricate care and skill and entrapped him among her silken threads? He still mourned her, that was obvious, still held her as a bright and shining light in his heart, loving and cherishing her memory with his every breath. Her vision remained blurred with tears as an overwhelming sense of despair sank its merciless talons into her.

She had never thought of herself as a jealous woman, nor had occasion to be, but the terrible pangs she now endured were more searing than she could have imagined. She had not foreseen this wrenching anguish of loss and suffering of the heart brought about by her husband's love for his first wife. Tears spilled from her eyes, soaking the pillow. She was glad that he had gone, glad that he could not see first-hand how his words had hurt her. Just when she had begun to look forward to a shared future, she could only envy the woman who still occupied a place in his heart where she would so desperately like to be.

Being the youngest of three siblings, for the most part ignored by her parents in favour of her older brothers, all her life Melissa had felt the need to be needed, valued and appreciated. Violet had filled the void in her life. And now, just when she hoped everything would work out right for her, she'd discovered that Laurence's first wife continued to have a hold over him. After telling herself she would be the perfect wife, to look after his home and family to the best of her ability, she was left with a man lovesick for a dead woman. She called herself a fool for her unrealistic illusions. Most of all she grieved for the painful destruction of the hope in her heart that the knowledge of her feelings for Laurence had shattered.

She could not ask him about Alice. Her pride forbade it. She knew now that he would never return her love and therefore she would not risk her heart any further. But, she asked herself, what did the future hold for her now? As she wiped the tears from her eyes, strength, renewed and resolute, grew. Leaving Laurence was not an option and she could not return to High Meadows. She had married Laurence and was determined to hold her course. But, she thought, he would never make her weep again.

Unfortunately, she could not control her feelings, but she could control how she acted upon them. Alice cast a dark shadow between them and she vowed that while his first wife held sway over his heart, she, Melissa, would not share his bed—yet, she thought, annoyed by the sudden weakness that crept over her, he was her husband. How could she deny him? How could she resist him?

Nursing her own hurt on the other side of the door connecting their rooms, Melissa would have been surprised had she known how Laurence suffered in turn over what had just happened and how he reached for the brandy decanter, pouring himself a generous slug in an attempt to drown his pain when he considered his recent harsh treatment of his wife. His wife! He had never intended marrying again, not after his first marriage had ended in tragedy, but he'd had no choice in the matter. The pleasure he had just experienced in Melissa's bed swiftly darkened into a sour irascibility. So, he thought, that was the way she would have it. She could not have spoken plainer. It had not occurred to him that the beautiful temptress who had surrendered so readily in his arms, who'd returned his passion with such intoxicating sweetness, might no longer be won over so easily.

He'd closed his heart and mind to protect his own feelings, but it had only created an insurmountable barrier between them. His wife had also erected a high barrier around herself, but not for one minute did he believe it was impregnable. Melissa was a warm and passionate woman—he was confident that he could succeed in luring her into bed any time he chose. But for the time being he would do as she asked. She was right. Everything had happened in a rush of late. Perhaps it would be prudent to take things a day at a time.

Before they had sat down to dinner she had apologised for prying into his past and been generously reassuring in response to his disclosures. His dead wife was a subject he tried not to think about, but Melissa's reminder had brought it all back and he gave in to the memories as he lay awake and restless in bed.

When morning dawned, he left the house to take care of some business matters without seeing Melissa. He was beginning to discover the whole tenor of his life was changing with Melissa now in it. Constant awareness of her presence kept him in a perpetual state of confusion. The intimacy they had shared made it even harder to detach himself. She was no longer just a woman he had made love to almost two years ago. She was a woman, a mother, a wife. His wife. Enough was enough, he decided. He couldn't be ruled by the past. It was time, finally, to see what life with Melissa had to offer him.

With each new day the bond between Laurence and his daughter grew stronger. Utterly enchanted by the child, who always went trustingly and gladly into his arms, he doted on her. As young as she was Violet liked being with her father and she always met his overtures with ecstatic gurgling. Watching her, in her childlike innocence, talking to her, feeling her little fingers curl round his, Melissa observed him playing the fool for his daughter's entertainment.

The child would gaze up at him, her eyes wide open, and call him Papa.

Melissa often found them asleep together in a chair before the fire in the nursery, Violet curled up against his chest. The charming scene would bring tears to her eyes and a twinge of envy, wishing she was the one resting her head on Laurence's chest. At other times Violet would put her arms about his neck and hug him, then begin to wriggle, for the attention span of such a young child was limited. She would scramble away and totter about the nursery. Laurence would sit for a while and watch her, his expression conveying a rare softness and pleasure. Melissa sensed there was something inside him that was still crying out for his son. Deprived of his beloved Toby, she hoped Violet had come to replenish the aching hollow left inside him by his son's death.

Where Melissa was concerned, his eyes were always guarded. They were polite with one another, pleasant even, both of them doing their best to begin the process of making something of their lives together. Melissa didn't wish him to see how desperately she wanted him. Her heart yearned for a two-way affection, where all the emotion wasn't only on her side.

When he had taken her to bed there had been no intention on his part other than to seal their vows and on hers to accept it. How could any woman fail to respond to the sheer masculinity of this man? The gleam of those magnificent eyes, the curve of his lips which gave an enchantment to his stern features. She sighed as her heart sank under the weight of hopelessness. She was a fool if she expected anything other than kindness and respect from him. It would have to be enough. She would have to take the utmost care not to show him what was in her heart.

When he was at home he would disappear into his study where he would pore over accounts, assessing profits from his many business assets, even though he employed accountants and lawyers to do it for him. He would remain in his study for hours at a time, occasionally leaving for wherever it was he went to conduct more of his business. He was always rushing and he always had something else to do, somewhere else to be. There was an energy about him that kept Melissa charged. One time she accompanied him across the hall, telling him that he worked too hard and enquiring if he would be home for dinner.

Laurence's eyes snapped to hers, his mouth curving into a humourless half-smile. 'I can't say. As soon as it is possible we will be leaving for Surrey, but I have many business transactions to take care of which can only be done here. Owing to the war in France, there is an economic crisis. If I am not in London to discuss matters at first hand with my business managers and bankers, the implications could prove disastrous.'

The length and speed of his strides made it necessary for Melissa to all but run to keep up with him. She watched him stride away from her and hurry down the steps, his overcoat flapping behind him. Ever since she had known him he was always in a hurry. Even when he wanted his horse or the carriage it was always 'Hurry up, man!' to the groom and he never lingered at the table when he'd finished a meal. It must be very exhausting being Laurence Maxwell.

During the day she could immerse herself in things to do to distract her mind, drawn by circumstances into a daily routine of household actions and decisions that she would have once thought to be totally alien to her character. With Mrs Evans's help she began to learn everything there was to know about the running of the house, which would also benefit her when they went to Winchcombe. She spent a great deal of her time with Violet.

Laurence often didn't appear for dinner. Melissa would hear him moving about on the other side of their connecting door during the night, but he had not come to her bed since that night they had arrived in London.

Eliza was Melissa's godsend. She followed fashion faithfully and was always beautifully dressed—Melissa felt plain by comparison—a small hat perched on top of her elegant coiffure. She was grateful for the time Eliza took arranging her wardrobe. Laurence had insisted that she be fitted out for every occasion and that no expense was to be spared. Melissa was shocked to find Eliza took him at his word and escorted Melissa to the largest and finest of shops, visiting some of the most fashionable modistes in Bruton Street and Bond Street.

Melissa stared about her with interest, thinking

how her mother would love all this. Eliza was clearly a valued customer. After exchanging polite remarks the proprietor would summon her assistants. When Melissa and Eliza were accommodated on chairs they unrolled the choicest wares for their inspection. Sapphire and dusky rose and rippling turquoise, satins and silks, cut velvets and embossed brocades were displayed.

'I seem to be putting you to so much trouble,' Melissa remarked when they were in the carriage taking them to Mortimer House in Piccadilly, where Eliza and Antony were residing with Sir Gerald Mortimer, Eliza's brother. It was close to the Strand and they were both in need of refreshment. Eliza had told Melissa her brother was out of town visiting friends in Brighton and was not expected back until the following day. The only time Laurence had mentioned Eliza's brother had left Melissa in no doubt that he had no liking for him and might not be at all pleased to discover she had visited his house. She recalled him telling her that he had nothing to recommend him in either character or manner, which had aroused Melissa's curiosity. She felt some expression of gratitude was due after one particularly heavy shopping trip to Covent Garden and the Strand. 'I realise my wardrobe is hardly up to London standards and it is indeed kind of you to give up so much of your time for me.'

'I enjoy doing it, so indulge me, Melissa. Laurence is Antony's closest friend so it is the least I can do. Besides, you won't have seen the papers but the society columns in *The Times* and the *Gazette* are full of your marriage to Laurence. The journalists are having a field day. Everyone was beginning to think he would never marry again.'

Melissa had read some of the comments in the newspapers with interest and amusement at some and anger at others. There was a great deal of discussion about her background, which was so significantly lower than Maxwell's. Statements about her life were bandied about, along with the news that she'd had a lengthy affair with Laurence before they married which had resulted in a child. Comments were made about her looks, her lack of a substantial dowry and her connections, which were hardly worthy of Lord Maxwell's lofty position. All this pointed to her complete unsuitability as his bride and led to some papers wondering if Laurence Maxwell had suffered some kind of mental problem following his first wife's death.

'The papers have written some hurtful things about me, that I do know. I do my best to ignore them, but after leading such a private life I hate knowing I am being discussed by people who do not even know me. Most of it isn't true, but I suppose the scandalmongers will have their day.'

'They will, that you can be sure of. For Laurence Maxwell, to turn up with a wife—well—everyone has been speculating what you will be like. You will be watched, studied and gossiped about so you must prepare yourself, for much of that gossip will not be favourable. People can be cruel at the best of times, full of envy and avarice.'

'Then I will simply have to face up to it. What else can I do?'

'Have you fallen in love with him, Melissa?'

'In all honesty I don't know how I feel. Laurence—he—he makes me feel things I have never felt before. I like being with him. I like it when he smiles and laughs. I—do care for him, Eliza—deeply.'

Eliza smiled. 'There you are, then. If it isn't love you feel now, it soon will be.'

'I know you mean well, Eliza, but I know very little about my husband. He—he refuses to speak of his first wife.'

'I can see how difficult all this must be for you, but don't be too hard on yourself. Laurence can be rather overbearing and intimidating at times, but it is not intentional,' she added in an attempt to soften Laurence's character. 'He works hard and demands too much of himself—especially since the death of Alice—and he expects others to have the same drive and determination.'

'Yes—I have seen that for myself.'

'His life has not always been easy. Financially his family was not well off—which was due to his grandfather who was a spendthrift. He has made all his money himself. According to Antony, from an early age it was clear to everyone that Laurence had been gifted with a superior intelligence. He learned fast and prospered, bringing some pride and honour back to the Maxwell name. Through hard work and determination he owns ships that fly his flag and land both here and abroad, where minerals of one kind or another are mined. Your husband, Melissa, is one of the wealthiest men in the country.'

Melissa stared at Eliza in dazed disbelief. 'As rich as that? I knew he was wealthy, but I find the extent of it astonishing.'

'He has a brilliant mind for business and invests his money wisely—although the war in France is causing him a good deal of worry. Some men gamble—Laurence is a businessman. He thinks too much of his money to throw it away at the tables. I'm not saying he isn't averse to a game of cards or dice now and then, or that he doesn't enjoy it when he does, but he plays purely for enjoyment. Although I suppose you could call him a gambler of sorts—thriving the way he does on taking risks on investments, driven by the thrill of the wager.' She looked at Melissa steadily. 'You—know that Laurence had a son, don't you, Melissa?'

Melissa nodded. 'Yes—Mrs Evans told me, although I suppose I would have found out eventually. I—I wish Laurence had told me himself—before we married.'

'Why? Would it have made a difference to your decision?'

'No—of course not. It would just have been nice to know, that's all.'

'Yes, I can understand that, but try to make allowances for him, Melissa. He—doesn't find it easy to talk about Toby. He was such a lovely little boy—

Violet resembles him.' Eliza glanced away, choosing her words with care when she next spoke. 'Laurence tries to give the impression that he doesn't need anyone. He has learned to deal with tragedy and adversity in his own way. His scars are deep. If he weren't so strong in mind and body, I doubt he would have survived after the accident.'

'Will you not tell me about Alice? Unless you feel you would be betraying a trust…'

'I wouldn't be doing that—even though Laurence might see it that way. I had hoped he would have told you how it was between him and Alice by now. To enable you to understand him better, it's as well you should know. They fought—often bitterly. When she died along with their son, he took it hard—he blamed himself for what happened—for not being there. Afterwards he took himself off to France to sort out his affairs, not caring whether he lived or died. It's no secret what happened. Alice hurt him very badly. She was beautiful—and ambitious—a social climber. Her father was a government official. When she met Laurence he seemed like a good proposition—even though she was involved with someone else at the time. Money and status and Laurence's indelible mark of success proved irresistible to her. She married him for what he could give her.'

'She—she didn't love him?'

Eliza sighed. 'I knew her well—I couldn't bring myself to dislike her—but I don't believe she did. Her—her heart was engaged elsewhere. Unfortunately, that particular gentleman couldn't give her the material things that Laurence could. Alice did well out of the marriage—Laurence showered her with jewels and gave her anything she asked for. The trouble was that work had always played a large part in his life and he spent long periods away from her—leaving Alice to do as she pleased. That was when it started to go wrong. The only good thing to come out of her marriage to Laurence was Toby.'

'Laurence must have been beside himself with grief when he died. What a terrible tragedy. How—how did the accident happen?' Melissa asked in a small voice, dreading what Eliza would tell her, but needing to know.

'Unfortunately the carriage was travelling too fast and it overturned—killing both her and Toby.'

Melissa's eyes glazed with tears. She felt devastated by what Eliza had revealed to her, which went a long way to helping her understand Laurence and how hard it was for him to talk about what had happened to him. He had lost so much. In his own way he had isolated himself from the world because his wife had destroyed everything he had held dear, everything he had loved. His son.

She swallowed down her tears. 'I didn't know—I never thought... Never imagined it was anything like this. Alice must have been quite mercenary to marry someone just for wealth and social position. How miserable and hurt Laurence must have been to discover it. I know how proud he is—and how much his pride must have been mangled when he learned what had happened.'

'He was. Very badly. He lost himself in his work with a blind, instinctive faith as his only hope for survival. It is a subject he always avoids talking about, but since that time he has held virtually every woman he has come into contact with in complete contempt. From the moment he married Alice things did not go well for him—in his private or business life. His liberty became important to him and I hope in the future his life will be conducted in less turbulent waters.'

'Thank you for telling me, Eliza. I appreciate it.'

'Don't give up on him, Melissa. Whatever went on between the two of you in the Spring Gardens cured him—it was the first time he'd shown any true interest in a woman since Alice. It worked far better than anything else could have. I don't know what it is you've done to him, but whatever it is, it's a good thing. He needs you, Melissa—though he may not know it yet. He needs someone to save him from himself—to heal wounds that are deep, to teach him how to love and be loved in return.'

'He will have to learn to trust me.'

'When he does that, he will give you the world. I promise you.'

Melissa turned her head and looked out of the window to hide her discomposure, her mind on Laurence. There was a tight feeling in her throat and she felt as if she wanted to cry. She swallowed hard. The very idea of Laurence needing her was an unsubstantiated idea, one that struck a deep and responsive chord in her heart. No one had ever needed her before, only Violet, but the needs of a child were different to the needs of one's husband. The fact that she might help Laurence by being his wife seemed incredible and strangely appealing. Eliza said Laurence blamed himself for the death of his wife and son—whether he was or not, he had been deeply affected by it and the pain he'd suffered had left scars deeper than any physical wound.

His suffering aroused her protective instincts. Her feelings for him went deeper than compassion. She wanted to help him, to soothe his grief. From the start she had been physically attracted to him and she'd thought before that she might love him; now, knowing what she did about his past tragedy, she was certain that she was in danger of irretrievably losing her heart to him.

True, he was frequently moody, distant and unapproachable, but the more she contemplated the matter, the more convinced she became that Eliza was right—Laurence needed to feel wanted and loved and Melissa was absolutely up to the task.

Chapter Six

On arriving at Mortimer House Melissa was shown into a drawing room overlooking a wide terrace and a well-tended garden beyond. The house was elegant and spacious, but it displayed none of the awe-inspiring opulence of Maxwell House.

'Antony isn't home, Melissa, so we will enjoy our refreshment in peace. It's such a lovely day I'll arrange for tea to be sent out to the terrace.' Eliza glanced at the open French doors. 'Walk out to the garden if you like. There are some rather lovely roses Gerald is rather proud of.'

Melissa did as Eliza suggested and drifted outside. The sweet scent of roses and summer flowers was heavy on the air. Sauntering across the lawn, she was surprised when a man appeared from an arbour, holding a single yellow rose in his elegant hand. Wearing a short wig of exquisite whiteness, he was tall, dressed in a blue-coloured frock suit of heavily embroidered silk—a fine lacy jabot spilled from his throat in a frothy cascade and lace ruffles dripped over his wrists and over well-shaped hands, caressing elegant, bejewelled fingers. On seeing her his bland expression gave way to reverent admiration before walking gracefully towards her. He tendered her a polite bow, looking at her with the impartiality of a true connoisseur, looking for flaws that others would miss and finding only perfection.

'Now who can you be?' he enquired with unconcealed curiosity, his voice as smooth and seductive as the softest silk, his eyes absorbing every detail of her face and figure. 'I don't recall seeing you at any of the soirées I have attended.'

Melissa bobbed a little curtsy, suddenly finding herself lost for words. He was attractive, with sultry features and dangerously hooded eyes, and he exuded all the confidence of a conceited charmer.

'I am Melissa Maxwell. Eliza was kind enough to invite me for refreshment.'

'Lady Maxwell?' His expression immediately became shuttered. 'Well, who would have guessed. I heard Laurence had married again. I am happy to meet you.' His expression became more open as he executed a courtly bow. The lascivious look he gave her as he took her hand and placed it to his mouth, his lips lingering too long on her slender fingers, going way beyond that of ordinary interest, irritated Melissa. 'You have only recently come to London, I believe—which is why we have not met before now. I do hope the scandal that has followed you to town doesn't bother you? The gossips can be cruel—for myself I never could resist a damsel in distress.'

'Hardly a damsel, sir, and I am certainly not in distress—and, no, the gossips don't bother me.'

'Ah—a lady after my own heart. However, society is not as discerning as I, but I reckon you will withstand whatever it throws at you with Laurence to fend off any malicious asides. What an attractive young woman you are. I have no doubt that when you do go out in society you will ruffle a few feathers and cause quite a stir.'

Unable to resist such charming flattery, especially when it was spoken by a man whose eyes twinkled with such wicked mischief, Melissa responded with a smile. 'There are many beautiful ladies in town, sir. I am quite certain I will not cause a stir at all.' He was approximately the same age as Laurence, she guessed, but there the similarity ended. This man was much more slender, with a brooding air and an immaculate look. 'I'm afraid you have me at a disadvantage.'

'I apologise. Allow me to introduce myself. I am Gerald Mortimer—Eliza's brother—at your service, my lady.'

Melissa got the impression he was watching her closely to determine her reaction. 'She told me you were in Brighton.'

'I was—but I decided to return a day early. I was surprised to learn that Laurence had married again.'

'Have the two of you known each other long?'

'Indeed—almost all our lives. We are neighbours in Surrey. Your husband has not spoken of me?'

'Only in passing, but then we have only recently married and I don't yet know many of his acquaintances.'

'But you do know Sir Antony and that he's my brother-in-law.'

'In which case,' Melissa said with a smile, 'I shall expect to see you at Winchcombe some time in the future.'

He hesitated. 'I wouldn't be so certain of that. Your husband and I are not exactly on the best of terms.' At her curious frown, he added, 'Perhaps you should not be seen speaking to me. Laurence would not approve.'

'I make my own friends,' she said, irked that he should think Laurence would deny her the right to converse with whomsoever she pleased. Yet perhaps she should not encourage him. The conversation was highly improper, and faintly disloyal to Laurence, but she was curious to know more. 'I confess that I am intrigued. Why would he not approve of me speaking to you?'

He smiled. 'Perhaps you should ask him.'

'I shall make a point of it.'

He looked beyond her, raising his hand to Eliza who had appeared on the terrace. 'Please allow me to escort you to my sister. Come, take my arm. She does not look best pleased to see me—or perhaps it is because you are with her reprobate of a brother.'

'Perhaps she has good reason to call you that,' Melissa murmured with a delicate lift to her brows. Not wishing to appear rude, she lightly placed her fingers on his arm, which was offered in such a way that it was a masterpiece of gracious arrogance.

He laughed outright, showing teeth as white and strong as those of a wild animal. 'You read me too well, dear lady—my reputation has gone before me,' he said as they walked towards Eliza, his heavy lids drooping over his eyes suggesting at intimacy, and a salacious, lazy smile curling his full lips. 'Not that it worries me overmuch.'

'I cannot imagine it would,' Melissa replied, forming her own judgement of him and sensing he possessed an unpredictable nature, of which her instinct told her to beware.

Seeing the smile fade from her lips and a wariness enter her eyes, Sir Gerald chuckled under his breath as they climbed the steps to the terrace, where Eliza was waiting for them. She looked uneasy and a worried frown creased her brow.

'Really, Gerald. You were supposed to be in Brighton,' she uttered, her tone one of reproach.

'I was, Eliza—as I've just been telling the adorable Lady Maxwell. I simply became bored of the company and decided to return to London a day early. You have no objection, I hope?'

'No, of course not—only I wish I had known,' she answered crossly.

'Had you known I would have been denied the pleasure of meeting this charming lady.' Seeing Melissa's expression, he laughed. 'Do not look so shocked, my dear. Damn me if I can remember when I last saw a prettier face than yours.'

'Oh, I'm sure you can if you try,' Melissa remarked, her wonderful amber eyes filled with wry amusement, noting that his voice lacked sincerity and that he spoke with well-regulated practice.

'If you are to go out into society, then you must get used to flattery. You mustn't mind me flirting with you. Most ladies who attend soirées and the like expect it and are mortally offended if they find themselves ignored.'

'That may be so, Gerald,' Eliza said acerbically, 'but Melissa is a married lady—*Laurence's* wife—and you should behave yourself.' Sitting at a round ornate table where a maid had placed refreshment, she began pouring the tea. 'If you want tea, Gerald, go and get yourself a cup and saucer.'

'Now why would I do that when I have servants to do my bidding? It is, after all, what I pay them for. However, I'll settle for something stronger shortly.'

'I expect you will, although I imagine you are awash with it already.' Handing Melissa her tea, Eliza told her to help herself to the delicate cakes which looked so tempting Melissa couldn't resist taking one. 'I feel that I must apologise for my brother, Melissa. He can be irritating and quite insufferable at times. Don't take anything he says seriously.'

Not at all put out by his sister's chiding and not in the least interested in partaking of a cup of tea, Sir Gerald pulled out a chair and sat down, stretching his long legs out in front of him and crossing them at the ankles before helping himself to a pinch of snuff and settling back to listen to the ladies discussing their morning's shopping expedition and observe the charming Melissa Maxwell more closely.

Eventually, feeling ill at ease with the stilted atmosphere that was prevalent between brother and sister, Melissa announced that she would have to leave.

'I'll walk you to your carriage—or my carriage as the case will be,' Sir Gerald said, getting up.

'Are you always so noble, sir?' Melissa asked.

He grinned. 'You may depend on it.'

Unable to shake off the continued attentions of Sir Gerald, they made their way to the front of the house where the carriage was waiting to take Melissa home.

Still holding the yellow rose, Gerald handed it to her, telling her he couldn't think of any other lady he would rather present it to.

Eliza glowered at him. 'Do not believe a word that trips off his tongue, Melissa. Gerald is a notorious womaniser and his intentions less than honourable.'

'And I would be grateful if you did not cast aspersions,' Gerald protested, seeming to be more flattered by his sister's rebuke than offended.

Melissa suddenly noticed Antony in the street, having just alighted from a carriage—Laurence's carriage—and seated inside was the familiar figure of her husband.

Her smile froze as her gaze became fixed on them. Laurence's gaze barely rested on Melissa before sliding to Sir Gerald, his mouth drawn into a ruthless, forbidding line. There was a tightening to his features as his eyes narrowed and swept over him like a whiplash. The look that passed between them crackled with hidden fire and for just a moment Melissa saw something savage and raw stir in the depths of her husband's eyes, before they became icy with contempt.

Melissa intercepted a silent communication between Antony and Eliza, noticing how Eliza paled and drew in her breath quickly, her hand rising to her throat as her eyes were drawn towards Laurence.

'What is this?' Antony said lightly. 'You're back from Brighton earlier than expected, Gerald.'

'Yes—that's precisely what my sister said. I hope you don't mind. It is my house when all is said and done.'

Antony was clearly discomfited by that. His gaze flitted from his wife to Laurence. 'Laurence—I'm truly sorry about this, but...'

'Forget it, Antony.'

'Pardon me—I forget my manners,' Gerald said, stepping forward, eyeing Laurence coldly. 'Would you not care to come inside for a shot of refreshment?'

Laurence subjected him to a look of severe distaste and chilling contempt. 'You are impertinent, Mortimer, and not worth the shot.' His eyes sliced to his wife. 'If you are ready, Melissa, say goodbye to Eliza.'

Filled with confusion by Laurence's show of rudeness, Melissa was puzzled by his behaviour, but recalling that he had not spoken favourably of Sir Gerald in a previous conversation and witnessing the

ous possession washed over his skin, jolting him with its intensity.

Because of the short time they had been married, he had respected her wish for some time to herself, some time to get used to the marriage. Bur she was still his wife and he did not intend living a celibate life much longer. Night after night he would glare at the closed door that stood between his room and Melissa's, imagining her on the other side—in her bed. There were times when his need of her was beyond all bearing. The longer the situation continued the more difficult it would be for them to come together. The situation clearly would not right itself so it was time he did something about it.

'Melissa,' he said, softening his tone, 'you're free to do whatever you want—and I'm glad you've found a friend in Eliza—but I don't want you going anywhere near her brother.' As soon as he had seen them together a part of him seriously objected. Melissa meeting a man she might be drawn to would mean sharing her as he had Alice, with all the heartache and pain this would cause. Alice and Gerald had been lovers for a long time. She and Toby had been killed on the day she had left Laurence for Gerald. He would not go down that path again. 'There is another matter I think we should discuss,' he said, deliberately putting Alice out of his mind. 'We have received an invitation to attend Lord and Lady Cranston's summer ball. I think we should go.'

'You do? Eliza mentioned something about it, but

dislike he so clearly felt, she thought Laurence must have good reason to cut him so deliberately.

'Yes, of course.' Turning to Eliza, she smiled. 'Thank you for your help, Eliza, and the refreshment.'

'Don't mention it, Melissa. I loved it, shopping together. You have some packages in my carriage. I'll see that you get them. And don't forget we will be calling on you the day after tomorrow to take you riding in Hyde Park.'

'I won't. I'm looking forward to it. It will be good to be back in the saddle again.'

Gerald stepped towards Melissa as she was about to climb into the carriage, making a bow worthy of the most elegant of courtiers. 'It was truly a pleasure to make your acquaintance, Lady Maxwell,' he said, the most charming smile pasted on his attractive face. He almost crowed with the achievement of acquiring her acquaintance, which, considering the way Laurence was glowering at him fit to do murder, was perhaps not the most tactful of things to do.

With a mask of feral rage, after snapping orders to the driver, Laurence glared across at his wife as the carriage moved away from Mortimer House. Melissa waited for the onslaught of her husband's fury although she did not consider she had done anything to justify it. She deeply regretted if she had done anything to upset him and it would be no easy matter placating him.

Drawing a quick breath, in an attempt to dispel the fury that the encounter with Sir Gerald had caused him, settling into the corner Melissa smiled across at him, trying to remain calm and in control of herself.

'After our shopping trip to the Strand, Eliza invited me to Mortimer House for refreshment. You are clearly displeased about it, Laurence. Why?'

'That is not the reason why I am displeased, Melissa. It is the fact that Mortimer was also present—although I suppose you would have to meet him some time. I saw the way he looked at you, which you must have observed for yourself. It would seem you have an admirer and I suspect it amuses you to have a flirtatious exchange with such a blackguard.'

'Is he really as bad as all that?' She tried to sound unconcerned while deep inside her anger stirred at Laurence's stubborn refusal to explain the reason for his dislike of Gerald Mortimer. 'He is handsome enough, I suppose, but he does not tempt me.'

'I'm relieved to hear it.'

'There really is bad blood between you, isn't there?' Melissa said quietly.

Laurence hesitated a moment, his silver-grey eyes thoughtful as he considered her question. His mouth tightened. 'You might say that. The man is consumed by his own obsessions. It's unhealthy that he should exhibit such an unrestrained interest in another man's wife.' He glanced distastefully at the rose she was still holding. 'Get rid of it.' Without waiting for her to do so he snatched it from her grasp and tossed it out of the carriage. 'I think it best that you avoid him whenever possible—that you keep away from such destructive, immoral influences, for it is clear to me

that your lack of understanding of society's ways and your inexperience only adds to your attraction in his eyes. As you will have observed for yourself, he and I are not the best of friends. You will not visit Eliza at his house again.'

'But—what are you saying? How can I not do so without upsetting her? And—Antony is your closest friend.'

'The discord between Gerald Mortimer and myself is of long standing. Eliza and Antony fully understand it—although for the life of me I cannot understand why she took you to Mortimer House.'

'Her brother was supposed to be down in Brighton. It wasn't her fault that he returned earlier than expected. I'm sorry if I've upset you. I won't go there again.'

Laurence stared at her, the anger draining out of him. He was struck afresh by her loveliness. It was easy to forget he hadn't wanted to marry her. What was difficult was controlling his physical reaction to her nearness—an exercise of fortitude, he thought wryly, that was proving to be exceedingly trying. He'd never imagined he would find himself confronted with this apparently insurmountabl barrier—the barrier Melissa had erected around he self like a stone wall. But if she thought to conti withholding herself from him then she was taken. He recalled the way she'd smiled at G Mortimer—he would like to see those lips cu just that way for him, he decided, as a breath

I didn't pay any attention to it at the time. I—thought you wouldn't want to go.'

'I don't normally attend society events. When the invitation arrived, I confess I only gave it a cursory glance and was tempted to tell my secretary to send a polite refusal, despite any social occasion at Cranston House reputed as being exceptional. It was Antony who persuaded me to accept it. He and Eliza will be going and I think you would enjoy attending such a prestigious event before going to Winchcombe. Invitations to any event Lord and Lady Cranston hold are as coveted as jewels.'

'Eliza said something of the sort, but I imagine the invitation has been issued out of politeness to you.'

'I trust you have read the newspapers and are aware of what has been written about us—about our marriage?'

'Indeed. It was hard not to.'

'No doubt you find the comments hurtful.'

'Yes, I do. Very hurtful. I didn't realise people could be so cruel.'

'Believe me, Melissa, the press, along with the malicious tongues of society, are capable of damaging any relationship. I think we should accept the invitation.'

'Show a united front, you mean.'

'Something like that. As my wife you will have to face society some time. You will meet and make the acquaintance of many of my friends, which will be a good thing, for we must go out into society and return their hospitality as it would be an advantage to you. It is also important to me that we put the right face on our relationship so I suggest the sooner we are seen together the better.'

'And you think attending a ball is the solution? I will attend, but with everyone talking about me it will be a nightmare. I shall encounter curious strangers who will watch my every move, searching for something else to gossip about.'

'You can do it. I have every faith in you.' He spoke in a tone that brooked no argument.

'And it doesn't concern you that I shall be flayed alive by wagging tongues?'

Unbelievably he laughed outright at that. 'Not a bit. The ball will be a complete crush, which will be to your advantage. You'll survive.'

'And I have no doubt that you will enjoy every minute of my suffering,' she muttered.

'I may be many things, Melissa, but I am neither cruel nor sadistic. Be assured that I will not leave your side all night—unless you really do feel that you cannot face it. I will not force you to go.'

'No.' She was adamant. 'How pathetic and desperate that would seem. I am fully aware that in the eyes of the *ton* I am a shameless wanton and unfit to mingle in polite society. I may have broken all the rules governing moral conduct, but I have no intention of hiding away for ever.'

Laurence gazed across at his wife, her face flushed with the heat of the day and the thought of facing society at a grand ball. He felt admiration for her honesty and courage in admitting her fear over the coming event and her determination to face it out.

'Your case is extreme, I grant you. Normally social prejudices exclude young women who have transgressed from the *ton*—not that you were aware of that or would care one iota if you did, when you willingly gave yourself to me in the Spring Gardens. But for what it's worth, you won't be alone. Antony and Eliza will be there also to give their support. You cannot imagine the influence we will have.' With a reassuring grin he explained, 'I do have enormous consequence and I will not permit anyone to say an unkind word against you.'

'Thank you. That's reassuring to know.'

'As my wife these are the people you will have to associate with and it is absolutely imperative to me that you learn to get on with them, which is why it is important that we socialise.'

'As the wife of such a high-profile figure, I realise I must conform. I am not complaining. I will yield to the temptation to allow myself to enjoy the evening, which already holds the promise of enchantment.'

Laurence arched his dark brows and eyed her with dry amusement. He liked her use of the word conform. Dare he hope she would be willing to conform in other areas of their marriage before too long? 'The object is to brave it out. You have spirit enough for that. As my wife, no one will dare disrespect you. I will not have my wife being a social outcast.' He grinned suddenly as he appraised his wife. 'No one will dare give you the cut direct in front of Eliza. She can be quite formidable and will terrify everyone into accepting you.'

Melissa found herself responding to his smile which she returned. 'But what to wear? I suddenly find that I have so many sumptuous gowns to choose from that I shall have to consult Eliza to help me.'

Laurence was already imagining her attired in such a way that she would outshine the rest. 'Normally I would advise glamour in favour of subdued elegance, but since it's your first outing we don't want to go over the top. I'm sure between the two of you that you will find something exquisite.' A frown suddenly creased his brow as a thought occurred to him. 'You do dance, don't you, Melissa?'

She laughed. 'Of course I can dance. That was one thing my mother insisted upon me being taught, so worry not, Laurence, I won't disgrace myself or you by making a hash of it on the dance floor—although it's quite a while since I practised so you will have to watch your toes.'

'Have you visited your Aunt Grace, by the way? You told me she lives in Kensington.'

'Not yet, but I thought I might pay her a call in a day or two.'

'When you decide to go you must let me know. I would like to meet her.'

Pleased that he wanted to meet her extended family her face broke into a smile. 'I would like that—and I know Aunt Grace would love to meet you, too.'

'Then go ahead and inform her of our visit.'

* * *

It was a brilliant, warm day when Melissa ordered the servants to have one of the horses saddled while she changed into her riding habit. It was the day Antony and Eliza had offered to take her riding in Hyde Park and she'd been looking forward to it enormously.

Pulling on her gloves as she crossed the hall, she was pleasantly surprised to encounter Laurence. Looking extremely fetching in a sapphire-blue riding dress, with a matching hat cocked at an impudent angle atop bunches of delectable curls that bounced delightfully when she moved her head, she stopped in front of him.

The heat of his gaze travelled the full length of her in a slow, appreciative perusal, before making a leisurely inspection of her face upturned to his.

'I've just been round to the stables. It had almost slipped my mind that it's today you are to ride out with Antony and Eliza until the groom told me you had instructed him to saddle one of the horses. You look lovely, by the way—enough to outshine all the fashionable ladies you will see in the park.'

'Are you coming with us?' she asked.

'I wasn't going to, but I changed my mind.'

'Oh—please don't feel that you have to.'

'I want to. Why should my wife have all the fun, I asked myself? Come, we'll go to the stables together and I'll introduce you to the horse I've chosen for you.'

Melissa followed, looking at Laurence admiringly, thinking how attractive he was, with his darkly handsome face and the breeze lightly ruffling his shiny black hair. With a tall hat tucked underneath his arm, he was resplendent in an impeccably tailored dark brown riding coat. His gleaming white neckcloth was perfectly tied and his narrow hips and muscular thighs were encased in buff-coloured breeches, disappearing into highly polished tan riding boots.

Melissa hadn't been to the stables before. Grooms were hard at work cleaning stalls and grooming horses, of which there were many. Some of the men tipped their hats politely to her when she appeared. Taking her elbow, Laurence propelled her towards a snowy white mare an elderly groom was holding.

'This is Ben. He's been with us for more years that I care to remember. He's in charge of the yard and making sure everything runs like clockwork,' he explained.

'I'm pleased to meet you, Ben. Riding is one of my greatest pleasures so I imagine we will be seeing much of each other.' She gave Ben a friendly smile, casting her eye down the long row of stalls. 'I have no doubt you have your work cut out with so many horses to look after.'

Ben's face compressed into a multitude of wrinkles as he grinned at her. 'We manage nicely, Lady Maxwell.'

'Let me introduce you to Lady. Lady is to be your mount for today,' Laurence told her. 'She's a reliable mount that I'm sure you'll enjoy taking out for your first tour of the park.' Standing back, he looked at her. 'Now, give me your opinion of her.'

'I'll be able to do that when I've ridden her. What is your opinion of her, Ben?'

'She's a good horse, my lady,' he said, scratching his head. 'She's a gentle mount—level-headed and sure-footed. She won't let you down.'

'I'm relieved to hear it.'

The mare rubbed her head against her, her soft dark eyes alive with intelligence. She stroked the velvety nose as Lady blinked her large eyes, arching her elegant neck and nickered softly, relishing the attention. Ben handed the reins to Laurence and went to fetch His Lordship's horse. Melissa wrinkled her nose at the saddle with distaste, having forgotten she would be required to ride side-saddle.

'I'd rather not be seated on that, but for decency's sake, I suppose I must. Although how on earth anyone can be expected to communicate with the horse on that, let alone stay on, is a mystery to me. I shall probably become unseated at the first hurdle—which I have no doubt you will blame on my poor horsemanship and not the saddle.' Peering askance at her grinning husband, who she was beginning to suspect was finding some humour in her apparent aversion, Melissa smiled gingerly. 'If I take an undignified tumble, I am sure it will fill Your Lordship with morbid delight,' she retorted tartly.

Laurence laughed. 'Heaven forbid! I imagine you are too good a horsewoman to do that. All the other ladies seem to manage it. Don't tell me you have never ridden side-saddle?'

'Not if I can help it,' she replied, running her hand

over Lady's glossy flank. The horse tossed her head in appreciation of her touch.

'If you're afraid to ride Lady side-saddle—if it's more than you can handle—simply say so,' he suggested generously, a lazy, challenging, taunting smile tugging at his firm lips.

Melissa merely glowered at him, affronted that he should dare suggest such a thing. 'I love to ride—but this silly saddle will take all the pleasure out of it. Still…' she sighed out loud '…it's a serious handicap, I confess, but because I have no wish to embarrass you and drive you to murderous fury today by insisting that the saddle be changed, I suppose if I am to play the game by society's rules then I have no alternative but to get used to it.'

'Very sensible. I'm happy that you're beginning to see things my way,' Laurence said with a wicked grin.

She scowled at him. 'Don't count on it. Does Lady have any peculiarities that I should know about before I risk life and limb?'

Laurence lifted an eyebrow lazily. 'She's as docile as a lamb.'

Melissa wasn't overly thrilled with all the reassurances she was receiving. 'Not too docile, I hope.' There was such a thing as being too docile, which usually meant boring. 'Come, help me into this monstrous instrument of torture.'

Placing his hands on her waist, Laurence lifted her effortlessly into the offending saddle, watching as she hooked one knee around the pommel and placed her booted foot in the stirrup before settling her skirts.

A groom brought the mount Laurence was to ride that had been readied for him. It was a striking chestnut stallion, with a rippling black mane and tail. His neck was wonderfully arched, his head and large eyes seemingly without flaw. The horse's sleek coat gleamed. Laurence swung himself up into the saddle with ease and with measuring awe Melissa could not help admiring the way he handled the spirited mount.

'Ready?'

Meeting his calm gaze, she felt an unfamiliar twist to her heart, an addictive mix of pleasure and excitement. She nodded, taking the reins firmly in her gloved hands.

Together they rode out of the yard, Laurence's skittish mount dancing sideways, elevating his white hocks in a flashy, high-stepping gait.

A large company was already congregated in Hyde Park. It was a place where the rich and famous came to see and to be seen. It was composed of ladies and gentlemen of quality, mounted on some of the finest horses that England could produce. The park was a hive of colourful activity, the atmosphere jovial and relaxed.

They met up with Antony and Eliza as arranged. They were in the best of spirits.

Edging his horse close to Melissa, Antony managed to take her gloved hand and place a kiss on her fingers. He grinned, a warm, enchanting grin. 'You look divine, Lady Maxwell. Marriage clearly agrees with you. You look delectable.'

Hearing every word of his friend's flattery, Laurence laughed. 'Hands off, you reprobate. Look to your own wife—who is rather stunning.'

Eliza, radiant and vivacious in a topaz riding habit, a matching hat adorned with a cheekily curling feather, favoured Laurence with a broad smile. 'Why, thank you, Laurence. I fear there are times when my husband fails to notice. It does him the world of good to be reminded.'

The four of them proceeded to the Ring. Since there were so many carriages attended by liveried footmen and bewigged coachmen and horses circling, they had no choice but to join the elegant parade and pad along at a sedate pace within the enclosed lane. Curious looks were cast their way. Eyebrows were raised, eyes assessing and lingering overlong on Melissa, and a buzz of whispers ensued, for it was the first time Lord Maxwell had been seen with a woman since his first wife's demise and, of course, as Eliza pointed out, London would be alive with gossip about her tomorrow.

Eliza, always a popular figure at the best of times, paused now and then to pay her respects to friends and acquaintances. Noticing Melissa's strained profile and sensing her frustration at being hemmed in, Laurence brought his horse alongside Lady.

'I suspect you would rather be riding free than struggling through this melee. Come with me. There's a remote region of the park where you can ride away from the crowds. It offers more freedom than the Ring. We'll meet up with Antony and Eliza later.'

Together they rode away from the Ring, cantering side by side at a leisurely pace. Laurence firmly restrained his powerful stallion who longed to gallop. They came to a quieter area of the park with a long stretch of green turf.

'You ride on,' Laurence said. 'Enjoy the gallop.'

'Will you not come with me? I'll race you.'

He laughed. 'I think not. My mount against your quiet little mare? You couldn't possibly win.'

Melissa wasn't prepared to stay and argue. Impatient to be off, she nudged her mount with her heel and she was away.

Laurence watched her go, pausing to drink in the sight of her, supple and trim in her blue habit. Their weeks of marriage had taught him to see beyond the outer shell of this lovely, vibrant woman and to read the true depth of the person hidden within. He realised that for all the pleasure he had derived from their coming together, some deeper, richer emotion was taking root in his heart. As yet he could put no name to it—it had a quality that was outside the realms of his experience. Still, whatever it was, it was pleasant.

As he indulged himself admiring his wife from afar, he watched as she galloped over the green turf, urging her mount on even faster. She rode like the wind, with the blind bravado of a rider who had never fallen off. She seemed to leave all her cares behind her like the gauzy blue scarf tied around the crown of her hat. It rippled gracefully behind her like the pennant on a ship's mast and the long skirts of her riding habit billowed along her mount's flank as she rode with more proficiency in the side-saddle than she had given herself credit for. The clash of his emotions as he watched her surprised him. He let her ride her fill before approaching her.

Having slowed her horse to a walk, the reins held loosely in her gloved hands, allowing the animal to choose the route and hearing the jingle of a bridle and the snort of a horse, Melissa turned and saw Laurence riding towards her. His warm, silver eyes looked at her in undisguised admiration as he drew alongside, a smile curving on his firm lips.

'Did you enjoy that?' She looked so vital, her eyes shining and her cheeks flushed from her exertions.

'I enjoyed myself thoroughly,' she replied, leaning forward and patting Lady's neck. 'I felt able to breathe again. What a spirited little mount Lady is.'

'My compliments, Melissa. I know few men who ride as well as you.' He fell in beside her.

'I'm sure you exaggerate, Laurence. You are being kind, but I do indeed love to ride.' The genuine warmth and admiration in his voice and in his eyes flooded her heart with joy.

'I know you do. Any time you want to ride out, if I am not available take one of the grooms. Lady enjoyed it, too, I wager. She looks perky. It will have done her good to get out. Is she to your liking?'

'Oh, yes. She's not as fast as Freckle, but we get on well enough. She's a lovely horse.'

They returned to the Ring at a leisurely walk. Antony and another gentleman were having a heated discussion about the merits of their respective horses, while Eliza chatted with the gentleman's wife. When Laurence came alongside him, Antony broke off his conversation to speak to him.

'I wondered where you'd disappeared to.'

'Melissa wanted a good gallop so I took her to the other side of the park. Have I missed anything?'

'You might say that—although it's probably a good thing you were otherwise occupied.' He indicated a gentleman walking away from them. 'You've just missed Gerald, you'll be pleased to hear.'

As if he knew he was being discussed, the gentleman paused and turned to look back.

Laurence scowled and Sir Gerald's lips curled with something akin to dry amusement mingled with dislike, and he nodded ever so slightly in acknowledgement, which Laurence did not deign to return. Undeterred, Sir Gerald casually turned and went on his way.

Antony sighed. 'So, things are still no different between the two of you, I see.'

'Should they be?'

'No, I suppose not. What happened between you affected all of us, Laurence,' Antony said with mild reproach. 'Eliza in particular finds it difficult to come to terms with it all. Alice was her friend and Gerald her brother. When the two of them met before you appeared on the scene, none of us could have foreseen the tragedy that was on the horizon.'

'How could we? But it is done now. No good will come of going over it. I am sorry that Eliza has been so deeply affected by what happened, but it is impossible for things to go back to what they once were.'

'No, I don't suppose they can.'

A laughing Eliza and Melissa came to join then, ending any further conversation about Gerald Mortimer. It was a merry group that left the park. After promising to meet up at the Cranstans' ball, they dispersed to their respective homes.

Chapter Seven

The day of the ball finally arrived. After making sure Violet was settled in the nursery Melissa gave herself up to Daisy's capable hands. On entering her chamber she was surprised to see one of her favourite gowns freshly ironed and spread out across the bed.

'Your husband instructed me to prepare something suitable for the ball. He said it had to be elegant and not too fussy. He also said the neckline was not to be too daring. I hope you approve the one I've chosen for you to wear.'

It was a sumptuous gown in deep rose-pink—almost the same colour as the gown she had worn to attend the dinner at Beechwood House. Caught halfway between annoyance and amusement at Laurence's high-handedness, Melissa laughed. 'Absolutely, Daisy. It was the very gown I would have chosen myself. Did he suggest the colour also?'

'Yes, as a matter of fact he did. He said this particular colour would enhance your complexion and suit your shade of hair perfectly.'

'I am indeed touched that my husband has taken such an interest in what I should wear. He has excellent taste.'

As she prepared for the evening's entertainment—her first London ball—excitement and trepidation caused her stomach to flutter. She was finding it harder and harder to retreat into cool reserve when she was near Laurence, especially when memories of the night they had lain together intruded and she remembered the joy of it, but she was happy and relieved that their relationship seemed to be on a better footing following their ride out in Hyde Park.

There were times when she knew Laurence wanted her. She saw it in his eyes when he looked at her, in his expression, and she deeply regretted the harsh words they had exchanged when he had left her bed on their first night in London. Perhaps tonight would go some way to making their marriage happy and solid and in time help to heal the wounds of the terrible loss of his wife and son.

Hopefully an evening at Cranston House would turn it around.

Returning home after a busy schedule of business appointments in the city, Laurence had just enough time to dress for the evening's entertainment and toss back a large brandy. Striding into the hall, he paused. Melissa was just coming down the stairs. Nothing had prepared him for the first sight of his wife dressed for the ball.

With a stunned smile of admiration, he took in the

full impact of her ravishing deep rose gown, his bold eyes moving over her with unhidden masculine appreciation. The skirts fell from her waist into panels that clung gently to her graceful figure and ended in a swirl at her toes. The bodice was slightly off the shoulder, showing to perfection the creamy flesh of her throat and a tantalising hint of the gentle swell of her breasts. Her hair was drawn back in a sleek chignon, its lustrous simplicity providing an enticing contrast to the sophistication of the gown. The effect was regal and enchanting. His heart wrenched when he looked on her unforgettable face—so poised, so beautiful that he ached to take her in his arms. Never had he seen her look so provocatively lovely, so regal, so glamorous and bewitching.

He had noticed the change in her that marriage and motherhood had brought about—she was not the charming innocent he had left behind at the Spring Gardens. The transformation both unnerved and enthralled him. The breathtaking woman who stood before him dressed so finely, her eyes alight with excitement for the evening ahead, was a lady fit to take her place in the most glittering houses in the land. Laurence had the odd sensation that Melissa had become someone else, but there was no mistaking those brilliant amber eyes or that entrancing face.

As he moved towards her, the scent of her gentle perfume wafting over him, his decision to have her in his bed tonight no matter how many objections she raised became an unshakeable resolve. He was certain she wanted him; he had seen it in her eyes.

Taking her hand, he helped her down the last steps, his gaze warming appreciatively.

'You look enchanting. I see Daisy obeyed my instructions to the letter. The gown is beautiful—the colour suits you—but perfection can only be attained when one works with the best of raw materials. After tonight, you'll take the shine out of all the London belles. You will be the envy of every woman there,' he said softly.

Melissa met his gaze and her heart swelled. If she was envied tonight, it wouldn't be due to her appearance but because she could claim this handsome man for her husband. Buoyed by confidence stemming from his warm compliment, she returned his smile, while deep inside she felt something tighten and harden with trepidation. Her cheeks were tinted a delicate shade of pink, her eyes alight and warm, her parted lips moist.

'Thank you, Laurence. I'm glad you approve of what you see. It gives me confidence for what is to come. I think I am going to need it.'

'I'm just relieved to see you have not taken to your bed with a fit of nerves.'

Despite her dread of the evening before her, Melissa had to bite back a guilty smile over that remark. 'I have to confess that I did consider it. Eliza and Daisy talked me out of it.'

Laurence nodded his approval. She was brave, immensely so. 'Everyone of importance will be at the ball. Hopefully, afterwards, when everyone has taken a good look at you with me, the gossip will die a swift death and you can get on with the business of being my wife.' Taking her gloved hand and drawing it through the crook of his arm, he escorted her out to the waiting conveyance, his mind already drifting ahead to the moment when that glorious mantle of shining dark hair would be spilling over the pillows of his bed and his bare chest, and her supple, silken body would be writhing in sweet ecstasy beneath him.

Seated across from Laurence in his black town coach drawn by four fiercely black horses, Melissa's face had reddened at his remark, reminding her of her duty which she had avoided of late—not for much longer, it seemed, for she was certain his words contained a deeper meaning. When she had met his eyes looking up at her from the hall, she had felt her heart slam into her ribs and her thoughts scattered. An increasing comforting warmth suffused her. A strange sensation of security, of knowing he was at hand and would be throughout the ball, pleased her. He had a certain flair in his mode of dress—a splash of claret in his waistcoat beneath the black coat, an artful twist to his pristine white cravat and a flourish to the ruffle at his sleeve.

Arriving at Cranston House, a stately Georgian mansion which was an outstanding example of opulence on a grand scale in the heart of Bloomsbury, it seemed as if everyone in London had been invited. The streets were congested with carriages depositing the cream of London society outside the open doors. Footmen in powdered wigs and claret and gold livery met each vehicle and escorted the guests into the brilliance of the interior.

Lord and Lady Cranston greeted them warmly. There was much fluttering of fans, bobbing of curtsies and bowing of elegant heads. Guests filled the large marble-pillared hall—debutantes in gorgeous pale-coloured gowns accompanied by their chaperons and young men dressed in black, with brightly coloured waistcoats and pristine white cravats.

Laurence escorted Melissa up the grand curved staircase. Exotic blooms on marble pedestals adorned the rooms and passageways, their scent exquisite. Gaming tables had been set up in reception rooms for those who preferred to pass the evening in dice and cards, and another two reception rooms had tables arranged for the customary light supper served before midnight. They paused to gaze down on the scene in the brilliant ballroom with its highly polished parquet floor and Venetian mirrors. The light from hundreds of glittering candles in glittering crystal chandeliers lit the soaring space while delightful music lightened the drone of conversation.

Melissa had never seen anything like it. Silks and satins in bright colours paraded before her. Perfumes drifted and mingled into a heady haze as bejewelled ladies took to the dance floor with their partners. Slowly they made their way down to the ballroom. A sea of people seemed to press towards them and voices erupted as heads turned and fans fluttered and people craned their necks to observe the new arrivals. Although they wouldn't dream of giving Laurence the cut, they looked at Melissa with raised brows and severe disapproval.

Noting Melissa's pallor, Laurence took a couple of glasses of sparkling wine from the tray of a footman. Handing one to his wife, he smiled at her. 'Here, drink this. It will put some colour into your cheeks. It will also help you to relax and make you feel less like running away.'

Melissa took a deep breath and did as she was told. After taking a gulp of her wine, she squared her shoulders. 'I've never run away from anything in my life and I'm not about to start now. My reputation may have taken a public flogging, but if I have nothing else I still have my pride.'

Laurence could not argue with that. She did have pride, lots of it, and he hoped she would face them all down with her head held high.

'Are you ready?'

Taking a deep breath Melissa nodded. 'Yes—although I am sure pistols at dawn would be far less nerve-racking.'

Laurence chuckled, taking her hand and tucking into the crook of his arm. 'But not nearly as effective. Now come along. Before the night is over everyone will love you.'

Melissa very much doubted it, but she let him lead her into the ballroom. She was dazzled and confused by this impeccable *ton*ish company. Every influential head turned to the new arrivals and conversation became hushed as eyes strained to have a look at Lord Maxwell's new wife. What they saw was a dark-haired beauty draped in an exotic, extravagantly expensive rose-pink gown that clung to her voluptuous body. Her thick, glossy hair was caught up in an array of curls entwined with a narrow ribbon matching her gown. The style emphasised her sculpted face and generous lips. No one looking at her would believe that her knees were trembling and her stomach churning with panic.

Laurence gently squeezed Melissa's hand, aware of her nervousness.

She was aware how female eyes turned to her husband. His commanding presence was awesome, drawing the eye of every woman in the room. A group of people moved to speak to him and she noticed how everyone was hanging on his every word, doe-eyed young debutantes gazing at him dreamily, and that there was a tension about the group that seemed to begin and end with him.

'What I see right now,' he said quietly during a moment of privacy, nodding his head towards his right, 'is at least a dozen besotted young bloods looking as if they would like to trample over me to get to you.'

'Then I'm relieved you are here to protect me. I can't see anything of Eliza and Antony,' she said, her eyes doing a quick scan of the throng.

'They'll arrive soon, I'm sure of it. Eliza probably can't decide what gown to wear.'

'Yes, maybe you're right.' She smiled up at him. 'When are you going to ask me to dance?'

He pretended shock, stepping back. 'Lady Maxwell. That is a shocking thing to ask. A lady never asks a gentleman to dance.'

'No? Then I would like to set a precedent. Would you care to dance with me, Lord Maxwell, or should I really shock everyone and set the tongues wagging even harder and approach one of the gentlemen you referred to? I'm sure they would not refuse to dance with me.'

Laurence gave her one of his lazy smiles. Pride of ownership was evident in his possessive gaze and Melissa's heart soared when she saw it. He had never looked at her like this before—as if she were a tasty morsel he was planning to devour at his leisure.

'Is that so?' he said with an assessing smile as he studied her upturned face. 'At least your brazen challenge has put some sparkle into your eyes. It's unfortunate that my advances didn't have the same effect.'

Melissa made the mistake of looking at his lips. She studied them for a second, then shook off the awareness that suddenly gripped her. 'How would you know that? The times when we have been… Well—if my memory is correct it was dark so how would you know if my eyes had a sparkle or not?'

Leaning towards her, he laughed softly, his mouth only inches from her ear. 'Then I think it is time we got to know each other better. The next time we find ourselves in bed together, I shall make sure the lamps are turned up—all the better to see you. But for now you win, Lady Maxwell. I would be honoured to dance with you.'

Without more ado he headed for the dance floor.

* * *

Melissa felt light-headed even before Laurence began spinning her in the dance. He was different tonight. She was not used to him being all courtly and romantic—she might even begin thinking he truly cared for her, when it was only a façade to show society that they were in accord. He did not love her, but she knew from the hurt in her heart that she was in danger of falling deeply, irrevocably, in love with him.

The group of young bloods with flirtatious grins raised their glasses in a salute as Melissa drew level with them and Laurence quietly fumed when he saw her acknowledge their homage with a bright smile.

'Do you have to smile at them?' he retorted sharply.

'I was only being polite.'

'Forward to the point of being fast is how I would describe it. I do not want my wife smiling and fluttering her lashes like an accomplished flirt.'

'And here was I thinking that smiling and flirting is an accepted, highly desirable mode of social behaviour,' Melissa teased quietly.

'For an unattached debutante I grant you, but not when the lady doing the flirting is my wife.'

Melissa suppressed a wry smile. If she did not know better she'd think he was jealous. She abandoned her waist to his encircling arm. It was steady and firm as a rock. Afraid that she would stumble over his feet, she looked down.

'Look at me, Melissa. Not at the floor.'

'I am trying not to tread on your feet.'

Laurence was not unaware of the attention they had initially created. 'I am certain I shall survive it. Focus your eyes on me and follow my lead. We have an audience. Hold your head up, look into my eyes and smile. Let them see that we are a devoted couple.'

She compromised, focusing her gaze on his cravat, trying not to think of all the people staring at them. After looking at them attentively, the couples on the dance floor renewed their interest in the music.

'See,' he said, his palm firm against the small of her back, his breath warm and smelling pleasantly of brandy on her cheek. 'You have fed everyone's curiosity and now they are getting on with enjoying themselves.'

'I am glad of the opportunity to show them I'm no maid fresh from the country with mud on my boots and straw in my hair,' she responded, smiling broadly with a light-hearted toss of her head.

'Don't get carried away, Melissa,' Laurence murmured with a note of caution, smiling nevertheless. 'It's true there have been rumours drifting about town about my new wife. Most people who have not had the opportunity of seeing you have imagined a rather plain young woman who set out to capture herself a rich husband. Nothing has prepared them for how you look tonight.' His eyes rested warmly on her face.

'Then I can only assume that the trouble I took to present myself at my best has been worth it.'

Melissa's fear of making a mistake on the dance floor proved unfounded, for Laurence was a superb dancer and her body soon remembered all the steps she had been taught. Of their own volition her feet followed where he led and her mind opened to the sensations of the music. His eyes shone with a purposeful light and, like the man himself, his movements were bold and sweeping, with none of the mincing steps of many of the other gentlemen participating in the dance. She was aware of the subtle play of her skirts about her legs and the hardness of her husband's thighs against hers. As he whirled her about in wide, graceful circles she seemed to soar with the melody. It was as if they were one being, their movements perfectly in tune.

The closeness of Laurence's body lent Melissa's nostrils a scent of his cologne, fleeting, inoffensive, a clean masculine smell. Her heart began pounding in her chest as if she had been running. Laurence had not touched her since their first night in London and she was not used to it, she told herself, that was all. But she remembered the times when he had and the unbelievable pleasure of it always took her by surprise. She did not look at him, but she could feel him watching her. With her hand resting on his shoulder, she could feel the hard muscles beneath the superfine of his coat, his strength, his power. She knew every chiselled contour of his chest, for had it not pressed against her own when they had lain naked together in bed? Heat pooled in the centre of her stomach at the memory and she forced herself to focus on the dance.

They made an uncommonly handsome couple. Whispers were exchanged between onlookers and further questions and conjectures made. Between the pair, however, so involved were they with each other that anything other than the music and their combined thoughts and sensations each aroused in the other went unheeded.

Laurence looked down at her, at her flushed cheeks and shining eyes. Suddenly his arm tightened about her waist, forcing her into even closer proximity. 'You are very quiet, Melissa. Have you nothing to say?'

Tilting her head back, she met his gaze. 'Do I have to say something?'

'It is customary to engage in some form of conversation with your partner.'

She smiled teasingly. 'Very well. I will say that you dance divinely.'

Laughing softly, he swept her into another dizzying swirl. 'That is what I am supposed to say to you—and you do, by the way—dance divinely.'

'Thank you. I appreciate the compliment. What else should we talk about?'

'We could engage is some mild flirtation.'

'Why on earth would we do that? We are a married couple, Laurence. Besides, you have just told me that flirtation is for debutantes and not married ladies.'

'I did—but it is appropriate for a lady to flirt with her husband if she so wishes. If you don't know how, I could teach you,' he murmured, his lips curving in a devilish smile. Staring down into her amber eyes, he momentarily lost himself in them. Desire surged through his body and he pulled her closer still. 'I'd like to try—maybe later.'

Melissa was given no time to reply for the dance ended and when they left the floor Antony and Eliza—attired in a gorgeous lime-green creation—claimed their attention.

Eliza's face brightened when she saw Melissa, and she immediately took her hand and drew her to the side of the ballroom.

'Forgive our tardiness, Melissa, but we had to wait for Gerald to return from his club. We'd promised to wait for him. Of course he arrived home with no sense of having done anything wrong—which is so like him. But forget about Gerald,' she said, looking Melissa over and obviously pleased with what she saw. 'That dress so becomes you, Melissa. It's a good choice.'

'Laurence suggested I wear it.'

'Did he? I am surprised to hear it. I never imagined he would concern himself with what you should wear. Tonight's event must be important to him—to you both.'

'Yes, I believe it is. He wanted to present me to society—to break me in, so to speak. It was nerve-racking at first, but I think everyone is beginning to lose interest in me.'

'Has Laurence introduce you to anyone?'

'A few, although we only arrived half an hour ago ourselves.'

'Then come with me and I will introduce you to everyone who is someone and who will be just dying to meet you.'

* * *

And she did. After another half an hour and beginning to wilt, Melissa managed to escape to the ladies' rest room. She tried to make her way back to Laurence, but several gentlemen who were eager to speak with him wedged their way in front of him, making it difficult for her to reach him. Left more or less to herself for the time being, she took the opportunity to slip through the French doors and step out on to the terrace. She was about to move down the shallow steps to the garden below when a blue-satin-clad gentleman seized her arm. Surprised, she looked around and found herself staring into Sir Gerald Mortimer's smiling face.

'Why, Lady Maxwell, I cannot believe my good fortune on finding you alone.' His eyes passed over her appraisingly. ''Tis exceedingly good to see you again. I trust you are well.'

'Very well, thank you.'

Sir Gerald's eyes lingered appreciatively on her face. 'My dear lady, you are simply ravishing.'

Melissa politely disengaged her arm and put a reasonable distance between them, knowing how Laurence would not approve of her talking to Gerald Mortimer.

'You have no escort?'

'Yes—my husband. He is just inside the door,' she informed him, glancing into the room and hoping Laurence wouldn't choose that moment to come outside. 'I just came outside for a breath of air—in fact,

I think I'd better be getting back before he comes looking for me.'

Sir Gerald pursed his lips in mild disdain. 'I can well understand his reluctance to let you out of his sight—even more so if he found you talking to me.'

Melissa's spine stiffened and she was rather amazed at the rush of indignation she experienced at this slur against her husband. 'Not at all. It is simply that this being my first big event since coming to London and, since I know no one, he is anxious that it goes well and I enjoy myself.'

'And are you? Enjoying yourself?'

'Yes, very much. I've just been talking to Eliza. She's very kindly introduced me to people of her acquaintance. She seems to know everyone present.'

He flashed her a charming grin. 'She's very popular, my sister, and always has a circle around her gossiping away. It always surprises me how they find so much to talk about.'

'She is indeed friendly—as is her husband.'

'They do make a handsome couple, don't they?' he remarked, catching sight of his sister and her husband accompanied by several friends as they strolled arm in arm along a garden path, happily engaged in conversation. 'Eliza is five years younger than I. Unlike myself, she is on speaking terms with your husband—which is down to the fact that she is married to his closest friend. There is something about marriage that always enhances the beauty of a woman—and my sister has certainly blossomed since her marriage to Antony.'

Melissa sent a cool glance skimming over him. 'You are not married, Sir Gerald?'

For the first time his cheerful demeanour disappeared and he smiled rather sadly. 'No, I'm afraid that happy state of affairs has passed me by.'

'That is nonsense. There are any number of young ladies I am sure would be perfectly happy for you to approach them with an eye to marriage.'

His gaze was slow and pointedly bold as he perused her exquisite radiance. 'Sadly, all the ladies who catch my eye are already attached. I did mention that I am your nearest neighbour in Surrey, didn't I?'

'Yes, you did, but why do I feel that you are attempting to change the subject, sir?'

His smile turned bitter. 'Perhaps because I am. It is painful for me to reflect on the past.'

'Please, enlighten me? I get the distinct feeling that it somehow involves my husband.'

'I am not the one to tell you.'

'Which makes me suspect that it might have something to do with my husband's first wife. Am I right?'

'You are extremely perceptive, Lady Maxwell.'

'You did know her?'

'Yes, I knew her.'

'What was she like?'

'Very beautiful.'

'And? There must have been more to her than that.'

'Yes,' he replied, his gaze drifting past her, his thoughts suddenly so far away. 'She was so full of life, her grace and elegance unsurpassed.'

Melissa looked at him curiously. 'Were you enamoured of her, Sir Gerald?' she dared to ask.

He gave her a sad smile. 'Everyone who came into contact with her was drawn to her. Her allure was like a magnet.' His gaze focused on her once more. 'I hope your wedded bliss to Laurence Maxwell lasts longer than Alice's did. If your husband would permit me, I would compliment him on his excellent taste—at least in choosing a wife—although he should be chided over his neglect of you.'

A deepening, angry pink hue was creeping over Melissa's face. 'He doesn't neglect me at all. Laurence takes care of me very well. I have no complaints.'

'I am happy to hear it.' His eyelids lowered as he savoured the beauty of her ire aroused. 'You are a very gracious and lovely lady,' he commented. 'Will you walk with me a while? The gardens are by no means large, but they are quite lovely—especially in the moonlight.'

'No, Sir Gerald,' Melissa protested, widening the distance between them. 'I cannot walk with you. I am not unaware that there is discord between you and my husband and he would be most put out if he cannot find me.'

'Then perhaps you had better say nothing to him about our meeting.'

'Are you suggesting that I deceive my husband?'

'Not at all. I merely wish to keep from causing trouble for you. Your husband would not be at all pleased to know you had spoken to me, or met me here, even if it was a chance encounter.'

'Melissa?'

Her name was spoken sharply. Sir Gerald's head snapped round and his eyes widened as they came to rest on a clearly irate Laurence Maxwell.

'You are bothering my wife, Mortimer.' Laurence's voice was low and fierce.

Sir Gerald drew himself up straight. 'I am a gentleman, Maxwell, and I can hardly leave a beautiful young lady unattended amid strangers. I saw no help for it but to keep her company.'

'My wife has all the company she needs. She is quite well escorted.'

Gerald smiled. 'Your wife is very beautiful, Maxwell. She is also high-spirited.'

'I am more aware of that than anyone else.'

'Were she not already married to you, she would, I am sure, prove extremely entertaining in a chase.'

A corner of Laurence's mouth lifted in a strained smile. 'Since when has a lady's married status ever stopped you? It never has in the past and I doubt things have changed. My advice to you is to have a care, Mortimer. I am quite adept with firearms; you might get clipped.'

'I'm no amateur myself, Maxwell.' Abruptly he inclined his head and strode back into the house.

Melissa watched him go, perplexed by their angry exchange. There was far more to their heated discourse than she understood, but she strongly believed that it had something to do with Laurence's first wife.

Laurence stood watching her with his arms folded across his chest. Melissa found it hard to meet his gaze. She felt like a child caught out in some misdemeanour. For the sake of her pride she could not tell him how he disrupted her thoughts and that her emotions were stirred by the fact of his nearness. Shielding herself against the displeasure he so clearly felt because he had found her speaking to Sir Gerald and her thoughts occupied with so many disturbing questions, she chose to attack rather than reveal her weakness.

'You're displeased because I was talking to Gerald Mortimer,' she said. 'I know you don't like him, but you treated him most rudely.'

'Rudely?' He laughed in sharp derision. 'He got off lightly. The man was ready to drag you off into the garden and I assure you he had nothing honourable in mind.'

Her eyes sparking militantly, Melissa glared up at him. 'Don't be ridiculous, Laurence. He wouldn't have done anything of the sort. He behaved towards me as any well-meaning gentleman would.'

'It's obvious to me that you need serious counselling on the definition of a gentleman. Mortimer is a rake of the first order and I don't want you to have anything to do with him.'

'I am sure you have your reasons, but you must believe me when I say I did not encourage him at all.'

His eyes softened and he nodded slightly. 'I do believe you. I know Mortimer and what he is capable of. He probably sought you out simply to provoke me.'

'Then don't let him. Short of cutting him, which would have been noticed and remarked upon, there was nothing I could do but converse with him.' Seeing that they were drawing attention and having no wish to continue the conversation, she spotted Eliza climbing the steps to the terrace. 'I think it's time for supper, Laurence,' Melissa said over her shoulder. 'I promised Eliza I would join her.'

'You, too, Laurence,' Eliza invited. 'Find Antony and come and join us.'

As the evening wore on and everyone seemed to have lost interest in her, Melissa began to relax and, for the first time since before the birth of her daughter, she began to have fun. She was welcomed by many, particularly the gentlemen, who were effusive in their compliments. On the sidelines, Laurence watched Eliza introduce his wife to more of her friends. Now, everyone wanted to know her.

'She seems to be doing all right,' Antony said, coming to his side. 'She's a success. I knew she would be. How can anyone resist her?'

'Indeed!' Laurence said, frowning as he watched his wife surrounded by a coterie of admirers, so many that Laurence hardly had an opportunity to speak to her himself. It hadn't taken her long to win them over. She was clearly enjoying herself. She seemed to light up the room with her charm and her artless sophistication. Every so often she would turn her head in his direction, her eyes alight with laughter and her mouth smiling broadly.

'She's an extraordinary young woman. She has a way with her. Her charm and beauty, as well as her casual unconcern about the rumours concerning her past, have gone a long way toward persuading many of the guests of her innocence. You're a lucky man, Laurence. Who would have thought it would come to this when the two of you met in the Spring Gardens. Come tomorrow she will be proclaimed the new rage.'

'I don't doubt it, Antony, but not for long. I intend taking her to Winchcombe before the week is out.'

'I'm surprised you haven't taken her before now.'

Laurence sighed, his expression thoughtful. The truth of it was that he was in no hurry to leave for Surrey. Winchcombe was filled with everything he had lost—his marriage, his son. It was a graveyard of bad memories. Giving Antony no indication of his thoughts, he said, 'Business has kept me in the capital until now. I think it's time Melissa saw her new home.' He looked at his friend. 'Are you to remain in London?'

He shook his head. 'We're heading back to Hertfordshire.'

'And Mortimer?'

'I believe he intends staying in town—he likes the social life here. He doesn't get down to Surrey much these days.'

Laurence was relieved to know that. 'Thank God I won't be encountering him for some time then.'

'You shouldn't—although,' Antony said quietly, 'it saddens me when I think what good friends the two of you used to be. I ought to tell you that he's considering closing up the Surrey house.'

Surprised to hear this, Laurence looked at him. 'He would do that?'

Antony nodded. 'He says there's nothing there for him, nothing to return to.'

'But—it's been home to the Mortimer family for generations.'

'Gerald is not sentimental in that way. With no intention of marrying, he prefers to make his life in London. If it were not for Eliza and any offspring we might be blessed with to inherit it in the future, and without a son of his own to continue the line after him, I believe he would sell it. He intends to go down there to put things in order—and Eliza insists on going with him. Which means I will accompany her, of course, so we will see you there before we return to Hertfordshire.'

Laurence was relieved to know Mortimer would be far removed from Winchcombe in the future.

Continuing to watch from a distance, it was with regret that he relinquished Melissa to the gallants leading her on to the dance floor, with mingled jealousy and pleasure as one partner after another claimed the beautiful and vivacious Lady Maxwell's hand for a dance. He shouldn't be surprised at her success. Her victory pleased him, for her own sake, even more than his own. She didn't deserve to be ostracised and made to suffer because of past mistakes. It was clear he had no need to be concerned. After tonight she would have acquaintances clamouring to call on her.

Melissa smiled broadly when Laurence found his way to her side between dances and before another partner could whisk her away. He smiled back, a slow, smile that melted her heart.

'Every gentleman here tonight has danced with you. I think it's high time you danced with your husband again. Come, dance with me, Melissa,' he murmured his voice soft and deep. 'The ball will soon be over and I would have one last twirl about the floor with you before we have to leave.'

Mesmerised by the seductive invitation in his voice, Melissa let him draw her on to the dance floor.

'May I ask what your admirers talked to you about?'

'You may, but I will not tell you,' she teased coquettishly.

He nodded, studying her with tranquil amusement. 'Do I have reason to call any of them out?'

She smiled, her eyes glowing with repressed laughter. 'Several. But with so many, you would be hard pressed to beat them all.'

'Don't count on it,' Laurence replied, spinning her round with unnecessary force.

She laughed. 'Laurence, please slow down. You swirl me round so fast I'm beginning to feel quite dizzy.'

'You've drunk too many glasses of champagne.'

She was indignant. 'No, I have not.'

'Yes, you have. Is it four—or five?'

His smile was amused and slightly mocking and she was stung into a response. 'You were watching me?'

'I had nothing better to do.'

'You could have sought me out sooner.'

'What? And deprive all those besotted swains of the pleasure of your company? You've made quite an impression and, regardless of your marital state, you must prepare yourself to be pursued,' he teased lightly.

'And here I was thinking I would be safe at a ball with my husband,' she quipped.

Laurence caught her gaze, his eyes narrowing seductively. 'Safe? Safe with me?' he murmured, his warm breath fanning her face. 'Of course you are.'

Melissa searched his face, feeling her heart turn over exactly the way it always did when he looked at her the way he was looking at her now. She saw the glow in his half-shuttered eyes kindle slowly into flame and, deep within her, she felt the answering stirrings of longing, a longing to feel the tormenting sweetness of his caress, the stormy passion of his kiss and the earth-shattering joy of his body possessing hers.

It was two in the morning before the ball ended and Laurence assisted his wife up the steps into the coach. Taking his seat across from her, he sought and held her gaze.

'You have clearly enjoyed your first ball, Melissa, and I'm proud of the way you conducted yourself.'

A warm glow filled her at his praise. 'I enjoyed it enormously. I have much to be grateful to Eliza for. She hardly left my side all night—unlike my husband, who happily abandoned me after supper.'

'Not happily—I assure you. I enjoyed watching you—although I found it difficult seeing you dance with one gentleman after another. I trust you behaved yourself before I thought it was time to claim you for myself. You have the most disconcerting ability to look like an enchanting ingenue one minute and an alluring, sophisticated woman the next.'

'Oh! I'm not sure how to take that.'

'It was intended as a compliment,' he assured her, smiling slightly. 'You must forgive me for not making it plain. I'm out of the habit of bestowing compliments on beautiful women.'

'Then I can only hope you renew the habit. I rather enjoy being complimented.'

'I'll keep that in mind.'

When they arrived at the house, pleading tiredness, she declined Laurence's suggestion that she stay and have a glass of wine and excused herself. Earlier she had told Daisy not to wait up for her, that the hour would be late and she could manage to undress herself. The bed was turned down and her nightdress laid out. Quickly she divested herself of her clothes and slipped beneath the sheets. She was drifting on the edge of sleep when she had a strange feeling of someone entering the room.

Chapter Eight

Melissa's eyes snapped open. In the dim light from the lamp she had left burning, she was surprised to see Laurence. Having come through the connecting door, he was leaning against the door frame. He'd divested himself of his evening clothes and wore his robe, his arms crossed over his chest. With his tousled dark hair he unerringly drew her gaze as he stood motionless, his attention riveted on her.

Her head fuddled with sleep, she struggled to sit up. 'Laurence! What are you doing here?' Her mind was in complete turmoil. 'It's very late. You really should be in bed.'

Laurence's expression didn't change as he shrugged himself away from the door and slowly strode to a comfortable armchair close to the bed, one where there was no obstruction to the sight of her. Melissa watched him intently, unable to read his expression, but she sensed something was troubling him. She could smell brandy and his eyes were piercing bright.

'Why are you here, Laurence?' she repeated.

'I want to talk to you.'

'At this hour? Won't it keep until morning?'

'No. It has to be now—while it is on my mind.'

'What—what is it?'

'It's about Alice—my first wife.'

'Oh, I see.' Making herself more comfortable, she resigned herself to listening to what he had to say. She had waited too long for him to do that—she wasn't going to send him away. Perhaps after he'd told her, things would improve between them. 'What was she really like? Please, tell me.'

'I have no doubt Eliza has already told you something about her.'

'A little, but I cannot form an opinion about someone I didn't know.'

'I would spare you the unsavoury details if I could, but I want there to be truth and honesty between us. The more you know of her the better you will understand.'

'I understand she was very beautiful—I saw the evidence with my own eyes in the painting of her.'

'Yes, she was. Coming from a family of moderate means, she enjoyed the trappings of my success, but she soon became bored—particularly when my business affairs sent me away for long periods and when she was at Winchcombe, away from the London social scene. We were overjoyed when Toby was born, but it soon soured and she began wanting more. Alice's idea of marriage did not include the concept of fidelity. She was unfaithful and made no secret of the fact.'

'I thought that in most aristocratic houses adultery was taken for granted, always provided, of course, the affair is conducted with discretion.'

'Not in my house and not when the other party was known to me. Neither of them took the trouble to conceal the affair.'

'And—Toby?'

'He was mine. I am sure of that. You must have seen the likeness in the painting of him.'

'Yes. He was the image of you—and he had that curious little birthmark which Violet has—almost in the same place.'

He nodded. 'Exactly. My father had it also. When I failed to provide Alice with the excitement she craved, she began her affair before Toby was out of the cradle.'

'Would I be right in thinking her lover was Gerald Mortimer?'

His lips twisted with bitterness. 'You are very perceptive, Melissa. Yes, in answer to your question, it was.'

'I suspected as much. That is the reason for the enmity between you.'

'Before she became acquainted with me—or perhaps I should say my wealth—it was assumed she would marry Mortimer. She used to come down to Surrey with Eliza and Antony, which was when I met her. When they resumed their affair it soon became common knowledge. I never could come to accept it.'

'Did she expect you to?'

'She told me I should be more open minded, otherwise my possessiveness would destroy our marriage.' His mouth tightened. 'I suppose I should feel pity for Mortimer, for he was a pitiful figure, but I don't. I could never forgive him for what he did. I began to hate him, blaming him for everything that happened. That's not very admirable of me, I'll admit, but that's the way I feel. I have good reason.'

'It's understandable.'

'Alice told me to pursue my own interests without interference from her. We fought constantly—right up to her death. When she died she was leaving me for Mortimer—taking Toby with her.'

He fell silent and Melissa dropped her eyes in remorse for making him feel that he had to open up to her, to speak about his wife and her lover, reopening old wounds. 'I'm so sorry, Laurence,' she said quietly, 'but thank you for telling me.'

She took a steadying breath. It was hard to believe how his disclosure wounded her, as if she were the one who had been betrayed. To discover that his wife had a lover while she was married to Laurence—she felt as if a knife had been thrust into her chest. She could not fail to be moved by his past. It was hard to resist wanting to hold this beautiful, tormented man to her breast and offer him comfort. All her own insecurities came rushing back with disturbing force. Laurence hadn't wanted to marry her—certain he didn't love her. It was clear he was still trying to bury the demons that tormented him, but what then? Would he do as his first wife suggested and feel free to pursue these other interests? How could she hope to hold on to the affection of a man who could no doubt have any woman who caught his eye?

Standing up, Laurence moved to the bed, looking down at her. 'Perhaps it was my fault that she sought companionship elsewhere.'

Melissa smiled up at him, a smile that hid her uncertainties. 'Don't blame yourself. Would things have been different if you had stayed at home more?'

'Perhaps not. Alice would never have been satisfied. When I first met you I was still in mourning. I was lost and angry. I didn't know myself any more.'

'You were grieving. You had lost your son. To grieve is a natural process when you have lost someone you love.'

'Yes—that, too. I still am. The only thing I felt I had left in my life was work—it was at the beginning of the unrest in France. It's how I coped.'

Melissa knew this. Sometimes she heard him moving about his room in the night. Now she knew why. It was because he was unable to close his mind to the ghost of his son that invaded each night.

'If I could give everything away to have Toby back, I would, in the blink of an eye, because for the first time in my life I wasn't in control. The intense grief I suffered over Toby's death has lessened with time—I no longer feel adrift without an anchor, in a sea of despair, but it still has the power to attack me now and then. Nothing meant anything at all in the face of what I'd lost. But now,' he went on, 'you have given me Violet—giving me what I needed without meaning to. Just by existing she has taught me to love something beyond my son and I can't stand the thought of losing what I have found.'

'You won't,' she told him, wishing with all her heart that he had included her in his statement.

'At that stage I had no idea how long term the devastation to my life would be.'

'I understand,' Melissa said. 'And I know you must find it hard to trust any woman after what Alice did to you. I can see that the prospect of putting your faith in someone must seem daunting. You have to take it one day at a time. I'm sorry if I've made it difficult for you.'

'You haven't. I realise now that I have no desire to spend the rest of my life alone. For what it's worth you are nothing like Alice.'

'No, Laurence, I'm not at all like her. I have no intention of leaving you or having an affair with another man. I can see that you still carry your hurt and bitterness around with you.'

Laurence's smile was one of cynicism. 'Does it show all that much?'

'Yes, I'm afraid it does.'

'There are some things, Melissa, that cannot easily be put aside.'

'I know that and I wouldn't expect you to. But your marriage to Alice and what happened between you two is in the past and belongs there. Just like our own encounter at the Spring Gardens is now in the past.

But at least one good thing came out of it: Violet. She isn't going anywhere, Laurence. I promise you that.'

He moved closer to her, reaching out and touching her cheek with the tips of his fingers. 'You are right and I adore her unashamedly.' He smiled softly. 'You had everyone eating out of your hand tonight. Be prepared to be inundated with invitations to attend this and that by every notable family in London.'

Melissa grimaced. 'Really? I don't think I'm ready for that.'

'That's good because they will be disappointed.'

'On? Why is that?'

'It's necessary for me to leave for Plymouth shortly—I'm expecting one of my ships coming into port so I must be there. I'm going to whisk you and Violet down to Winchcombe in a day or so. I think it's time you went down to Surrey. You will enjoy getting to know your new home while I'm away.'

'I would like that,' she said, although she would miss him when he had to leave. 'How long do you expect to be away?'

'A week—possibly more.'

Melissa watched him. All her thoughts suddenly fled as he took her hand and carried it to his lips, kissing her fingers lingeringly. She understood the sudden heated look of desire in his silver-grey eyes. He wanted her.

'I have no wish to return to my room, Melissa.' His gaze shifted to the empty space beside her before settling on her lovely face. Whenever he thought of his wife his thoughts had a habit of turning to lust. 'I often think about the couple of times we have made love. I am impatient to repeat what we did.'

The suggestiveness of his husky tone made Melissa's heartbeat quicken. He couldn't be so disenchanted by her if he was talking about what would happen when he climbed into bed with her. Unconscious of the vision she presented leaning against the pillows with her hair tumbling over her shoulders in loose disarray, Melissa's cheeks flamed, but at the same time her heart missed a beat.

'I fear the nearness of you might soon destroy my good intentions—although if that should happen, I hope you would not object to any actions that follow.'

Melissa's colour deepened. The quiet emotion in his voice startled her and she averted her eyes. It was a challenge, softly said, and she found herself clasping her hands in front of her in an attempt to keep them from trembling. For the time they had been in London, his intention was to put on a grand front and she had done the same. But how easy it would be to let appearances slip into reality and for her to allow him back into her bed. Even if none of the gentler emotions such as love were present, could they not still have a good marriage?

Aware of her confusion, he took a step back. 'When you have need of my services, feel free to knock on the connecting door. You will find your husband more than willing to share your bed.' He chuckled softly. 'Your cheeks are flushed, Melissa. Are you unwell?'

'I am perfectly well—although I find myself at a

disadvantage. Since I am in bed and you are not, is it your intention to batter my defences and when I am so weakened climb into my bed?'

Laurence smiled inwardly. 'I believe I have got the measure of you, my lovely wife. I know that your outward demeanour is no indication of how you feel inside. You are a clever woman, granted, but you have not yet learned that resistance, or indeed any kind of opposition, only turns me in the other direction from the one which you might want me to take. The night we met, I remember you telling me it was your birthday.'

Surprised by the question, she glanced at him warily, wondering where the conversation was heading. 'Yes. My eighteenth.'

'A naive and virginal eighteen,' Laurence murmured, his gaze on her still-flushed face.

'Yes, I was—until I set eyes on a certain gentleman.'

'And you suddenly thought you were in love.'

She looked at him in helpless consternation. 'Yes, I did—I was sure of it—even though I was sexually illiterate.'

He laughed softly. 'I imagine passion is supposed to be the characteristic of most eighteen-year-old girls. Aren't all young ladies supposed to be in love at that age?'

'I don't know. I can only speak for myself.'

An explicable, lazy smile swept over his face. 'And when I came along and gave you your first lesson, was I a good teacher, do you think?'

A fresh blush stained her smooth cheeks. 'I don't know. I had nothing to compare you with.'

'Of course you hadn't. My motives weren't noble—although they were adult and perfectly natural,' he murmured. 'I don't like it that you keep yourself from me, Melissa. The situation cannot continue.'

'You would force me?' she retorted crossly.

Laurence threw up his hands impatiently. Her attitude had suddenly turned to defiance and that head-held-high hauteur she flaunted whenever she thought she was in the right. 'You know I would never do that. But four weeks we have been married. How much longer do you need? I consider myself a married man, not a monk. You are my wife and one day you will—I hope—bear me more children. Resisting the inevitable is like swimming against the tide. Perhaps if you were to itemise your grievances as to why you prefer to sleep alone, we could discuss them and come to an understanding.'

'I have no grievances to speak of. When we married, you were a virtual stranger to me and I knew very little about marriage—even less about being a wife. All I asked was that you give me time to get used to the situation.'

'For how long?' he retorted sarcastically. 'A month—six?'

Melissa sighed and shook her head slowly. 'You're angry, Laurence. I'm sorry if I've made you so.'

'Angry, no—frustrated, yes,' he uttered, striving to keep his raw hungry need for her at bay. 'In the beginning I wronged you, true, so wreak your vengeance on me if you must, but then be done with it and let me hear no more about it.'

'If you think that, then you could not be further from the truth. I do not wreak vengeance on you, Laurence. It has never entered my head. I have no cause to do that.'

'Then for what reason do you still hold me off?'

She sat up straight. 'I'm just cautious. I am a woman—my own woman, Laurence—and it's difficult sharing a man whose mind is filled with thoughts of another woman.'

'Another woman? And who might that be?'

'Alice.'

His lips twisted in a semblance of a smile. 'Careful, Melissa. You are beginning to sound unpleasantly like a jealous wife.'

'No, Laurence. I am not jealous of a dead woman. But I feel she will always be there—between us.'

He stood and looked at her, seeming bemused by her reply and unable to understand the logic of what she said. 'If you think that, then you are very much mistaken. It is now nearly three years since Alice died. You must not think of her as an impediment to our marriage. She will not be a shadow who will step upon your heels unless you let her. What do I have to do to convince you that you have a special place here, in this house and in my life?' On that note he disappeared into his own room, closing the door firmly behind him.

Melissa stared at the closed door, wondering what he was doing on the other side. Suddenly it came to her that she wanted to know, that she wanted to be with him, to sample the delights they could share in his own bed. The intimacy of their last coming together blazed across her mind and she found she had no control over her own thoughts.

Closing her eyes tightly, she was determined to sleep, but she had tasted the sweetness of his seduction—she knew the long, sleek length of his body, the firmness of his thighs pressed to her own and she desperately wanted to experience all that again. With a sense of urgency and without further thought, throwing back the covers she swung her slender legs over the side of the bed and strode towards the door her husband had disappeared through just moments ago.

Pouring himself a large brandy, Laurence stood by the window looking out, hoping to quell the familiar burning need for Melissa which had risen in his loins. It was easy to forget he hadn't wanted to marry her. What was difficult was controlling his physical reactions to her nearness. An exercise in fortitude, he thought wryly, that he had found exceedingly trying. He didn't know how much longer he could stand this living arrangement.

She was possessed of a strong determination, was waywardly confident and showed a capacity to think for herself. He admired her sweetness and her honesty and she made him laugh. He stared into the deep purple-blackness of the night, drinking deep of the brandy as he began to marshal his thoughts with a precision taught him by years of doing business with gentlemen and rogues alike. He had a choice to make. Either he could go on living in the past, or give in to the ever-strengthening bond between him and Melissa.

When they had met in the Spring Gardens she had imagined herself in love with him. His lips twisted grimly. He found it hard to believe that anyone could actually love him—not his money, not his power—but him. Melissa was the only woman he knew for whom he could ever imagine risking his heart again or baring his soul. Recalling how quickly she had melted in his arms with such ardour during the times they had made love, he did not have the slightest doubt of his own ability to eventually lure her into his bed again.

A few weeks in his bed, her spirit would be broken and he'd have her purring like a kitten. Yet, he thought, staring down into his glass and unable to suppress the smile that curved his lips, her courage and her spirit was what he admired most about her and God help him if he did anything to destroy that. She was also a natural-born temptress with the smile of an angel. She would never bore him, he was certain of that.

He realised he had come to care for her deeply. His growing need for her made him vulnerable and he could not bear the thought of being apart from her.

To his amazement a gentle tapping on the connecting door intruded into the quiet of the room. With enormous vitality his blood raced through his veins. Crossing to the door and flinging it open, he saw her standing there like a spirit of the night in a long, white, clinging nightgown, her glorious wealth of dark hair falling down her back. She did not move or speak, but gazed at him, her enormous eyes searching his face. Laurence couldn't believe his good fortune that she had come to him. His heart slammed into his ribs as he stared at her, tracing with his gaze the classically beautiful lines of her face, the brush of lustrous ebony eyelashes, and saw the invitation in her imploring amber eyes. Hope and disbelief collided in his chest.

The grin he gave her was positively wicked as his appreciative gaze slid over her. 'What took you so long?' he murmured. Then, taking her hand, he drew her inside and closed the door.

Drawing her further into the room, Laurence could find no words to break the spell. Melissa's lips parted in a low, wordless moan as his arms went about her, folding her in his embrace.

'You came,' he whispered, his lips against her hair.

'Yes. I thought it would be nice to try out your bed—to see if it's as comfortable as mine.'

'I'll remember to ask your verdict later, my love,' he murmured.

As he took her face between his hands, his lips touched hers, testing their softness, tasting, caressing, rousing until her arms crept up his chest and around his neck. Her lips quivered and opened beneath his—like a flower, he thought, its petals filled with nectar which she was offering to him. The kiss deepened, becoming one of urgent hunger, drawing from her soft sighs of contentment, of pleasure and anticipation of what was to come. Laurence bent and his arm went behind her knees, lifting her up and carrying her to his bed, placing her on the covers.

Discarding his robe, he lay beside her, drawing her into his arms, claiming her lips once more before trailing a molten path downward to her neck and the peaks of her breasts straining at the fabric of her nightgown. His hands moved over her, persistent, demanding, Melissa tempting his every move with a kiss, until Laurence pulled her beneath him, possessing her with naked abandon, sweeping her along with him every step of the way.

His senses fled, try as he did to prevent them from leaving. His breathing quickened and he was kissing her, loving the feel of her, knowing exactly what he wanted, what she wanted. Her body began to tremble and writhe against his and he heard a moan deep in her throat as he touched her. She clutched him with all of her body, welcoming his hands on her breasts. They were ripe and firm, like sweet plums. His fingers moved in a way which rubbed the nipples until they were hard. Leaning over her, he trailed his hand about her waist, over her thighs and down her legs.

She had the scent of a woman aroused, which called to the masculine in himself. His male body had wilfully taken over from the sensible man he normally was. His lips covered her sweet body, his eyes glittering with barely controlled desire. Their passion became more ardent and they rolled over the bed, wrapped together in the same pursuit as each other. There were moments when she was astride him, her slim legs on either side until he rolled her back and had her lying down. She was squirming in his grasp and the male part of him—the physical, lusting part of him—was delighted, denied of its pleasure for so long as he adjusted her lissom body to accommodate him and herself, positioning her legs apart, ready for him.

Melissa lay beneath him, the full weight of his body pressing hers down into the soft bed. Little moans escaped her throat at the ecstasy he aroused in her. She became helpless with desire, allowing it all to happen, wanting what he was going to do with primitive ferocity. She was vibrant with a bursting depth of passion, alive and trembling. His hands were searching and caressing. The female core of her began to soften with the physical pain of her own need.

For a second a small voice in her head seemed to make her pause and to savour what he was doing to her, but she was acting like a crazy woman. When she felt the sudden assault of his maleness, it was so intensely satisfying and pleasurable that she almost fainted from it. She could feel him inside her, thrusting deeper and deeper, possessive, commanding. Now there was no holding back. Clinging to him as the abandonment went on, she was almost delirious with the exquisite sensations and by the powerful response of her own body. It seemed to have a will of its own.

And then it was over. Laurence gathered her tightly into his arms as his seed spilled into her. Melissa felt a bliss so bright she thought she could not possibly endure it. He touched his lips to hers and whispered against her mouth, 'Thank you. You have no idea what this means to me.'

His words shivered through her senses. They had pleasured one another. Already she ached for it to happen again, already she had discovered the woman in her, the latent desire she had always known deep down was there. Repositioning them both under the covers, Laurence took her into his arms once more. His hand came up to stroke her hair, but he remained conspicuously occupied by his thoughts.

What was he thinking? Melissa wondered. Was he comparing her to Alice? When he remained silent her heart sank. If he sought his pleasures elsewhere with a mistress tucked away, it wouldn't worry her as much as sharing him with a dead woman—although she suddenly felt a sharp pang which she recognised as jealousy, for she would not think kindly of her husband conferring on another woman the physical intimacies he had shared with her. It was the hold Alice still seemed to have on him, that even though she was no more she still held such sway over his life, that deeply concerned her.

'Would you be angry if I asked you a question, Laurence?' she asked quietly, her head resting against his chest and feeling the steady beat of his heart.

He gave a heavy sigh. 'Not at all—not if it's important to you.'

'It is. Did you love Alice very much?'

Laurence's peaceful, relaxed state quietly vanished. Only Melissa would raise such a subject at such a time. The question was indelicate in the extreme—especially after making love. But then, Melissa had never been one to follow established rules of propriety and convention. Her head was tucked under his chin and he gently placed his lips against her hair, considering her question and how best to answer it.

'I suppose I did—when I married her—but she wasn't a woman a man could love easily. She was Eliza's friend. I met her at Antony and Eliza's wedding. I suppose I was flattered when I realised she was attracted to me. Unfortunately, my wealth attracted her more.'

'Did you know this before you married her?'

'Yes, I did, but I didn't want to believe it.'

'Yet you still married her.'

'I did—for the usual reasons—it was time I married and I was eager to produce an heir. Things changed when Toby was born. She began to demand more of me than I could give.'

His voice held a raw edge of pain that Melissa could feel. 'I imagine her betrayal hurt your pride.'

'Yes, but I must shoulder some of the blame for what happened. I left her alone too often and for long periods. That was when she turned back to Mortimer for comfort. Being a close neighbour, he was always sniffing round her when I was absent. I was outraged, but there was nothing I could do. If she had chosen Mortimer merely to repay me for my negligence, to arouse my jealousy, then I think I could have dealt with it better. But she genuinely loved him. I had no idea when I married her how deeply she was involved with him—that there was an understanding that they would marry. I was always too wrapped up in my own affairs to notice and if I heard a rumour too ready to discount it.'

'Why didn't she marry Sir Gerald if she loved him?'

'Because he couldn't give her what she wanted—financially—whereas I could.' Looking down at his wife, he placed his hands on her shoulders and held her away from him, seeing the concern she clearly felt for him mirrored in her eyes. 'Don't concern yourself with Alice, Melissa. I mourned her death—and that of our son. But that is in the past, where she will remain. Alice seems part of another life now, another existence. My life today is not bound up with memories of her—but Toby will never leave me.'

'I sincerely hope not. When she is of an age to understand, I would like you to tell Violet about her brother, for her to get to know him through you.'

'She will, I promise you.'

'I thought that you still loved Alice and that I compared unfavourably with your memories of her.'

'Do you think that what we have just done means nothing to me, my foolish one? You are the most delightful lover any man could be fortunate enough to take to bed. Don't ever underestimate your power over me, Melissa. In fact, you may test it again if you wish—right now.'

Before she could react, he had captured her lips once more. Hurt and angered by his casual assessment of their relationship, wanting to announce that she would prefer to be addressed as his wife and not likened to a lover, she was tempted to shove him away, but to do that would be to incite an argument and she didn't want to do that since she was already in danger of letting him see how desperately in love with him she was. Her heart yearned for a two-way love, not this one-sided affair, where all the emotion seemed to be on her side and where all his tenderness was simply borne out of a man's natural lust for a woman.

But she was his wife, his woman, he had made her so in his huge bed. For what was left of the night he showed her what her body was for, what it needed, showing her what pleasures could be had, showing her how to please him and herself, but he did not tell her that he loved her. He did want her—at least physically—his lustful wooing left her in no doubt of that. And the whispered overtures he had plied her with when he had coaxed her to yield to the delights to be found in his bed, of how his introduction to the more erotic rudiments of being a fully-fledged wife had quickened her own hunger once he had given her a taste of what to expect. But was it any different to what he would say and do to any other attractive woman?

He had told her that Alice was in the past, that she belonged to another life. That might be so, but the pain of his first marriage was still with him, she had seen it in his eyes. Over the coming weeks and months she would do her best to help him break free of the past, without grief or guilt eating away inside him. If it took her the rest of her life she would convince him that he had a right to be in love and to someone who would love him in return.

Laurence awoke the next morning in a state of sated bliss. His body was wonderfully content. The rumpled bed was warm and he was extremely comfortable beneath the sheets. Allowing his eyes to open slightly, he saw a silvery light filtering through the curtains and heard birds chirruping happily in early morning song. Remembering the night past, he stretched and breathed deeply, wondering if it had all been a voluptuous dream.

Turning his head on the pillow, he was surprised to find Melissa curled up alongside him, her hair spread in wonderful disarray over the pillows and as naked as the day she was born. Her face was turned towards him, her soft rose-red lips slightly parted and her dark lashes shadowing her cheeks as she slept. Reluctant to move lest he disturbed her, he luxuriated in the simple joy of watching her. A burst of elation exploded inside him when he remembered the beauty of her. As he inhaled her sweet scent, he knew that the memory and the peace of this moment would never leave him.

Gently he reached out and brushed the hair back from her face. He felt her respond and heard her sigh, then her arm reached out and came to rest on his waist, edging closer until their bodies touched. Her eyes flickered open and she smiled.

'Good morning, Laurence. Have you slept?'

Chuckling softly, he drew her even closer. 'Very

little, as a matter of fact. I was pleasurably distracted for the most part. How about you?'

'The same. Are you glad I knocked on your door?'

'Highly delighted. Feel free to knock on my door as often as you like.'

'I'll do that. Will you kiss me so that I know I haven't imagined what happened?'

'Why? Do you doubt it?'

'No—not if you kiss me.'

Laurence was only too ready to oblige. Afterwards, she rubbed her eyes and yawned. Struggling to sit up, she looked down at him, her hair covering her bare shoulders and caressing his chest.

'I think I should return to my own room. Violet will be waking soon—if she hasn't already.'

Laughing playfully, he drew her back down, reluctant to let her go. 'Violet has enough nursemaids pandering to her every need. Let them get on with it while my wife panders to me.'

Soon his laughter turned to groans of want as he found her lips and they rolled across the bed. Melissa was only too happy to fall in with his desire and her arms went around him as he kissed her throat, his lips slowly trailing down the length of her body. Her body sang vibrantly and she couldn't have left if she'd wanted to. Her breasts pressed against his chest and she arched her back when he entered her.

'My God, Melissa! What are you doing to me?' he murmured hoarsely, capturing her lips once more in a long, drugging kiss, proceeding to love her with a slow, languorous rhythm. His control eventually slipped away as he surrendered to the glory of this woman, his wife.

When the storm of their lovemaking had passed they lay together, Laurence's fingers tangled in her hair.

Melissa sighed and melted into her husband's embrace, unable to believe that she could feel such joyous elation quivering inside. 'I really must leave you now, Laurence.' Rolling on to her stomach and leaning on her elbows, she hovered above him, kissing his lips before sliding to the edge of the bed. Slipping her arms into her robe, she got to her feet and glanced at him, a provocative smile curving her lips. 'I look forward to seeing you at breakfast.'

Chapter Nine

Melissa's first glimpse of Winchcombe was impressive. The house was tucked away between tall trees and huge shrubs of rhododendrons. The gardens embraced the flora of the area, but behind the apparent relaxed efficiency she imagined a team of gardeners beavering away every day of the year to produce such a haven of peace and tranquillity. Trees lined the drive and a fountain could be seen in a large courtyard. The spouting water sparkled in the sunlight and gravel crunched beneath the wheels of the carriage.

'Oh, my,' she breathed, with a growing sense of unreality. Everyone who had told her about Winchcombe had stressed what a truly grand house it was, but never had she envisaged anything like this. Winchcombe Hall was certainly not a house of modest proportions. 'Why—it's a lovely house. Is it very old?'

Laurence smiled at the dazed expression of disbelief on her face, well satisfied with her reaction. 'I'm afraid it is,' he said, folding his arms across his chest, preferring to watch the myriad of expressions on Melissa's face rather than the approaching house. 'Built during Queen Elizabeth's reign—it survives relatively unaltered.'

'And all those windows,' she murmured, watching as the evening sun caught the two stories of huge windows, lighting them up like a wall of flame, contrasting beautifully with the green and yellow tints and fiery shades of the surrounding foliage.

'People were enthusiastic for enormous windows in those days. Glass was very expensive. People used it in large quantities to show how rich they were.'

'Goodness! Your ancestors must have been very rich indeed.'

The four bay mounts pulling the coach at last danced to a stop in front of the imposing stone-pillared entrance. The driver leaped down and held the carriage door open for them. Laurence handed Melissa down, followed by Daisy holding Violet. A servant wearing a dark green uniform edged with gold braid appeared in the open doorway, standing aside for them to enter. Other servants appeared and descended on the coach to strip it of its mountain of baggage.

Laurence turned to Melissa. 'Welcome to Winchcombe Hall, Melissa.'

Her eyes wide with embarrassed admiration, Melissa turned to him. 'It's so grand. You might have told me,' she uttered softly.

'I hoped to surprise you.'

'Well—you succeeded admirably.'

'I sincerely hope you will like living here.'

She gave him a jaunty smile and teasingly said, 'I shall contrive to endure the hardship. How many rooms does it have?'

Laurence laughed. 'Would you believe it—I have no idea. We'll count them together as some future date. Now come inside and let me introduce you to Mrs Robins and the staff. After that you will be shown to the rooms that have been set aside for you. It they are not to your liking, you can change them.'

'I wouldn't dream of putting anyone to so much trouble.'

'Why not? You are the mistress of Winchcombe. You can do exactly as you please.'

Side by side they entered the house. At a glance Melissa became aware of the rich trappings of the cool interior, the highly polished parquet floor and wainscoted panelled walls. An ornately carved oak staircase opposite the entrance cantilevered up to the floor above and a large atrium allowed the sun to flood in above them.

With a growing sense of unreality, Melissa was introduced to what she considered to be a veritable army of servants—she was certain she would never remember all their names. Asking to be shown to her rooms, she followed Mrs Robins up the grand staircase, closely followed by Daisy carrying Violet.

Later, when Melissa had bathed and changed her clothes and made sure Violet was settled for the night, Laurence came to escort her to dinner.

'Do you approve of the rooms we selected for you?'

'Yes—they're lovely.' How could she say otherwise? They were elegant and tastefully furnished. Mrs Robins had told her that they had been Alice's and it was to her relief they had been designed by Laurence's mother. 'I like the prospect from the windows and they are comfortable and not too far away from the nursery. They will do very well.'

'I'm relieved. Shall we go down to dinner?'

He held out his hand to her, and, instead of taking it, she walked straight into his arms. For one breathless moment his eyes studied her face while the pressure of his arms slowly increased, then he bent his head and captured her lips in a kiss of such tenderness and tormenting desire. His hands slid over her back, pressing her body closer to his and she kissed him back willingly and with all her heart.

With an effort that was almost painful Laurence dragged his mouth from hers and folded her to him. Melissa stayed in his arms, wishing she could remain there always.

'We should go down to dinner,' Laurence said softly, his breath warm against her ear. 'But before we do, I have something I would like to give you.'

Melissa pulled back in his arms and looked at him, her delicate brows pulled together in confusion. 'Oh?'

He smiled, taking her hand and placing a large sapphire and diamond ring on her wedding finger, above the gold band that already rested there.

'When we met everything happened with such haste that we had no time to get to know each other.

This ring belonged to my mother and her mother before her.'

'And Alice?' Melissa whispered, unable to take her eyes off the splendid gift and deeply moved that he had given it to her.

'I never gave it to Alice.'

Melissa didn't question the reason behind this as she touched the beautiful stone reverently. 'This—it—it is beautiful, Laurence—and extremely generous of you.'

'You are my wife. It is yours by right. There are more jewels locked away that are yours to wear on special occasions, but I wanted to give you this now.'

'Thank you. I'll treasure it always—and one day...'

'It will be passed on to Violet.'

She smiled and, reaching up, drew his face down to hers and kissed him again with all the love and gratitude that was in her heart.

In the days that followed, Melissa was content to settle down, although she would miss Laurence when he left for Plymouth. Hopefully he would soon be back home. Her day began when she parted from Laurence after breakfast, after a night in the candlelight, beneath the caressing boldness of his hands and eyes, when she was his woman, when her treacherous female body came breathlessly alive, willingly, and she clung to him in a great desperate yearning, her naked body achingly but pleasurably fatigued as she left their bed each morning.

Although Laurence had a very efficient bailiff and

a steward and a number of efficient workers on the estate, when he was home he insisted on familiarising himself with everything that was being done and the concerns of the tenant farmers were his own concerns. Because of this attitude, the farms were productive and His Lordship a popular figure when he was seen involving himself in the work.

Melissa was pleased that before he engrossed himself with his responsibilities of the estate and his many business affairs, Laurence went each morning to the nursery to see their daughter. He would gently swing her up into his arms, listening to her baby talk and looking with rapt attention at the angelic face. When he had finished his work, with Melissa he would make his way to the drowsy warmth of the nursery again, gently holding Violet in the crook of his arm until she began to fall asleep. Carefully he would hand her to the nursemaid before going to have dinner with his wife.

Melissa did her utmost to familiarise herself with the running of the house, happy to listen and take advice from Mrs Robins, the kindly, well-meaning housekeeper, who had been at Winchcombe for two decades. Melissa had never applied herself to any task of such magnitude, although her governess and her mother had attempted to train her in the duties expected of a lady of the gentry. It was a pity she had never paid them much attention, Melissa scolded herself, determined that she would learn everything she needed to know eventually. Winchcombe was a splendid estate, one she was proud to call her home, even though she might never be able to win Laurence's love.

There was a constant stream of neighbours who came to call out of curiosity. Most of them genuinely wished them well. She was delighted, too, when her father did as promised and sent Freckle, her beloved mare, to Winchcombe.

One bright morning she entered the dining room and found her husband already at breakfast. He stood up and came to pull out her chair. Her heart flipped over at the sight of him, tall and superbly built, wearing black knee boots, tight buckskin breeches and a loosely fitting shirt in thin white lawn, the sleeves full gathered. She sat opposite, impatient to be away to the stables to see Freckle. On the sideboard under silver covers were mushrooms, sausages and fluffy scrambled eggs, but she couldn't bring herself to eat anything. To pacify Laurence, who was unashamedly tucking into anything and everything the servant placed in front of him—like most men he always insisted on starting the day with a hearty breakfast—she managed to eat some bread and butter smeared with jam and drank a cup of coffee.

'You really should eat something more substantial this early in the day,' Laurence said, drinking his second cup of coffee. 'You'll need your energy if you intend riding out. Cook is most put out. She takes you not eating breakfast as a personal criticism of her fare.'

'Then I shall go by way of the kitchen and explain—again—that I never usually eat anything much until noon.' Pushing back her chair and placing her napkin on the table, she went around the table and kissed his proffered cheek. 'Are you at home today?'

'Until noon.' His handsome features became thoughtful as he contemplated his wife's face. 'We can have lunch together if you're back in time from your ride.'

'I will be. I'll look forward to it.'

'Good. I don't want my wife disappearing before my eyes because she refuses to eat.'

'You don't?'

'No.' The smile on his lips curled, and his mouth lifted slightly at one corner, lids drooping seductively over his silver-grey eyes. 'I want you strong and healthy. It's certainly an asset during our private times,' he told her. His words sounded provocative—exactly as he wanted them to sound.

Melissa laughed softly, relieved the servant had disappeared to refill the coffee pot for His Lordship. Leaning over him, she encircled him with her arms, resting her cheek next to his. Laurence was a potently sensual male and in the bedroom he was superlatively skilful and masterful. That aspect of their marriage could not possibly have been improved upon.

'You're incorrigible, Laurence. I think I'd better leave you to your breakfast lest you start getting ideas about revisiting your bedroom—and I am not prepared to forfeit my ride.' Kissing his cheek, she went to the door.

'Don't forget to take one of the grooms with you. He'll show you the best places to ride.'

Giving him one last smile, she left the dining room and went to the kitchen to pacify Cook.

The stables were a hive of activity when Melissa got there. She could smell horseflesh, old leather and damp hay. She'd sent orders to have Freckle made ready for her to ride out. Her beloved mare whinnied with delight when she saw her, prancing quite outrageously on the cobbles.

The groom objected when she told him she would go alone.

'But I must attend you,' he said. 'If you are thrown or...'

'I have never been thrown from a saddle in my life,' she told him, hoisting herself up into the saddle and settling herself, smiling at his refusal to be dismissed.

'But the master will not like it...'

'I don't suppose he will,' she said, knowing perfectly well that Laurence would be livid. He had told her not to ride alone, but he was beginning to discover he hadn't married a mouse or a puppy that would obediently roll over at his every command. 'I will be all right—truly. You have given me an excellent description of the area so I won't get lost. I shall be perfectly safe.'

Her manner was firm but kind, and the groom soon realised he was no match for her determination. Reluctantly he backed away. She had every intention of being alone on her first ride on Freckle in a long time and she didn't want anyone holding her back.

Nudging her horse into action, she was soon riding beyond the grounds of the house and taking to the gently undulating countryside. There were meadows on either side of her, the hedges bright with wild rose and elderberry, the buzz of insects on the warm air. There were cows standing knee deep in clover, their heads down as they pulled contentedly at the lush green grass, their tails swishing their backs to swat away the midges. She breathed in deeply and luxuriated in the feel of the gentle breeze caressing her face. It was good to be riding Freckle again. She had missed her as much as she missed her parents and she was determined to have them down to visit as soon as it could be arranged.

Calculating that she had ridden about three miles, she reined Freckle in on the top of a humpback bridge which spanned a fast-flowing stream, the road veering sharply to the left on the other side. Unable to resist the temptation of taking a closer look into the clear depths of the water, she dismounted and rested her arms on the wall, looking down. Becoming carried away by the gentle sound, she failed to notice the man leaning against a tree at the side of the stream. When she did she gasped, for it was none other than Gerald Mortimer, attired in sombre garb without the fancy frills and lace and without his usual wig. She hardly recognised him. His hair was fair with a hint of curl and drawn back in a simple queue. His horse was nibbling the grass close to the water and Sir Gerald was watching her calmly, his expression one of gravity. Shoving himself away from the tree, he slowly climbed the bank and walked up on to the bridge where she stood.

'Lady Maxwell. I'm surprised to see you here. Why did you choose this particular place to stop?'

'Because I have ridden far enough and the stream tempted me.' She looked up at him. 'Why? Is there some significance to this place?'

He shook his head. 'Are you settled at Winchcombe?' he asked, taking a different tack.

'Yes. It's a fine place. But what of you?' She looked at him closely. This was a different Gerald Mortimer to the one she had met in London. He was more serious, quieter—troubled, without his usual swagger and smug arrogance. His face was deceptively youthful, despite the fine laughter lines around the eyes and mouth. Quick to laugh and quick to smile. But it was the eyes that gave him away. They were a deep, arresting shade of green, and fathoms deep with sadness, the kind that comes from losing a loved one. 'I believe you are to close up your house. I can't imagine why anyone would want to make their home in London when they have all this on their doorstep.'

'Can't you? No, I don't suppose you can,' he said quietly. 'There's nothing left for me here. Eliza and Antony are with me. My sister is helping me prepare for the closure. I imagine she will be calling on you before she leaves.'

'I do hope so. You are our nearest neighbour, I believe.'

He nodded. 'Our lands join to the south. Perhaps you should leave, Lady Maxwell. Your husband would not be pleased to see you talking to me—not here.'

Nonplussed, Melissa looked at him. He was standing a little away from her, gazing at the far end of the bridge. That was when she noticed the stones had been dislodged and fallen into the stream. Then she knew. Its significance hit her.

'Oh, dear—I see. This—this is where it happened—the accident.'

He nodded, avoiding her eyes. 'It was here that the carriage left the road and overturned—the carriage carrying Alice and Toby.'

She didn't answer him. She couldn't. For a moment she was totally incapable of speech, her throat tight, her body numb. 'I—I'm so sorry,' she said at length. 'It was such a terrible tragedy.'

He looked at her. 'Why? Why should you be sorry? She was a stranger to you.'

'Yes, she was, but the tragedy has affected so many people.'

'It is painful for me to reflect on the past. Sometimes I imagine she is still here.'

'Is that why you are closing your house—because coming here reminds you of Alice?'

He nodded. 'Something like that. I miss her, you see.'

'Yes. Eliza told me you were fond of her.'

He looked down at the rippling stream, seeming not to hear her, his thoughts clearly far away. 'I loved her. She was my life. I have never loved anyone else—

I never will. She should not have died the way she did—she was so lovely. I loved her the moment I saw her—long before she ever laid eyes on your husband. And she loved me, too—she never stopped loving me. But she was blinded for a while by everything Maxwell could give her—things I could not. But she tired of him in the end. She was leaving Laurence, do you know that?'

'Yes. He told me. And—do you blame Laurence for the accident?'

He smiled sadly. 'No. I do not blame him. It was what it was—a tragic accident. The driver was going too fast—as you see the bend on the other side of the bridge is sharp. The carriage hit the wall and tipped over into the water. There was nothing anyone could do.'

'Did—did the driver survive?'

'He was in a bad way for a while, but he pulled through—unlike Alice and her son. I had no idea she'd intended leaving with Toby. I wish to God she hadn't.'

'I know Laurence wishes she hadn't either.' Reaching out, she took Freckle's bridle. 'I must be getting back. I managed to get away without a groom. Should Laurence find out I have disobeyed him he will not be at all pleased.'

Gerald folded his hands for her booted foot and hoisted her up into the saddle. For the first time he laughed. 'Well, well. You ride astride, I see. Do not let the ladies hereabouts see you. You will scandalise the countryside.'

'I'm sure I will,' she said, returning his smile. 'I do not favour the side-saddle—it's like an instrument of torture. I prefer the freedom of riding astride. I find it much more natural and comfortable—but I shall do as propriety dictates and make a point of riding side-saddle when I am in company to protect my good name. Good day, Sir Gerald. Please give my kind regards to Eliza and Antony. I look forward to seeing them at Winchcombe before they leave.'

Melissa rode back to Winchcombe deep in thought. She was deeply troubled by her encounter with Sir Gerald. That he had loved Alice had been plain for her to see and he felt her loss as great, if not greater, than Laurence. On the two occasions she had seen him he had been bold and alive and full of vigour. Today he had looked beaten, tempered by something which had taken all the arrogance and vitality from him. How hurt he must have been when Alice had married Laurence.

Her thoughts were so occupied with their conversation that she didn't at first see an irate Laurence striding impatiently at the entrance to the stable yard. He was obviously waiting for her and aware that she had ridden off without a groom in attendance. She drew the mare to a halt and jumped down, handing the reins to a groom who had coming running from the stables the moment she had ridden into the yard. Laurence had become still, watching her, like a soldier on sentry duty, waiting for her to pass. There was not a single trace of reason in his expression, only an undeniable aura of restrained fury gathering pace inside him, waiting to be unleashed on her.

Smiling at her husband, she began walking towards the house, trying to ignore the anger burning in his eyes. She was aware of him striding after her, his fury reaching her in waves.

'Melissa! Don't you listen to anything I say? I specifically told you not to ride out without the accompaniment of a groom, yet you blatantly flouted my authority. Are you out to incur my anger? Is that it?'

'What? More than I have already, you mean?'

'Don't be flippant,' he ground out.

Without slowing her pace, Melissa turned her head and looked at him. She could see that he was furious. The glacial look in his silver-grey eyes and the stern set of his features sent shivers down her spine. There was certainly nothing soft or lover-like in his tone, as there had been earlier when she had left him at breakfast.

'I didn't, Laurence, at least not on purpose. I simply couldn't resist riding out and a groom would only have held me back. I wanted to enjoy my first ride on Freckle without restrictions—as I have done all my life.'

'And if you had been thrown, hurt, I would not have known where to look. I am only concerned for your safety.'

She glared at him militantly, her face aflame with vivid indignation. 'Really, Laurence, there is no need,' she said with no hint of an apology for riding out alone. 'I do ride rather well, you know. I have been riding Freckle ever since my father gave her to me and she hasn't thrown me once.'

Gritting his teeth and taking a deep breath, Laurence took her arm, halting her in her stride. 'There's always a first time.'

'Then I will deal with it if such a thing does occur. You cannot expect me to become as your mother and your first wife have been, just because that is what you are accustomed to. We are man and wife, but that does not mean I shall do everything you tell me to do.'

'You won't?'

'Indeed I will not. I am not accustomed to being arbitrarily ordered to do this and not do that.'

'Then since Winchcombe is your home, don't you think you should get used to it?'

'No, Laurence, I will not. I have been brought up in a certain way and I cannot change overnight. In fact, I'm not sure I want to change at all. I like the way I am. I am your wife and will be your equal—not your chattel to be told what I can and cannot do.'

She was tilting her head imperiously, daring him to argue, but it wasn't in him to take up that particular point with her just now.

'Where did you go? Did you see anyone?'

'Yes, as a matter of fact I did.'

'Who?'

'Sir Gerald Mortimer.'

Laurence stared at her. The blood drained from his face, making the birthmark on the side of his face stand out starkly. 'Where? Where did you encounter him?'

She looked at him directly. 'On the bridge that spans the stream.'

Laurence's face turned even whiter. 'You met him there—where…'

'Where the accident happened. Yes, Laurence, he told me.'

'What was he doing there?'

'Visiting the place where Alice died.'

Laurence looked at her for a long moment, then turned and began striding towards the house. She followed, having to take little running steps to keep up with him.

'I didn't arrange to meet him, Laurence, if that's what you think. We met purely by chance.'

'You are not to see him again, Melissa. Do you understand? I do not want you to have anything to do with him.'

'I probably won't be seeing him again since he is to close the house—as you well know.'

'Not a moment too soon.'

What she considered to be her husband's unreasonable manner, and still affected by the deep sorrow caused by Alice's death that continued to torture Sir Gerald, stirred Melissa's anger. 'I know what happened, Laurence, and I cannot understand why you are being like this. Apart from riding without a groom in attendance I cannot see that I have done anything to merit your displeasure.'

'Can you not?' he seethed, stopping once more to glare at her. 'Devil take it, Melissa. You know nothing about it. It means nothing to you that the man you have decided to befriend was plotting to run off with my wife?'

She winced at his savage tone, but she refused to retreat. 'Your first wife, Laurence. And I am not befriending him, but I can see that he was as affected as you were when Alice died. He was devastated. He sincerely loved her—was in love with her when she married you. It broke his heart. Imagine how he must have felt—his terrible loss. And, since she was leaving you to go back to Sir Gerald that tells me she never did stop loving him.'

Laurence had grown quite still. The angry eyes that settled on his wife were a glittering silver-grey. 'My, my! What's this—my wife turning philosopher? It would seem you've had quite a chat with our neighbour. He's lost no time in filling your ears with his side of things. The man will not be satisfied until he's turned you against me.'

'Have some faith in me. He won't do that—not ever. I'm only telling you what I have learned about your first wife. What are you trying to do, Laurence—destroy yourself? You weren't responsible for the accident that killed Alice and Toby—no more than Sir Gerald was. She was the one at fault—the one who was running away.'

Laurence's face became hard and there was a ruthlessness visible in the set of his mouth. 'For God's sake, Melissa. They were lovers—lovers while she was married to me.'

'I know. You told me.'

'And do you not think I had cause to be angry

about that—that I was being cuckolded by my closest neighbour?'

Despair welled in Melissa's heart at the fury she had unintentionally aroused in him. 'Yes, you had every right to be angry—at your wife, at Sir Gerald, but not at yourself. Yes, you were often away and she had time on her hands. But that did not mean she had to resume an affair with the man she would more than likely have married had she not met you. It is because he loved her so deeply that he cannot bear to come down here, to Surrey, where he is reminded of her all the time.'

'Your concern for the man is quite touching,' he said, his voice dripping with sarcasm.

'I am not concerned, Laurence—not for him—although I do feel sorry for him. Alice treated him very badly. I am simply concerned about the way the tragedy has affected you.'

'Do not take me for a fool, Melissa. You flout my orders by riding off alone when I specifically told you not to and you secretly meet a man who has done nothing but wish me ill since the day I married Alice. I was forced to weather Alice's propensity for scandal, for seeking her pleasures outside the marriage bed, but I draw the line at allowing the situation to repeat itself with you.'

Melissa's anger surfaced at the injustice of his accusation. 'I did not meet Sir Gerald secretly! How dare you imply it was an assignation! We met purely by chance.'

'Then I suppose I shall have to believe you,' he bit back, turning on his heel and striding towards the house again, already regretting that he had to depart for Plymouth in the next few days, leaving her alone and vulnerable to the likes of Gerald Mortimer. 'I should hate to see any similarities to your predecessor.'

'I am not in the habit of lying, Laurence,' she fumed, running to keep up with him. 'And I do not wish to hear the name of your first wife ever again. All I can say is that the more I hear of her, and the more I know of you, the more I pity her and find myself feeling extremely sorry for her, having been in the impossible situation of being married to you. I do not blame her for leaving you—in fact, I'm amazed she stayed with you so long. You are a monster, Laurence Maxwell, and I wish I'd never set eyes on you.'

Her angry words brought Laurence to an abrupt halt. He endured her outburst, his face an impassive mask. He saw how flushed with anger she was under the heavy mass of her hair and that her eyes were bright with bravely held, angry tears. She looked lovely and he knew he had only to make one single, very simple movement to stop her and take her in his arms, to wipe the anger and pain from her eyes, but her words, her rage, had driven him into a tyrannical mood and no power on earth could have made him yield to that desire.

His eyes were merciless as he reached out and

grasped her arms, bringing her to a standstill once more. She lifted her head and stared at him, haughtily, jutting out her chin, and Laurence felt the anger pounding in his temples for she looked wonderful, defiantly, astonishingly so.

'Enough, Melissa. I think you have said quite enough.'

'I am not Alice. I am nothing like her. I would never play you false. I swear it.' She snatched her arm from his grasp and marched away from him, uncaring whether he followed or not.

Laurence did believe her, but he could not dismiss her involvement or her eagerness to defend the man who had done everything in his power to destroy his first marriage. He was furious that Melissa had met with Gerald Mortimer, but he was determined not to fight with her as he had with Alice when she had flaunted her affair quite shamelessly, taunting him with her lover like a weapon of revenge. He would not allow the nightmare to begin all over again.

Ever since he had made her his wife Laurence had enjoyed their exchanges of different views that often flared between them, but she could not, of course, continue as she had before they were wed, when she had been left to run wild with no firm parental guidance all her life. It simply would not do—she was his wife and the mother of his child. While she had been straining against the reins which marriage, or at least marriage to a man such as himself, would impose on her, he had admired her spirit, the hot depths of indignation in her eyes at being told what to do. She had been like a small bird sitting on his shoulder for the past weeks and he had enjoyed her occasional peck at him, but he had to draw the line somewhere.

Chapter Ten

The argument continued over into the splendid dining room where they ate their evening meal. The atmosphere between them was strained, Laurence's conversation curt, cool and distant.

It was the first night since Melissa had gone to his bed after the ball in London that they slept alone. Her encounter with Gerald Mortimer and Laurence's furious reaction to it cast a dark cloud over the following days. Melissa was incensed with her husband's churlish behaviour and heartily tired of hearing about Alice. She also found her husband's proprietary manner towards her unreasonable and immensely irritating.

Laurence thought about his wife constantly. She was quiet, withdrawn, polite and, when not with Violet, she was riding out with a groom in attendance. She made him feel that he was nothing to her and the irony of the situation, had it not been so wretched, might have made him smile ruefully.

There was a time not so very long ago when he had been largely indifferent to her feelings. Now, as though to punish him for his indifference, he was the one who loved—with a love that had grown steadily—and was rejected. He remembered the night of the ball. Radiant she had been, and laughing, vivid in a way that had told him she was happy. She had a spirit to match his own and she had grown, phoenix-like, out of the naive young woman he had made love to in the Spring Gardens. She was sharp and clever, yet for all that, still as vulnerable as she had been then.

But how exquisite she had been in the candle's glow of their bedroom, her flesh a warm rosy glow, her firm breasts coral-tipped, her body eager and willing with sensuality, his own body loving her. Many were the times he'd wanted to go to her, knowing she was behind the closed door that connected their rooms, the image of her both powerful and tantalising. He had wanted desperately to reach out to her, but his own stupidity over Alice, and his pride, had held him back. In all the years and his experience with women there had been no one like Melissa and in all the weeks they had been married they had been mostly out of step with each other, so they had never come together at the right moment.

A letter from Eliza was delivered to the house. She wrote how she and Antony were to return to Hertfordshire two days hence and they would be calling on them at Winchcombe before they left. Since Laurence was to leave for Plymouth they also wanted to see him before he left. There was something of extreme importance Eliza had to impart and it was necessary that Laurence was present. The worrying part about it was that Gerald would be accompanying them and Melissa couldn't help wondering how Laurence would react to this news.

They arrived mid-afternoon beneath a sky heavy with dark rain clouds. Antony and Eliza arrived in a carriage, but Gerald had opted to ride over since he might wish to leave in a hurry. Laurence wasn't best pleased that Gerald had accompanied them, but it was too late to do anything but grin and bear it.

Antony was noticeably quiet and, after greeting Melissa, he seated himself in a chair which stood apart from the others, as if knowing something unpleasant was about to occur and wanting to be no part of it.

When Gerald entered the room in their wake, Laurence regarded him with a sardonic expression. The atmosphere between them could be cut with knife.

Gerald bowed over Melissa's hand. 'It's lovely to see you again, Lady Maxwell.'

'Thank you for seeing us,' Eliza said, sitting on an elegant green and cream sofa. 'We're returning to Hertfordshire tomorrow so it will be a while before we're down this way for some time. We'll let you know when we're next in London. I hope you didn't mind us inviting ourselves, but we really couldn't leave without seeing you.'

'I'm glad you didn't,' Melissa said, studying Eliza closely and sensing that what she had to say to them was of a serious nature. 'Etiquette has its place, but friends should be able to visit one another whenever they wish. Don't you agree, Laurence?'

'Absolutely,' Laurence replied tightly. Doing his best to put as much distance between him and Gerald as he could, he took up a stance near the fireplace, one arm resting on the mantlepiece.

'How are you settling in at Winchcombe, Melissa?' Eliza asked. 'I expect you found it daunting at first.'

'I have to confess I did, but I like it very well. It's a lovely old house.'

Two maids entered, bearing refreshments. Melissa occupied herself with pouring the tea and handing out the delicate cakes. Gerald raised his cup to her politely. 'Thank you. Here's to you, Lady Maxwell', and to Laurence he said, 'I salute you, Laurence. Your wife is quite charming. You always did have good taste in women.'

The silver-grey eyes considered Gerald without any hint of expression, then with slow deliberation he placed his cup down, raising his eyes. Had it not been for the coldness in them, his reply might have passed for a flippant remark. 'I'm glad you admire my taste as such. But then, you always did.'

Eliza was quick to step in, like a bone between two dogs whose hackles are raised, her tone one of controlled reproach. 'Please stop it, you two. Do you have to be at daggers drawn all the time? This enmity between the two of you affects all of us. You are not only neighbours, you used to be such close friends.'

'The best,' Gerald drawled. 'And since my good neighbour is clearly displeased by my presence here today, Lady Maxwell, I shall put you in the picture. There was a time when Laurence and I spent a great deal of our time together. We were as close as friends could be. We were the same age. We went to school together, socialised together...' he looked at Laurence and grinned '...in fact, we seem to have done most things together, don't we, Laurence?'

'And then Alice came along,' Antony retorted, casting a look of exasperation at his best friend and brother-in-law. 'And we all know what happened after that.'

Understanding the antagonism between the two men, Melissa looked at Eliza. 'You mentioned in your letter that there was something of importance you had to tell us, Eliza.'

Eliza put her cup and saucer down and sat up straight, a determined gleam in her eyes. 'Yes. First of all I would like to say that I am heartily tired of the discord between Gerald and Laurence—the cause being Alice. I have held my tongue on this matter for far too long and I think the time has come for me to speak out. I ask myself time and again how two people can behave like children when they used to be as close as brothers. I know how much Alice hurt you both and it gives me no pleasure having to discuss that particular lady—after all, she was a very close friend of mine for a long time, but there is something

I think the two of you should know and I wanted to tell you both together.'

Melissa was unable to determine what she saw in Laurence's face—chagrin or irritation, or both—but she saw the muscles in his cheeks flex and she watched him impatiently shove his hands into his pockets. She got up, picking up the tray of tea things and carrying it to the sideboard, glad to have something to do.

'If you have something to say, Eliza, please say it,' Antony said, eager to be away from the hostile atmosphere that prevailed in the room.

'Yes,' Gerald seconded, getting to his feet and walking across the room, clearly agitated about what his sister was about to disclose. 'I think you better had, Eliza, although why you have waited until now to get whatever it is off your chest baffles me.'

'I've thought long and hard about telling you. I truly thought Alice had caused enough heartache for the two of you without adding more, but I've changed my mind. Having expected to marry her himself, Gerald went away when Alice married Laurence. He came back after Toby was born. You were away for long periods, Laurence. Alice was bored—she was always bored when she was away from the social scene in London.'

'I know that.' Laurence shot a glowering look at his rival. 'Winchcombe never appealed to her. She was always at her happiest when she was in London.'

Eliza shook her head, sighing. 'We all know what she was like—extravagant, selfish, spoiled by her adoring parents. She was always confident of her own power over other people—always used to getting her own way with a snap of her fingers. As soon as Gerald met her he became her slave. They resumed their friendship—the closeness they'd had before...' She faltered, biting her lip before turning her attention to Laurence. 'She began to hate you, Laurence. I'm sorry to be blunt, but that's what whatever drew her into marrying you became. Sometimes love makes people ruthless in a way that hatred doesn't—which was why she decided to leave you. You see, she realised she still loved Gerald too much to lose him and you were in the way.'

Laurence turned from her in an attempt to bring his thoughts into order, before looking at her again, his face hard and uncompromising. The resulting knowledge of the depth of Alice's hatred for him was deeply hurtful. Yet the moment it presented itself Laurence knew he couldn't rest until he had told them the whole of it. 'It would seem she hated me so much that she was prepared to take my son from me. She took my son, Eliza. She took my son and he died as a result of her stupidity and selfishness.'

'I know that,' Eliza answered quietly.

'I cannot believe she hated me so much that she would do that.'

Eliza fixed him with a fierce gaze. 'Can't you? I can.'

Laurence looked at her without speaking for a moment. There was more, he knew it, and he wasn't going to like it. 'Tell me.'

Eliza sighed and shook her head wearily. 'There—there's something you don't know, either of you,' she said, looking from Laurence to Gerald. 'Alice—she was with child—your child, Gerald. She told me in confidence before she decided to leave Laurence. People who are cornered do desperate things, which was why she decided walk away from her marriage.'

The silence that fell on the room was so profound that if anyone had entered at that moment they would have heard their hearts beating. Gerald's face became filled with honest puzzlement as his mind took its time to register what Eliza had said.

'Alice was to bear my child?' he said hoarsely. Eliza nodded. 'But—but why did she keep it from me?'

When Melissa caught sight of Gerald's face as he gripped the back of the chair he stood behind, she saw only raw, naked grief—the kind that could rarely be feigned.

'Why didn't she tell me?' he repeated brokenly, angrily. 'Why didn't you tell me, Eliza, instead of keeping it to yourself? You had no right.'

'I know. Alice would have told you—but for the accident. I could see how much you were suffering—which is why I didn't tell you. I—I didn't want to add to your grief. I'm sorry. I should have.'

'Yes, you should.' Gerald's shoulders slumped. 'I loved her. Dear Lord, I loved her so much. She was the only thing in my life I have ever loved. I begged her not to marry you,' he said, his heated gaze fixed on Laurence, 'but her mind was made up. It was your money that attracted her. You could give her everything she wanted—whereas I… My father left Eliza and me money and assets that would allow us to live in comfort for the rest of our lives—but it could not compare with your immense wealth.'

Laurence's mouth curled cruelly. 'Be that as it may, have you forgotten that on the night she died she was running to you? Had I known that she was carrying your child I would have divorced her. You see, nothing could have induced me to continue to live with a woman who was to bear another man's child.'

Eliza stood up, her hands clenched, her face an angry red. 'Please stop this. I ask you both to let this be the final chapter in Alice's life—for all our sakes.'

His shoulders sagging, as if all the life had drained out of him, Gerald lowered his head. 'I wish she'd told me—and you, Eliza. I cannot believe you did not tell me.' He said nothing more. It was a quiet sound that hung between them, without anger or emotion, but it held all the cruel anguish which he felt.

Laurence felt his erstwhile friend's pain along with anger at his first wife. Alice had left a harsh and bitter legacy they could never have imagined—or deserved. Strangely, he felt no satisfaction at what Gerald was suffering, a man he no longer considered to be his enemy, but could never be his friend again, only a bitter taste of self-loathing, despising himself with a virulence that was almost unbearable for having completely annihilated someone who believed he had every justification in the world to hate him.

* * *

Standing apart from the four other people in the room, on the outside looking in and feeling very much like an outsider, looking from one to the other, Melissa could feel the fresh anguish that was tearing both Laurence and Gerald apart. Suddenly the walls of the room seemed to close in on her, the atmosphere becoming more and more oppressive and claustrophobic. Feeling strangely isolated and different, as if she didn't belong, she slipped out of the room. Without giving what she was doing much thought, she went to her room and scrambled into her riding habit. As she made her way to the stables, the weather was turning. The sky was dark with gathering rain clouds and the wind had risen to match her mood.

She wondered how long it would be before they could all move on from this, from the damage Alice had done. There was nothing she could do, she knew that, so she must accept that and live for the moment. Not so long ago she had been happy to come to Winchcombe, but now nothing seemed clear to her any more. Not even Laurence. From the very first moment she had laid eyes on him he had done things to her mind and now all she could think of was him. But how could she be content now that she knew the heartache of real love?

The wind was strong, the rain having started to fall heavily as she headed away from Winchcombe. She'd ridden a long way when she realised how foolish she had been to rush out into the wild elements. Unfortunately the light had almost gone so she didn't see the overhead branch of a tree at the side of the lane. Her head slammed against it and a white flash burst in her brain as the reins were jerked from her hands and she was flung out of the slippery saddle. When a clap of thunder shook the earth followed by a flash of lightning that lit up the sky, her terrified horse bolted, leaving her lying on the wet grass.

It was the groom who had tried to prevent Melissa from riding off who came to the house to inform the master that his wife had left the house and ridden off alone. Until then Laurence hadn't noticed Melissa's absence. His visitors were about to depart, but Eliza insisted they wait until Melissa had returned to the house.

Little fool, Laurence thought furiously as he strode to the stables. As if they didn't have enough to worry about without her riding off when a storm was brewing. Within minutes he was riding in the direction the groom told him she had taken. The wind was strong and the rain lashing down from a leaden sky.

Momentarily stunned, her head tender where it had made contact with the branch, Melissa managed to stagger to her feet. Looking around for her horse, she strained her eyes in the gloom. Unable to locate Freckle and chiding herself for her recklessness in riding out in such dreadful weather, she knew there was nothing for it but to make her own way back to the house. Seized by a great weariness and hampered by the buffeting wind and rain and her skirts clinging to her legs, she made slow progress. Her boots squelched in the mud, but, undeterred, she stumbled blindly on.

She was only aware of another presence when someone grasped her shoulder. She spun round, her hair a wild, wet tangle plastered to her face, beneath which her eyes peered out like an animal from its den, blood oozing slowly from the cut on her brow mingling with the rain. Afraid and trying to run from the threat, she stumbled and fell. She saw the shape of a man as if through a long tunnel, his cloak flying wide behind him until he resembled a great bird swooping down on her. When she felt strong hands grasp her and pull her to her feet, with no idea who her assailant might be she struggled wildly.

'Please don't touch me. Let me go.' She continued to fight against the hands that held her, but she could not fight the force that had her in its grip. Her body went limp as she felt the fight go out of her. The rain clung to her eyelashes like tears.

'Please let me go,' she cried helplessly.

'Little fool,' Laurence growled, holding her close. 'What the hell did you think you were doing, riding off like that and in this weather? Let's get you back to the house.'

Unable to think clearly, her head aching abominably, Melissa sagged against him. The fear that she might be in the clutches of some wild beast receded when she smelt the familiar spicy tang of his cologne. It was Laurence and she was relieved that he had found her.

Laurence picked her up into his arms and held her against his chest, his face distraught as he looked at her lovely hair streaming across her face like wet seaweed. Somehow he managed to hoist her into the saddle and climb up behind her.

Melissa sighed and closed her eyes as a strong, steel-sinewed arm went round her and held her close.

When they reached the house Melissa had recovered sufficiently to slide from the saddle. Her legs felt wobbly, but she could stand without help. The rain continued to fall heavily, but she was so wet she was beyond caring.

'Let me help you, Melissa,' Laurence said, taking her arm. Her face was whiter than death and the wound on her forehead still oozed blood. 'You're hurt. We must get that wound looked at.'

'It's nothing,' she mumbled, stepping away from him and shaking her arm free. 'Leave me alone, Laurence. I'll make my own way to the house.'

'What were you thinking?'

'Nothing. I simply wanted to get out of the house—away from all of you and your constant, infernal talk of Alice. Will we never be free of her?'

Laurence didn't argue—now wasn't the time. 'Eliza is still at the house. When she was told you had ridden off she wouldn't leave until she knew you were safe. She's distraught—and rightly so.'

'I'm so sorry to have caused such concern, but as you see I am fine.'

She turned away, relieved to see Freckle had made her own way back, although she was still all a-tremble following the thunder and lightning that had caused her to bolt. Melissa went to her and, with soothing words and tender strokes, the horse began to settle. Leaving her with a groom to rub her down, she made her way to the house, Laurence close on her heels.

Eliza was waiting, anxious for her safety. 'What on earth has happened to you?' she asked, shocked by her bedraggled sight of her.

'I found her in the lane some way away,' Laurence told her, his brow furrowed with concern. 'She's taken a tumble from her horse—and is in quite a state, as you can see.'

'Goodness, Melissa. To go riding off on a night like this was suicidal. We'd best get you to bed and send for the doctor to take a look at your head.'

'It's nothing, Eliza, and I don't want the doctor. Please don't fuss. There's nothing wrong with me that a hot bath won't cure.'

'Well, then, come along. Let me help you to your room. We'll have you cleaned up and in bed in no time.' Eliza turned to Laurence. 'Leave her to me, Laurence. Antony is still in the drawing room. You look as though you could do with a stiff brandy. Gerald rode off shortly after you. I'll let you know when Melissa's settled.'

Melissa opened her heavy-lidded eyes, closing them quickly when they were assaulted by bright sunshine filtering through the curtains. A dull ache throbbed in her head and she felt strangely depressed and melancholy. She tried to understand the bitter desolation that held her in its grip and in that instant she remembered riding off into the storm the night before. She also remembered being knocked off her horse along with the bitter irony of Laurence finding her and bringing her home. Eliza had stayed with her until she had been bathed and put to bed. She must have fallen asleep because she remembered nothing after that.

Gingerly touching her head, she felt the small dressing Eliza had put there. Dragging herself up to a sitting position, eager to see her daughter, she rang the bell for Daisy.

The nursery was quiet when Laurence, looking for his wife, found her there. Violet was having her mid-morning nap. Her nursemaid was in the room next door, busying herself while her charge slept. Violet lay on her back, her arms flung out on either side, breathing softly. Melissa was leaning over her daughter. Tenderly she touched her cheek.

Aware that someone had entered, she half turned. Seeing Laurence, she turned to look once more at their daughter. Closing the door, he moved further into the room, keeping his stare fixed firmly on his wife.

'I didn't expect to see you up so soon. I went to your room last night, but you were sleeping. How are you feeling? You gave us all a fright. It was lucky I found you so quickly.'

'Yes,' she murmured with mild sarcasm, 'wasn't it.'

'Don't you ever go riding off into a thunderstorm

again—with no protection and with no logical reason for doing so as far as I can see. It was both stupid and irresponsible of you.'

'Yes, I know, although the weather was the last thing I was thinking about when I rode off. And please don't raise your voice, Laurence,' she said, stepping away from their daughter and beginning to fold away some small items of Violet's clothing that had been brought up from the laundry. 'We don't want to wake Violet. Isn't it today when you have to leave for Plymouth?'

He nodded. 'I wanted to make sure you were well enough first.'

'I'm fine, Laurence, as you can see,' she said, without pausing in her work. 'Please don't let me stop you.'

A look of irritation flashed across his face. 'Be sensible, Melissa. What you did was reckless and foolish. Anything could have happened to you. I was out of my mind with worry.'

Pausing, she looked at him, her eyebrows raised in what looked like surprise. 'Really? You must forgive me if I find that hard to believe. The last I saw of you, you were battling it out with our guests about Alice. I was knocked from my horse by a branch. I didn't see it in the dark. And please don't insult my intelligence by pretending to care for me when we both know the real reason you married me is over there sleeping.'

One black brow flicked upwards in a measuring look. 'What is this?' He caught her wrist in a firm grip. 'Will you stop what you're doing and look at me? Do not close down your thoughts from me and shut me out. We will finish this—this conversation before I go anywhere.'

'There is nothing to finish.' Melissa pulled her wrist away.

Turning his back on her, Laurence strode across the room as he marshalled his thoughts. When he finally spoke, his voice was quiet and ruthlessly controlled. 'There is. I dare not turn my back on you for fear you will do something outrageous. I haven't known a moment's peace since I married you.'

'I'm sorry to hear that,' Melissa said tightly, fighting against a wave of despair and taking refuge in attack. 'That's all I needed to hear after spending the weeks since our marriage treading around on eggshells lest I disturb or upset you in any way should I as much as mention your first wife.'

'Now you are being ridiculous.'

'Am I? I don't think so. I did not ask to be put in this position. My actions, be they right or wrong, have been dictated by events set by you, not by any desire on my part to cause you concern. I have never set out to thwart you or undermine you in any way. If I had followed my own wishes when you arrived at High Meadows, I would have refused your offer of marriage and sent you on your way.'

'I am sorry I inflicted my presence on you, Melissa, but under the circumstances—for Violet's sake—we had no other choice.'

'No? You're a clever man, Laurence—or so everyone is always quick to point out to me—so I am sure you could have worked something out. Our relationship has been difficult from the start, but I have done what I thought was right in an impossible situation.'

They faced each other, eyes locked, the air heavy with tension as the cruel words echoed around the room.

Laurence knew that the time had come for him to leave, that his coach was waiting to take him to Plymouth—he also knew that when he did so the gulf between them would only open wider. If they tried to hide from it, to pretend it wasn't there, it would always be there between them. It would seem he had misjudged her and the situation. She had married him and demanded nothing for herself, putting his needs and those of their daughter before her own. He had no right to take his frustration and the bitter failure of his first marriage out on her. She did not deserve it.

'It has been a difficult time for you, I realise that. Perhaps I've been too impatient—I haven't given you time to adjust to our marriage. Look, I don't want to leave you just now. I can put it off until tomorrow.'

Melissa could not explain the disappointment she felt and nor did she care to analyse why she should feel this way. 'No—there is no need. Some time apart might be good for us—time for us to work out what is most important and to put things into perspective. Go, Laurence. The sooner you leave the sooner you will be back.'

'Perhaps you're right.' His gaze feasted on her

lovely face. It was devoid of colour. Wisps of her rich dark hair had escaped from some of its pins and rested in curls on her forehead and around her neck. Her eyes were dull, with neither happiness nor contentment in their depths. But the way she held herself told him she was determined to maintain her dignity despite the raw emotions tearing them both apart. The gentle fragrance of her perfume drifted through his senses and he was seized by a strong yearning to hold her against him, as he had on the nights when they had shared a bed. With nothing left to say, turning from her, he crossed the room and went out.

Staring at the closed door, a lump rose in Melissa's throat and tears stung the backs of her eyes. Going to the window, she saw him climb into the waiting coach and watched until it had disappeared down the drive. Why had she been so disappointed a few moments ago when he had told her he could put off departing by a day? Was it because she had not wanted him to go to Plymouth at all? Or was it because she had wanted him to *want* to stay with her?

Her heart was breaking. She had wanted to tell him how she felt so many times, to reveal her true feelings, to tell him she loved him desperately. Instead she had blamed him for forcing her into their marriage against her will, that had it been left to her she would have done things differently. It was far from the truth, of course, but the feelings she carried in her heart would remain there until he found it in his own to return her love.

* * *

Laurence had been gone a couple of hours when a letter was delivered. It was addressed to her. Recognising her father's writing, she proceeded to open it as she slowly went to her room. His news was grim and wrung her heart. It was with a heavy heart that she informed Mrs Robins that she was leaving for High Meadow immediately, instructing Daisy to prepare her and Violet's things.

The coach took her back to Hertfordshire, the familiar homeliness and wild beauty of it unobserved, for she was encased in grief.

Chapter Eleven

Laurence had not been gone twenty-four hours when he returned unexpectedly to Winchcombe, leaving others to manage his affairs in Plymouth. Ever since he had left home he was unable to dismiss Melissa from his mind. She had made it plain that she did not care about his commitments elsewhere and certainly not about him. He felt his innards twist with the pain of it. She had made it clear that she didn't care whether he was there or not. Giving much thought to the troubles that assailed them, he realised that he may have been too hard and insensitive to her feelings regarding Alice and Gerald Mortimer.

On a sigh and with a whimsical smile tugging at the corners of his mouth, he admitted the truth of it. At thirty years old and with more turbulent water under the bridge than he cared to give any more thought to, he had fallen victim to a beautiful, courageous young woman who was in possession of an undesirable streak of fiery rebellion. He felt his body tense as the unfamiliar emotion drove into him like a physical force, becoming aware that his reticence had been eroded by that stifling, most destructive of all emotions, making the paradox of his passions and conflicting needs difficult to control.

Despite everything, he was now in no doubt that he loved Melissa deeply, that what they had together was real and transcended anything else that had come before. It filled him with a sense of wonder, want and hunger—this ultimate love that could only be understood by the two people involved.

The house was unusually quiet when he arrived at Winchcombe. Letting himself in, eager to see his wife and daughter, he bounded across the hall and up the stairs, reluctant to admit to the sharp disappointment when she did not appear to greet him. Thinking she would be in the nursery, he went there first. Finding the nursery devoid of both his wife and child, he turned enquiringly to Violet's nursemaid.

'Where is my daughter? Has my wife taken her out? The hour is late and it is past time Violet was in bed.' He strode to the window, fully expecting to see Melissa wheeling their daughter in her carriage.

'No, my lord—she—Her Ladyship—she's not here.'

Laurence stared at the girl as if she'd taken leave of her senses. The weariness drained from him as a cold mist of dread settled round his heart. 'Not here? Then where is she?'

'She—she left soon after you left for Plymouth,

my lord,' she replied, wringing her hands. 'She—she was upset—most distressed about something. She left in a hurry. Daisy went with her.'

'Where? Where did she go?' he demanded. He transfixed the increasingly nervous maid with a fierce stare that left her stammering and uncertain.

'She—she...'

Laurence stared at her hard as panic set in. He remained quite still, his breathing shallow. He remembered another time when his first wife had gone missing—taking their son with her—on a day just like this. The memory ripped across his brain as suspicion screamed through his body. No, he thought, she can't have. She wouldn't have done that.

'My lord—'

'Where is she? She must have told you where she was going?'

'Home, my lord. She said she was going home. I—I expect she will be there by now.'

Laurence took a moment for the words to penetrate his brain, then he stalked from the nursery and went in search of Mrs Robins, only to be informed by his butler that since it was her day off she had gone to visit her sister in the village. When asked if he knew where his wife had gone, the butler repeated what Violet's nursemaid had told him.

Remembering how quiet Melissa had been after her tumble from her horse and the angry words they had exchanged in the nursery before he'd left for Plymouth, when no one was forthcoming about her reason for going to Hertfordshire, he assumed the only possible reason was that she had left him. Then he contradicted his own suspicion, shaking his head as if to dislodge the outrageous thought. He could not believe such a thing of her. The suspicion was completely without foundation. Had they not lain together, made love together? Hadn't she given her body to him time and again with trusting sweetness and openness? He had come to believe that there was more than respect and tolerance in her feelings towards him, that she loved him a little and that their union would soon become one of far more value than that which he'd had with Alice.

But such thoughts as these did nothing to dispel his suspicion that she had indeed left him. He tried to keep a hold on his temper, which threatened to overwhelm him, and it was with a mixture of fear and exasperation that he immediately ordered his valet to pack some clothes and order the coach.

Incapable of any kind of rational thought, what he felt as the coach left Winchcombe was raw, red-hot anger. The closer he got to Hertfordshire did nothing to release the tension or the anguish in his heart.

When Laurence reached High Meadows, trying to rein in his impatience, he asked to be taken to his wife. The house was quiet, its walls exuding something of the old days that was stable and unchanging. He was told that the Baron and his wife were in their rooms. Melissa was also upstairs resting. He climbed the stairs for the confrontation with his wife, his face set in uncompromising lines, his eyes now glacial, hiding all trace of the fury that had threatened to shred his heart to pieces.

Letting himself into her room, he found her seated on the window seat, her knees drawn up to her chin, her arms wrapped around her legs as she gazed out over the countryside beyond the tangle of gardens. When he saw her he was torn between a desire to berate her soundly for leaving Winchcombe and a heady desire to pull her into his arms. His heart gave a joyful leap, having made up its mind that whatever had driven her to leave Winchcombe could be easily resolved and they would soon be heading back home.

Melissa turned her head when the door opened, expecting to see Daisy or her mother. Seeing Laurence, she stared at him in disbelief. A deluge of love filled her heart. She could only marvel that for whatever reason he had come to her when she needed him most. She wanted to fly across the room into his arms, but when the cruel words of their parting thrust their way into her mind that stopped her. Placing her feet on the floor, she stood up and straightened her skirts, waiting for him to speak. He looked dishevelled, his eyes haunted with something she could not identify. Why had he come? He was supposed to be in Plymouth.

His face was inscrutable and after a long moment he said, 'What in God's name do you think you are doing?'

'Me? What are you talking about?'

'When I returned to Winchcombe and found you gone—I thought…' Running his trembling fingers through his hair, he shook his head, breathing hard as he tried to control his feelings. Closing the door he strode further into the room, standing over her. 'I thought you had...'

Melissa's heart ached with remorse when she realised what it was that was clearly torturing him. 'You thought I had left you?' He must have been beside himself. Never in her wildest dreams had she imagined he would think she had done exactly the same thing to him as Alice.

'What else was I to think?'

'I told Mrs Robins why I had to come here.'

'She wasn't there and no one else knew.'

'I am so sorry, Laurence. Contrary to what you thought, I have not left you.'

His eyes blazed with relief. 'Then why did you leave Winchcombe the minute I'd gone out the door?'

'My brother is dead, Laurence. I received the news from my father almost as soon as you had left.'

The flat, almost detached tone of her voice made the statement even more compelling. Laurence stared at her, unable as yet to absorb what she had said.

'Your brother?'

'Henry.'

'When?' His voice was a whisper of compassion.

'We don't know the details, only that his ship was in a convoy of vessels heading for America when it went down in a storm. Apparently there were no survivors.'

Laurence was stricken. He knew just how close Melissa had been to Henry and how distressed she must be feeling. 'What can I say? I am so very sorry, Melissa. You must be devastated.'

'Yes. I wanted to be here to offer comfort to my parents. They have taken it extremely hard, I'm afraid. But I am surprised to see you, Laurence. You should not be here,' she told him. 'This does not fit into your work schedule. You had work to do—in Plymouth. You should do it.'

'My work can wait. There are others who can do it for me. My priority at this time is you. I deeply regretted leaving you and returned to Winchcombe before I'd even reached Plymouth. I was worried about you. You were hurt when you were knocked from your horse—and the bitter words we exchanged before I left played heavily on my mind. Let me help you, Melissa.'

'You? How can you help me?' She did not look at him.

He winced at the coldness of the question. 'I would like to try.'

'Why? Why would you want to do that?'

'I am not a monster, Melissa—which you accused me of being, as I recall. I know how you must have suffered since you received the news of your brother. He was very dear to you, I know that.'

For the first time since he had entered the room she looked at him properly. 'Do you? Do you really, Laurence?'

He moved closer to her, looking down into her face upturned to him. 'You are still shocked—to lose your brother—for him to die so young and so suddenly.'

'Yes, you are right. He was too young. He had everything to live for, but we always knew this might happen. It was forever at the back of our minds.'

'Of course it was, but it's a shock all the same when it happens. I do know all about that, Melissa. I would be only too glad to do anything I can to ease your grief. I would take you in my arms and hold you, console you—share your pain—to take the hurt and sadness from your heart until there is no room left for it.'

Smiling thinly she turned from him, moving slowly back to the window and looking out, a faraway expression in her eyes. 'I'd hoped to find consolation once before in your arms, Laurence, until I realised I would have to compete with a dead woman for it. Don't worry about me. I'm perfectly all right—really. I'm tired, that's all—but I appreciate your offer. You really should return to Winchcombe.'

'I'm not going anywhere. I am here for you. Will you take me to your parents? I would like to offer them my condolences.'

'They're resting. Henry's death has affected them deeply. Come, we'll go downstairs. I'll get you something to eat. You must be tired after your journey. I'll have a room prepared for you.' Halfway to the door she stopped and looked at him. 'So—am I to understand that you returned to Winchcombe for me?'

He nodded. 'I missed you, Melissa. When I thought you had left me I was beside myself with anguish and every other emotion you can put a name to. I was crushed. I could not imagine the rest of my life without you. You have become a part of me—like my flesh and blood. I came here to berate you—to beg your forgiveness—but now I know why you left I am not so insensitive that I don't know what you must be going through. There are things to be said, matters to be settled between us, but they can wait until later.'

'Yes—yes, they can. Now is not the time.'

Laurence paid his commiserations to her parents. The loss of their son had clearly devastated them. They were glad that he had come to be with Melissa. She was pale, withdrawn, a drifting copy of her former self. Her grieving for her brother was done not in his presence, but in private. A feeling of helplessness, a feeling so strong welled up inside him like a great river which has been dammed. He was not sure at that moment what it was he felt, he only knew that it was something he had never felt before. The longing, the absolute need for Melissa to stir, to show some sign that she cared for him, to give him permission to take her in his arms where he could comfort her, protect her, took him over completely.

Since the angry words they had exchanged at Winchcombe, he had been more disturbed than he cared to admit over the accusations she had flung at him about Alice. The revelation of how much Melissa had come to mean to him, how much he loved her, brought a surge of remorse, mingling with the torment of his cruelty towards her. He remembered how she had been that day he had encountered her after she had ridden off alone—magnificent in her anger, courageous in her defiance and filled with an incredible sweetness and innocent, tender passion.

Everything must have become too much for her when she had suddenly snapped and he had seen her spirit revived. She had been quiet over the days following their bitter words, subdued, enduring his coldness towards her. How could he possibly have likened her to Alice—with her viciousness and spite, goading and taunting him—who had laughed in his face when she had confessed her adultery?

Melissa was none of these things. In fact, she was everything that Alice was not. With the revelation of how deep his love was for her, it was as though his mind had finally become free of its burden of pain and sorrow at the same time. As she moved about the house comforting her parents and making arrangements for a small memorial service to be held in the village church for her brother, Laurence felt she didn't even realise he was there half the time, but he could keenly feel her despair.

Antony and Eliza had returned to Hertfordshire so he rode to see them most days and spent a lot of his time with Violet, who was a great comfort to him.

Robert arrived in time for the memorial service. His wife, not wanting to leave her father who was not in the best of health, was to travel down with their two children at a later date.

The meeting between Laurence and Robert was cordial. Of medium height and dark haired like his sister, Robert Frobisher was a serious-minded person who was deeply upset by the death of his older brother.

The memorial service was a subdued affair, attended by those who had known the spirited Henry Frobisher. It was a comfort to Melissa that Antony and Eliza were there. The Baron was quiet, holding in his grief, his wife weeping softly beside him. Melissa remained by her parents' side as friends and neighbours came to pay their respects. She grieved tearlessly, but Laurence could see the strain of the past days was beginning to tell on her.

The day which had been full of sadness was over. After saying goodnight to her parents and brother and making sure Violet was asleep, Melissa went wearily to her room, knowing Laurence would be there, waiting for her. He had been a constant support from the moment he had arrived, patiently watching her, considering her needs. Now, as she knew he would be, he was seated by the hearth.

Laurence got to his feet. 'Melissa?'

She looked at him for a long moment, his voice penetrating the inner sanctum of her mind and the ice about her beginning to melt. 'Laurence?' she whispered. 'Oh, Laurence.'

Quite suddenly her face crumpled and she began to move across the room towards him, her gaze held by his. There was something in his expression and miraculous intuition in his compelling silver-grey eyes which touched her heart.

He saw the great wash of tears spring from her eyes and flow across her face, and his heart jolted for her pain. His expression was soft, his love for her shining through the brilliance of his eyes. He came closer and took her by the shoulders, wrapping her in his strong arms.

'I've got you, Melissa. Weep all you want.'

She cried silently, huge tears spilling over her lashes and coursing down her cheeks. It was agony for Laurence to watch her anguish, raised from the vast reservoir of despair threatening to drown her. Sitting on the edge of the bed with her, he kept his arms around her. He could feel the alert tension in her slender body. Eventually her tears ceased, but she seemed content to remain in his arms. The warmth of the room wrapped itself around them so that it seemed that they were alone in a world without substance or reality.

'Are you feeling better now?' Laurence asked, his lips against her hair.

As if awakening from a deep trance, Melissa nodded. The storm of tears had ceased and with its passing some of her tension had been washed away. Having dealt with adversity from the day of their marriage, she was too weak to fight Laurence when he was being kind and understanding—besides, he felt so warm and strong, his arms comforting and his voice soothing. His mere presence gave her a sense of security and safety. Laurence was both surprised and touched when she nestled closer and buried her face into his chest. It was as if she wanted to hide herself in his embrace.

After a while she raised her head. It seemed a lifetime passed as they gazed at each other. In that lifetime each lived through a range of deep, tender emotions new to them both, exquisite emotions that neither of them could put into words. As though in slow motion, unable to resist the temptation Melissa's mouth offered, slowly Laurence's own moved inexorably closer. His gaze was gentle and compelling when, in a sweet, mesmeric sensation, his mouth found hers. Melissa melted into him. The kiss was long and lingeringly slow.

Raising his head, Laurence gazed at her in wonder. Her magnificent eyes were naked and defenceless.

'Will you stay with me?' she murmured. 'I don't want to be by myself tonight.'

'I'm not going anywhere if you don't want me to.' Releasing his hold, he turned her face up to his, stroking her hair back. 'Shall we go to bed?' he asked, cradling her face in his hands and tracing her cheekbones with his thumbs.

'Yes,' she whispered, 'I would like that.'

In no time at all they had divested themselves of their clothes and slipped between the cool sheets. Melissa felt the strength of his arms and the warmth of his masculine body. She could feel the hard muscles of his broad chest and smell his maleness and the spicy scent of his cologne. A tautness began in her breast, a delicious ache that was like a languorous, honeyed warmth. She had missed his presence in her bed so much.

As he sensed the change in her Laurence's arms slackened. His senses were invaded by the smell of her. It was the soft fragrance of her hair—the sweet scent of roses mingled with musky female scent—that made his body burn. Her body began to tremble with longing to be where it belonged, where it had always belonged had Laurence known it. Now he did as she placed herself in his protection, a safe refuge. Her body clung to his and they did not speak for there was no need of it now.

Melissa awoke the next morning to an enormous feeling of contentment, her body warm and rosy, drugged with love. Her eyes were dark and languorous with the unfocused stare of a woman who has been completely fulfilled—not only in the flesh, but in the heart and mind. They had made love repeatedly, a loving that neither of them had ever known, which they could swear had never been there before. It was a pairing of their hearts and bodies which had at last come together at exactly the right moment. When Melissa looked into Laurence's eyes she saw an expression she had looked for every time they had made love and despaired of ever seeing. Now, at last, it was there, a difference in him. His eyes were clear and in them, shining and glorious and uncomplicated, was his love for her.

Without relinquishing their hold on each other,

they talked of the days passed, of Violet, Melissa's parents and the previous day's memorial service.

'It was good of Antony and Eliza to come,' Melissa murmured. 'Tell me what happened to Gerald after Eliza told him about Alice. I saw how devastated he was by the news that she was to have had his child.'

'It's hardly surprising. After what happened to Toby I would like to say he got what he deserved, but between that and how I really feel there is no connection whatsoever. We both lost a great deal and I am not proud of what I did. He did to me what I did to him by marrying Alice in the first place when he was already in love with her and had good reason to think they would marry. I took everything from him and it shames me to say that. I experienced no satisfaction at the outcome.'

He spoke with a solemnity that puzzled Melissa. 'When he left Winchcombe, how did the two of you part?'

'He left without saying a word. He was overcome with grief when Eliza told him about the child.'

'It's understandable. What will you do—leave things as they are?'

Shaking his head, he tightened his arm about her naked form. 'I will call on him when I am next in London—perhaps when we return to Winchcombe. I am honour-bound to put things right between us. I believe he loved Alice as much as he was capable of loving any human being—and she loved him, despite being married to me. That was one thing I learned that night—something in my conceit I always doubted. I wronged him, I admit that.' Looking down at Melissa's upturned face, he drew her close, looking deep into her eyes. 'It is time I laid Alice's ghost to rest, although Toby will always be with me. Where Gerald is concerned—you do see why I must go and see him, don't you?'

'Yes, yes, I do,' she replied. 'And I'm glad. And now Robert has arrived we can think about returning to Winchcombe.' Her expression was one of sadness. 'It will be hard, though, leaving High Meadows and my family again. I had a happy childhood and all my good memories are here. All the things I associate with my brothers—they live here.'

'Of course they do, but you will make new memories—at Winchcombe with Violet.'

'And you.'

'Yes—the three of us,' he murmured. 'From now on I intend to spend less time away—I will let others do my bidding. I don't deserve you, my darling, or your forgiveness. I have treated you very badly.' Combing her hair back from her face with his fingers, he tilted her face to his and kissed her lips tenderly, all the love that had been accumulating over the time he had known her contained in his kiss. 'I love you,' he murmured, his breath warm against her lips. 'Though I would have been the last man to admit it, I think I have loved you ever since we met in the Spring Gardens.'

Catching her breath, Melissa raised her brows in amazement, silently questioning, hoping.

'I have come to realise just how much you mean

to me,' he went on. 'When I thought you had left me something died inside me. I have reflected long and hard on what you said about Alice—that you did not wish to hear her name mentioned ever again. I don't blame you. I remember how angry I was that you had said that, but later I realised how difficult it must be for you when everything around you must remind you of her. When she died I told myself that I did not need any woman's love—that I did not want it. But I can see now that I was wrong. I want your love, Melissa. All of it. So you see, my darling, you have caught me in the tenderest trap of all.'

'You have it, Laurence. I have loved you from the moment I saw you arrive at the Spring Gardens. I had no experience of such emotions that compromised all my thoughts. I watched you to the exclusion of all others. I did not understand it, but it was as if some invisible thread connected us. The night was dark, but you shone in my sight. I watched you until I caught your eye. I had eyes for no one else after that.'

'There we are, then.' On a sigh and with a whimsical smile tugging at the corners of his mouth, Laurence admitted the truth of it. Love tightened his throat. What he felt was so exquisite it pained him to draw breath. 'What we have transcends all else. I want to give you the world because you have given me so much in return. You are a rare being, Melissa Maxwell, and I love you.'

Melissa kissed him gently. 'Thank you, Laurence. That is the nicest, most wonderful thing you have ever said to me.'

Epilogue

Melissa and Laurence stood looking down at the grave where Alice and Toby had been laid to rest. It was the fourth anniversary of their deaths. Though it was winter the weather was mild, with primroses and violets pushing through the soil, soon to be followed by daffodils. Violet carefully placed a small posy of flowers beneath the headstone. Standing back, she tilted her head on one side to see if she'd done it right.

Melissa held the much-welcomed new addition to their family in the crook of her arm—Thomas Henry Maxwell, a lusty boy now three months old, who bore a strong resemblance to his sister. Standing by her side, Laurence put his arm about her waist and kissed her cheek before caressing his son's brow with his fingertips. He then laughed as he watched Violet return to the grave to rearrange her posy into what she considered to be a better position.

Melissa smiled up at her husband, into his eyes which were shining and clear, his face uncomplicated by the past and filled with happiness, contentment and his love for her and their family, which was returned by her with all the fierce joy in her heart.

* * * * *

If you enjoyed this story, why not check out these other great reads by Helen Dickson

Carrying the Gentleman's Secret
A Vow for an Heiress
The Governess's Scandalous Marriage
Reunited at the King's Court